Bile burned Jordan's throat as he forced his clenched fists open.

He could barely handle the thought that anyone, but especially their father, would hurt Jacob and Lacey. That the man would actually threaten their aunt Nell, the woman who was taking such good care of those kids.

Jordan took a minute before he spoke; the last thing Nell needed was another angry guy. "So you're going to adopt them," he said in a mild voice.

"Yeah. But I love them, too. I *want* to adopt them."

How could he possibly sell the house where they lived until the adoption went through, and Nell and the kids were safe? Jordan closed his eyes, hoping the whole situation would magically disappear. But a minute later, when he opened his eyes, Nell still looked as if she was expecting her world to bottom out. Damn it. There had to be another way out of this mess.

Dear Reader,

Many of us live on a plateau for years, raising children, working, playing. But sometimes life takes a sudden turn, and we have to come out of that stasis and deal with mercurial situations. Not many people embrace change when it's thrust upon them. Nell Hart and Jordan Tanner are no exception. They're both so focused on their individual goals, when circumstances draw them into each other's orbit, neither is prepared for the impact that has on their lives.

I love writing stories about ordinary people in extraordinary circumstances. Although it's a stretch to say Nell Hart is ordinary. She's kind and compassionate and fierce in her loyalty to those she loves. She does, indeed, have heart. Jordan Tanner does, too, he just doesn't know it. His fast track to success gets derailed when Nell and her soon-to-be-adopted niece and nephew become part of his daily life. It doesn't take him long to realize money can't compare to the richness of family and community.

I had fun writing about the people who live at 879 Dunstan Lane. Nell stole my heart—there's that word again!—from day one. And who doesn't love a man who is kind and gentle with children? I hope you enjoy their story.

I'd love to hear from you. You can email me at kate@katekelly.ca or visit my website www.katekelly.ca.

Sincerely,

Kate Kelly

A Deliberate Father

Kate Kelly

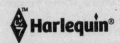

TORONTO NEW YORK LONDON
AMSTERDAM PARIS SYDNEY HAMBURG
STOCKHOLM ATHENS TOKYO MILAN MADRID
PRAGUE WARSAW BUDAPEST AUCKLAND

Recycling programs
for this product may
not exist in your area.

ISBN-13: 978-0-373-71751-4

A DELIBERATE FATHER

ABOUT THE AUTHOR

Growing up in New Brunswick, Canada, Kate Kelly had long red braids and freckles. Ah, you say, Anne of Green Gables. Not quite. Sunday mornings, outside the church they both attended, Mary Grannan, the author of the Maggie Muggins series, would greet Kate with, "Good morning, Maggie Muggins. How are you today?" Kate doesn't remember what she replied on those occasions, bedazzled by the wonderful, outlandish hats Mary Grannan wore. Kate has had a lifelong love affair with books, but writing came in fits and starts. She didn't take it seriously until her forties. Now she can't get along without it. She has the good fortune to still live on the east coast of Canada with her husband (the children have flown away). She writes, grow herbs and perennials and sails when the wind blows her way.

To June Kelly.

Wish you were here.

Many thanks to Lina Gardiner,
the best critique partner ever!

To Norah Wilson, what a ride it's been!

To the Domino Divas, my gang!

And, of course, to my guys, Adrian, Reed and Rei.

CHAPTER ONE

JORDAN TANNER PULLED UP across the street from the faded purple monstrosity and uttered a dozen different curses, each one ending with *Great-aunt Beulah*. Not that he wasn't grateful to have inherited the house—mausoleum, whatever—but he harbored no illusions. As the last Tanner standing, this legacy had come to him through default.

Rain beat against the windshield of his Lexus as the wind tore down the deserted street. The oak he'd parked under groaned from the assault. He should move his car away from the trees. But Dunstan Lane was entirely lined with the old giants, and he knew a stall tactic when he saw one.

Jordan climbed out, unfurled his umbrella and studied his new home through the pelting rain. Not home. *Residence*. Home was his I-can't-believe-I-finally-made-it condo forty minutes down the highway. All he had to do was ride out the next few months in the butt-ugly Victorian until the place sold. Then he would return to his real life.

A movement on the roof three stories up caught his attention. Curious, he crossed the street and peered upward. A small woman, maybe a girl, scampered over a dormer, stopped near the edge above him and raised her arms to the sky. You didn't have to be Einstein to know that was a curse ripping out of her mouth.

He tossed the umbrella aside and broke into a full out run. How long would it take him to get to the top floor? And then? Then he'd figure it out. Talk her down. Break into the third-floor apartment if he had to and find a way onto the roof. No one was going to kill themselves today. Not on his property.

He pounded up the fire escape, stopping only to sight the woman. She was squatting now, even closer to the edge, and swinging something in her hand. He pulled his head down and pushed on, his breath searing his lungs. Waste of energy to shout. Probably some crack crazed teenager. Probably one of his tenants. He hit the landing outside the top-floor apartment. Nailed to the side of the house was a ladder that went the rest of the way up. *Thank God.*

He grabbed the bottom rung as he spared a quick check on the crazy lady. Yup, still there, but she had turned away from the edge, her attention focused on the shingles.

"I wouldn't do that if I were you, mister." A thin voice wafted out from a window that opened onto the fire escape.

Jordan shot a look behind him but the curtains obscured whoever had spoken. Another nutcase, no doubt.

"There's a woman on the roof," he hollered over his shoulder as he hoisted himself up the first rung. "I think she's going to jump."

A small boy poked his head out the open window. "She's fixing the roof. You better wait until she comes down." The anemic-looking child pushed his heavy framed glasses farther up his nose and looked him over. "You got a cold beer?"

"Excuse me?"

"She thinks cold beer is yummy. If you give her one, she might not yell at you."

Jordan stepped back onto the landing and leaned over the railing until he caught sight of the woman. Now that he was taking time to notice, yeah, that was a hammer in her hand. The soft thump of hammer meeting nail reached him as he watched her duckwalk away from the edge.

He hunched his shoulders against the relentless rain. "Does she always work on the roof during a storm?"

"Not always." The kid looked like he was having a midlife crisis at the age of, well, whatever age he was. Somewhere between eight and twelve. His thick black glasses swallowed his face, giving him a pinched look, as if he spent a lot of time scraping the bottom of the peanut butter jar. He started to shut the window.

"Hang on a sec. What's your name?"

"Jacob." He banged the lower edge of the window with his fist. It slid down another two inches.

"Jacob, I'd like to ask you a few questions." Like how rotten the old house was, and exactly who lived in it. Beulah's solicitor hadn't mentioned children. And where was the caretaker? Could it possibly be the tiny woman repairing the roof?

"I'm not supposed to talk to strangers," Jacob said through the glass.

Of course he wasn't. But Jordan would probably get more out of the kid in five minutes than a wily old caretaker. He hadn't talked to his aunt for at least ten years but that didn't mean he'd forgotten her. Beulah had been borderline crazy, in his opinion, and like attracted like. The five apartments in the house probably housed all sorts of misfits. Like the woman on the roof for instance. "If we introduce ourselves, we're not strangers. I'm Jordan."

He pasted on his I'm-a-nice-guy smile, the one he used right before he told his clients how much it was going to cost them to save their companies. Jacob sent him a withering look. "That's not the way it works."

Okay, the kid wasn't stupid. Time to talk business. "Give you a couple bucks if you answer some questions."

"About what?"

"About the—*umph*." Jordan crumpled to his knees as someone ambushed him from behind. An arm wound around his neck, cutting off his air supply. What in blazes? He grabbed the slender arm and tugged. If he could get to his feet, he could fall backward and shake off—

"I've got a hammer in my hand," a voice grated in his ear. "You move, and I'll use it."

The woman from the roof.

"Call 9-1-1, Jacob. Tell them we have an intruder," she said.

"Perry will come when he hears our address," Jacob shouted through the window.

Roof Lady swung her hammer under his nose. "What kind of sicko sneaks up a fire escape in the pouring rain and offers a child money to talk to him?"

Jordan eased back on his heels, his attacker plastered to his back like Spider-Woman. "You don't want to call the police."

Her grip tightened around his neck. "Are you a friend of Tony's?"

"I'm Jordan Tanner, Beulah Winer's nephew."

Her arm went slack, and he heard her suck in a sharp breath.

"Oh, boy." Jacob slammed the window all the way shut.

She climbed off his back. "Mr. Tanner?"

"Yeah." He got to his feet and wiped the rain from his face as he turned around on the small landing. The woman barely reached his armpit. With her huge green eyes and small pointed face, she reminded him of a drowned kitten. He looked pointedly at the hammer in her hand until she slipped it into the hoop on her tool belt.

She crossed her arms over her chest. "You're early," she said in the same voice his secretary used when he was late.

"Why are you up on the roof when— You're the caretaker." The conclusion he'd been trying to avoid couldn't be ignored any longer. Round one to Beulah Winer. He'd assumed she'd left him the house because he was the last living member of their not-so-illustrious family, but only five minutes in, and it wasn't stacking up that way.

He'd hoped the house would provide the means of cementing the financial security he'd always dreamed of and very nearly achieved. But he'd failed to take into account the fact that his great-aunt was the benefactor. There was a good chance Beulah had left him the house to torture him.

"That's right, I'm the caretaker." Roof Lady elbowed past him and after a couple of thumps, yanked the window open and slid through. Jordan barely had time to register her trim butt before she turned and eyed him. "Do you have any ID?"

"You've got to be kidding." Hadn't she been listening? He owned the building.

"You were lurking outside my window, trying to bribe my kid with money. I'm calling the cops if you can't prove who you say you are." She grabbed the phone from the kitchen counter and cradled the handset under her chin. Her right hand stole down to rest on the head of her hammer.

"I thought—" he got out through clenched teeth as he wrestled his wallet out of his soaked pocket "—that you were a jumper." He flipped his wallet open and held up his driver's licence. "Jordan Tanner, at your service."

BEULAH WINER HAD BEEN MEANER than a swarm of wasps on a hot summer day. And just as crazy. She hadn't been particularly fond of Nell—she hadn't been fond of anyone as far as Nell could tell—and Nell had returned the favor. Like everyone else living in the house, she'd made a wary peace with the spiteful old lady, had even helped her as much as Beulah allowed. In return, Nell had found a safe harbor for the past two years. A safe harbor that was quickly sinking out of sight.

"You thought I was going to jump off the roof?" She slid the phone back on the counter. With a sinking stomach she studied his driver's licence. Even with his hair plastered to his head and rain trickling down his face, Jordan Tanner still managed to look as self-assured as his photo. He had a stubborn chin and clear blue-gray eyes with a black rim around the iris.

"I didn't see the hammer from the street," he said as he pushed his dark hair off his forehead. "All I saw was a…woman up on a roof in a storm."

Nell narrowed her eyes. Okay, so she was drenched. And of course he had to arrive before she had a chance to change out of her overalls and get rid of her tools, but— What was she doing? The only thing that need concern her was getting Mr. Tanner in and out of the building and her life as quickly as possible. And if that meant playing nice for the next hour or so, she could do that. She didn't have to like it, but she could do it.

She bit back a smile as she demurely motioned for him to crawl through the open window. She knew she should suggest meeting him at the front door, but watching him clamber through the narrow opening was much more appealing. He shot her a hard look, as if to say he knew exactly what she was up to, then in one graceful move, somehow managed to maneuver his wide shoulders through the small frame. She took a step back when he straightened to his full height, the room dwarfed by his size. She should have guessed he'd rise to the challenge.

"If you give me your suit jacket, I'll hang it up in the bathroom and grab us some towels. Unless you want to go home and dry off. Come back later." Hard to keep the hopeful note out of her voice.

"I'd prefer to look around now."

With a heavy heart she accepted his sodden jacket and trudged off to the bathroom. Of course he wanted to look at the apartments today. From the little she'd been able to squeeze out of the tight-lipped solicitor who'd handled Beulah's affairs, Tanner was a business consultant who lived in Seabend, the upscale seaside community just twenty minutes out of Halifax. Seabend had become so crowded with trendy coffee shops and boutiques, Nell barely recognized it anymore. The only reason Waterside hadn't developed in the same way was because they were another forty minutes down the road, making them a solid hour from the city. Tourists trickled through in the summer, but they stuck to the waterfront where a few stores had sprouted. Thankfully, people like her, who lived a few blocks back in the old neighborhoods, were left undisturbed. Heaven forbid Tanner should waste time making a second trip here. She rolled her eyes. God save them all from consultants.

In the bathroom, she scrubbed her face with a towel

and studied her reflection in the mirror. Her eyes were huge, and if anyone bothered to notice, they'd see the slight tremble at the right corner of her mouth.

She gripped the edge of the sink with both hands and leaned into her reflection until her breath steamed up the mirror. *You will not be afraid. You will go out there and tell that man he needs you to run this place. You will....* She rested her forehead against the mirror. She couldn't lose her apartment. Jacob and Lacey had finally started treating the place like home. She'd never find another one for such a low rent in this neighborhood. If they had to move, her little patched-together family would suffer—and so would her chances for adopting her niece and nephew.

The thought that Jacob and Lacey could be taken away from her, that she might not gain custody, was unacceptable. She wanted to howl every time she thought of the kind of life they'd have with their abusive father, Tony. The adoption should have been final ages ago, made easier because she was a relative. But Tony had contacted Child Welfare a few weeks ago and expressed concern that his children weren't receiving the best care. In Nell's opinion, his real concern was getting parole, and if he had to use his children to get it, he would. As a result of his bogus complaints, she and the children were now being subjected to an intense home study. It scared her to think of what would happen to Jacob and Lacey if he was granted custody after he got out of jail. Who would take care of them?

She was determined to be pleasant to Tanner. *Mr.* Tanner. She couldn't afford not to be.

She slipped into Lacey's bedroom, yanked off her wet clothes and dragged on her green silk blouse and black slacks. Her hope of impressing upon Tanner that they were a normal family had been blown out of the water when she'd attacked him on the fire escape. But at least she could look halfway decent while she showed him the apartments. Running a hand through her damp hair, she hurried toward the kitchen. Jacob had probably disappeared into his room, and she didn't like the idea of Tanner exploring on his own.

Halfway to the kitchen, she skidded to a stop. Standing in the middle of her tiny living room, Tanner looked almost approachable in bare feet. Nell paused briefly to evaluate her new landlord. Jordan Tanner was a big man, over six feet tall, and yummy enough to make her want to take a second look. From the way his dark hair spilled elegantly onto his forehead, her best guess was his cut wasn't the fifteen-dollar special from the local barber. The faint lines around his eyes suggested he was in his mid-thirties. His white dress shirt had damp splotches on it, and he'd loosened his conservative gray tie so it hung at a crooked angle. He'd removed his wet socks and shoes, and his bare feet gave him an oddly vulnerable appearance.

He turned as she walked into the room. Her toes tingled as he surveyed her from top to toe. "Sorry about earlier. I should have known better than to offer Jacob money. Seeing you on the roof rattled me."

"Apology accepted. I probably overreacted." There was no *probably* about it. She'd almost beaned the guy with her hammer. "Maybe we should start over. My name is Nell Hart." She held her breath as she stuck out her hand. He could make her life miserable if he chose.

A smile broke out on his face, and she swayed toward him as her hand disappeared inside his warm clasp.

"So." She pulled away and rubbed the goose bumps on her arms. "This is my apartment, obviously. It's a two-bedroom. It's not very big, but good enough for us. You're welcome to look at the rest of the rooms." She clamped her runaway mouth shut and led the way out of the crowded living room. His dazzling smile had loosened something inside her, like her good sense.

She wondered what he thought of her living space in the same breath that she wondered what difference it made. When they'd moved in, she'd painted the walls white, minimized the furniture and taken down the curtains to give the living room a bigger feel. But it was never going to be anything other than a small room with too many people using it. "They're the kids' rooms, so—"

"Kids? As in more than one?"

Her back stiffened as she knocked on Jacob's door. "That's right. Jacob and Lacey."

"Two bedrooms, two kids. Where do you sleep?"

"We're working on that. Jacob? Mr. Tanner would like to see your room."

"Call me Jordan."

She sent a weak smile over her shoulder. A shiver worked through her. Too much man, standing far too close and smelling delicious. Like spice and mystery. Breaking the cardinal rule of entering without permission, she burst into Jacob's room.

Her nephew's bedroom was in its usual frightfully well-organized state, except the blankets had been pulled off his bed. He'd made a tent in one corner by draping two blankets over his desk. She knew he was hiding inside; she could hear him breathing.

Nell felt crushed. He'd built his first tent the day after her sister, Mary, had died. He'd emerged to attend the funeral, but it took her another two weeks to coax him out again with the promise of ice cream and a visit to the science museum. For months after his mother's death and his father's incarceration, Jacob ferreted out quiet, dark spots to curl up in, seeking asylum. A habit he'd stopped until now.

She'd tried to hide her anxiety about the inevitable changes headed their way, but obviously she hadn't succeeded. Jacob had enough to carry on his thin shoulders; she'd wanted to protect him from additional worry. Like her, he'd had to grow up too hard, too fast. "What's going on, Jacob?"

"Just reading."

"Everything okay?"

"Yes." He sounded so forlorn.

Tanner leaned against the doorjamb and studied the room. "I remember making tents like that when I was a kid. This isn't a bad room. Could use a second window."

Or better yet, a replacement for the existing window so she wouldn't have to cover it with plastic in the winter. Not that Tanner was ready to hear the gritty details. She had a feeling he was still trying to wrap his mind around the fact that his caretaker was a woman with two children. Just wait until he found out about her low rent. At least he'd made it sound normal that Jacob was hiding under his blankets. Maybe it was normal. Maybe she was overreacting.

"Lacey's room is across the hall. It was clean last time I looked." Melody had taken Lacey shopping for the afternoon. Nell had tried to coax Jacob to go with them, but he'd refused. She opened the door a couple inches, peeked in and breathed a sigh of relief.

The room was tidy. Sort of. If you looked past the brightly colored ribbons and scarves that festooned the walls and furniture. Lacey had wanted a complete refit, but the budget had stretched only to visiting second-hand stores to hunt for small pretties. She hated saying no to the kids; they rarely asked for much and had accepted her frugal lifestyle with such quiet dignity it sometimes frightened her. She wanted them to stamp their feet, to whine and demand that they get to be kids just like their friends. But they were still too scared, too battered from the curves life had thrown at them.

"It would make a great office," Tanner commented, looking over her shoulder.

Nell's mouth twitched. Instead of pointing out the

room was already occupied, she snapped the door shut. "Would you like to see the downstairs apartments now?"

He looked at his bare feet. "Is there an inside staircase?"

As tempted as she was to lead him back out to the fire escape, she succumbed to her good sense. "This way."

She trotted out of the apartment and down the two flights of stairs, taking a sadistic satisfaction in the knowledge that Tanner was doing the grand tour in bare feet. "This was your aunt Beulah's apartment," she explained as she unlocked a door on the first floor. "You probably know that." Not that Nell had seen him in the two years she'd lived here.

"Auntie and I weren't close," he commented drily as he followed her into the apartment. "Not bad. Refinished hardwood floors. Lots of light. It's changed a lot since the last time I saw it. That was years ago. Did you do the renovations?"

"I did the floors and painted the walls and helped install the new windows."

He walked through the empty apartment, switching lights on and off as he went. "Even the kitchen's half-decent."

Nell busied herself with checking the tap at the kitchen sink. She'd discovered it dripping yesterday and had replaced a washer. Not that she doubted her work; keeping busy was her way of staying out of trouble. She hated to admit it, but even wet and wrinkled, Tanner looked like trouble.

"I know a nice young couple who are anxious to rent the apartment." She followed him into the master bedroom.

He whirled around to look at her. "Do you? How much do you think I can charge for a three-bedroom?"

"Fifteen hundred is a fair price for this community."

"How much are you paying?"

Uh-oh. Either the solicitor, Mr. Swinburg, hadn't told him or Tanner enjoyed watching her squirm. "Five hundred. Plus heat."

He frowned. "For a two-bedroom?"

"Beulah and I had an arrangement."

"Which was?"

Was, not *is.* She squared her shoulders. "I can do small carpentry repairs and I'm good with plumbing. And after two years I know all the quirks of the furnace."

She felt as if she were being interviewed when he leaned against the wall and crossed his ankles. "And you fix the leak in the roof only when it rains?"

"I told your aunt when I moved in that she needed a new roof. But if something didn't directly affect her, she often chose to ignore it."

He wiped a hand over his face. "I don't suppose you do roofs, as well?"

"No, but I could help someone who knew what they were doing."

"What else needs replacing?"

She looked around the apartment. "The windows down here are new but the ones upstairs aren't so great. The furnace will last you another few years if you baby it along. The foundation is solid. The house needs a fresh coat of paint." She didn't specify inside and out. As for the wiring, that could wait until he asked.

He wandered back to the living room, looked around and sighed. "There are three other apartments?"

"There are two one-bedroom apartments on the second floor, both rented. And there's a small bedsit beside this apartment. It's tiny."

"Is it rented?"

"No." *Not officially.* Nell held her breath, praying he wouldn't want to look at the room. She'd meant to ask Rodney to make himself scarce today, but once the storm had moved in, she hadn't had the heart. He was too old to sleep outside, and he was still running a bit of a fever.

She hadn't planned on bringing him home two weeks ago. The first time, she'd spotted him squatting on the sidewalk in town, she almost hadn't recognized him. The older man had lost so much weight, and it had been years since she'd seen him. Rodney Stiles was a face from a past long dead and gone; hearing his familiar voice, although weakened, had stirred up powerful memories. She gave him all the change she had and continued on her way. But she couldn't stop thinking about him, about how cheerful he and his wife had always been when they delivered the weekly egg supply to her parents' convenience store. Rodney's wife, Lucinda, had smelled like cinnamon. She'd told Nell she had strong, capable hands, and that she'd make a good farmer.

The next time Nell went to Seabend, she brought along a blanket and jacket for Rodney. When she found him on a bench in a small park, he looked like he was a dried-up old twig the wind had blown along the sidewalk. He accepted her gifts, but she could tell he was embarrassed. While eating the hot lunch she insisted he have, she learned Lucinda had died a few months earlier. Since then he couldn't stand living at the farm. A week later, rain settled in for a few days, and Nell returned to Seabend and found him huddled in a doorway, shaking. Whatever the cause of his shakes, he needed help. She convinced him to go home with her for a few days, just until he was feeling better.

"Who lives on the second floor?"

Nell snapped back to attention. "Mrs. Trembley. She says she's seventy-four, but I suspect she's older. She and your aunt were...friends." If bickering could be called a sport, they'd been the champions. With Beulah's passing, Mrs. T. had started to fade. She no longer had color in her cheeks from the heat of an argument. And she'd stopped dyeing her hair because who else could she goad by saying she looked ten years younger?

"Friends." Tanner closed his eyes as if he had a headache. "Rent?"

"Four hundred," she murmured.

His eyes shot open, their dark beam accusing. "What did you say?"

Nell fisted her hands on her hips. "Your aunt may have been...difficult, but she was kind in her own way." Unlike her nephew, apparently. "Mrs. Trembley is old, and she doesn't have a family. It's only a one-bedroom. You couldn't get much more for it than four hundred."

WELL. WELL. LITTLE MISS NELLIE had a temper. With anger flushing her cheeks and those disturbing green eyes sparking, she was beautiful. Earlier, he'd been mesmerized by the overalls she'd had on. She'd worn a cropped shirt under them, and the brief, teasing glimpses of her flat midriff disappearing into the dark folds of the overalls had been, to put it mildly, distracting.

Thank goodness she'd changed because Nell Hart's smooth skin was the last thing he should be thinking about. Instead of the financial asset he needed, he'd inherited a houseful of charity cases and a crumbling mansion. Somehow, something would have to change. He had to make this—for lack of a better word—apartment house, a paying venture. It was the only way he'd be able to sell it for the price he needed.

"Melody Northrop lives in 2B."

"And?"

Nell smiled. "She's single and beautiful and pays six hundred a month."

He tucked away his answering smile. It was the first time Nell had offered information willingly. Jordan recognized the tactic; get the bad news over with, then soften it up with some good news. He'd let the caretaker bit blind him; she was clearly a great deal smarter than he'd thought.

"That's a relief to hear." But not exactly inspiring. Hard to believe in his neighborhood, which was only forty minutes away, one-bedrooms cost between two and three thousand a month. But as the real-estate agent had pointed out, this was Waterside, not Seabend. Not only were they close to the ocean here, but when the wind blew from the right—or wrong—direction, the smell of manure on the farmers' fields was also very much apparent.

That was the strange thing about the east coast of Canada. Million-dollar homes rubbed shoulders with old homesteads. People with money were moving into the area, but the farming families were still reluctant to sell off their acreage, even if it meant living in poverty. That kind of sentiment was frustrating, but opportunities were finally opening up. In twenty years, Waterside would be the next Seabend. If Jordan handled the sale the right way, the house could be a potential gold mine.

For now, six hundred for a one-bedroom was acceptable. Five hundred for a two-bedroom was not. Even for an in-house handyman. *Handywoman*. As he watched Nell check the lock on the living room window, he wondered if Aunt Beulah had grown soft in her old age. From the little he remembered about his aunt, the crusty old wing nut had been as tightfisted as they come. What had Nell Hart done for the old lady that an off-site handyman couldn't? She was a major impediment to the sale of the monstrosity. With the poor condition of the house, he'd be lucky to find a buyer for it, but no one would be willing to take on the house plus a live-in caretaker. She had to go, and he, lucky man that he was, would have to tell her.

"You could probably get a bit more for this apartment. It is a three-bedroom."

He went to the door and waited for her. "I'd like to see the bedsit now."

"I need some time to clean it up. It's not ready." She gripped the window ledge as if she expected him to drag her from the apartment. Interesting. What or who did she have stashed in the bedsit? Jordan started to smile. Miss Nellie could prove to be an entertaining diversion during his temporary stint here.

"I need to see if it's big enough for me to live in. Otherwise, I might have to evict someone." If he had a mustache, he would have twirled it. He didn't plan on evicting anyone—yet. One way or another, he'd fit into the bedsit.

"What?"

"I'm moving in until the house sells. I'm a hands-on kind of guy." He made sure his smile had a bite to it, just enough to make her wonder whether he was joking or not.

"But that's..." Not going to work. Definitely not for him. He wasn't looking forward to leaving his condo to live in this firetrap. And by the look on Miss Nellie's face, it wasn't working for her, either.

CHAPTER TWO

"YOU'RE LEAVING ALL THOSE clothes here?" Alex asked as he stared into Jordan's closet.

Trying to ignore his headache, Jordan zipped up the suitcase. "I'm only going to be forty minutes away. I'll be dropping in from time to time."

He'd arrived home last night in a black mood to find Alex waiting for him with a bottle of Scotch to celebrate their first joint business venture. As he watched his friend shove his clothes to one end of the closet and start hanging up his own suits, he tried to recall how he'd allowed Alex to convince him to sublet his condo. Alex insisted he was doing him a favor by taking the place off his hands for the next few months, but Jordan had seen him working a deal too many times not to know when he'd been played. Which was exactly why he wanted Alex as a business partner; the guy knew how to work the angles. He wasn't sure how he felt about him moving in on his personal turf, though.

"The sooner you clear out the riffraff, the sooner we sell, and you can move back here." Alex hummed as he hung up one of his suits. "It's a good idea for you to move in. Sounds like you have a lot of house cleaning to do."

Jordan scooped up an armload of books he'd selected a couple days ago and stacked them in an empty box. "You're working with a real-estate agent to get the house listed, right? And coming up with our own list of potential clients, as well?"

"I am, but you'd get a higher price if the house showed a profit. It's the live-in caretaker who's the worst. She either has to go or start paying market rent."

Jordan's queasiness spiked. Not only was he going to live on Dunstan Lane to monitor the situation and the repairs, but he had to find a way to get rid of Nell and her kids. Yeah, he was really looking forward to the next few months.

"Just keep your eye on the ball," Alex cautioned. "In the past year alone there were three businesses we could have bought into if we'd had the capital. Selling the house is going to make it possible for us to branch out on our own. Don't forget that."

"Not going to happen." Not after he'd worked so hard to get this far. He was often accused of being too focused, but without backup, he couldn't afford to relax. The consquences were immediate, sometimes permanent. He'd moved on from his poverty-stricken childhood. The only direction he planned to travel now was up—after selling the house.

"Good. So, any chance Sandra will show up at your door?"

"No." Jordan stacked a few more books in the box.

"I thought things were heating up between you."

"They're not." And he didn't understand why. Logically, Sandra was the perfect woman for him. She was a consultant at the same firm as him and Alex, but worked in marketing, while he was a turn-around consultant. Often they worked on the same account. Jordan went in first, assessed the company's problems, looked for ways to improve efficiency and cut costs and helped the owners write a new business plan. Sandra was all about strengthening the clients' brand, keeping them in front of their intended audience.

They worked well together, enjoyed each other's company, and had the same drive for successs. If that wasn't enough, she was a beautiful woman, and she'd let him know she wouldn't mind if they spent more time together outside office hours. It should have added up to the perfect relationship. He couldn't put his finger on exactly what else he needed, but something held him back from committing to her. It made him uneasy to think about it, so he tried not to. In any case, he wasn't ready to get involved in anything serious at this point in his life. He had business to attend to.

"She's smart, she's foxy and she wants what you want. Money, success and all the trimmings. You're nuts, man. Unless you've been holding out on me. Should I expect any other girlfriends showing up at the door?"

"No." Jordan stalked into the bathroom to escape Alex's cheerful tone. Bad enought the guy was moving onto his turf while he was stuck at the old Victorian, now he was angling for his woman, too.

WHEN JORDAN DROVE UP to the side entrance of the Victorian two hours later, dark clouds scudded across the sky, threatening more rain. Everything looked sodden, even the closed-up sunflower that peeked around the corner of the building.

One of Nell's projects likely; she seemed like the sunflower type. She'd managed to skinny out of showing him the bedsit yesterday when Mrs. Trembley had started thumping on the second-story floor with her cane. The elderly tenant declared she'd been waiting hours to meet him and wasn't willing to wait a minute longer. He'd been polite but distant and had cut the interview short, having had a bellyful of 879 Dunstan Lane by then. He couldn't wait to get back to his condo where he didn't know his next-door neighbors. Didn't have to know them, didn't care to know them. No clutter, no fuss. Just the way he liked it. Except with Alex living there now, the place didn't feel like his anymore. He'd forgotten how lousy it felt not to know where you belonged.

Using the key Nell had given him yesterday, he opened the outside door to the room that was to be his home for however long it took to sell the house. At least the bedsit had its own private entrance. The other tenants shared an inside hallway and staircase, but he could come and go without having to talk to anyone.

He sighed; there wasn't enough space to breathe, let alone live inside the room. Everything looked too small and drab—the bathroom wedged in one corner, the tiny kitchenette strung along the back wall. Worse, all the complaining in the world wasn't going to change the fact that he'd elected to stay here.

He kicked a chrome, sixties-style kitchen chair that didn't look as if it would hold his weight. Okay, he ate out more nights than not, so the kitchen wasn't a big deal. And as long as he had lots of hot water and good pressure, he could handle banging his elbows against the sides of the shower. The bed, a lumpy couch that pulled out into a double—or so Nell had assured him—didn't begin to pass muster. He'd have to buy a new mattress. No telling what was living in this one.

He dropped his suitcases in front of the only closet as water pipes screeched overhead. He shuddered and shoved open a window. The room smelled of damp clothes and disinfectant; it needed a good scrubbing. That was a caretaker's job, right?

His mood brightened until he remembered he had to tell Nell about the rent increases. With the expense of raising two small children, he imagined paying a higher rent was going to put a serious dent in her budget. With that in mind, he'd decided to hold off for a couple more weeks before tackling the issue of her caretaker position. It didn't make sense to keep her on staff when all he had to do was hire a tradesman from time to time to do repairs. Eventually, he'd have to let her go.

Best-case scenario, he'd come up with a solution before he had to fire her. He had a lot of contacts and planned to start looking for a better job for her as soon as he found out what skills she had to offer. Who could resist more money and a nicer place to live? He knew at least two people who owned newly renovated apartment buildings. One of them owed him big-time.

"Anyone home?" A quick rap of knuckles, and the outside door popped open. "Sorry to barge in. It's started raining again." A gorgeous redhead burst into the room, followed by a small girl who hung back in the doorway.

The leggy redhead thrust a bouquet of flowers toward him. "Welcome. I'm Melody from 2B. Close the door, Lacey. You're letting the rain in." She strode over to the kitchen and started going through cupboards as if she lived there. "No vase. I was afraid of that. I'll run upstairs and get one."

She dashed for the door. "Oh, this is Lacey. Lacey, this is…I'm sorry. I've forgotten your name. Jason? Justin?"

Melody from 2B smiled, and the day brightened. "I'm, ah…Jordan Tanner." Way to go, forgetting his own name. "Nice to meet you." He shook her hand. "And, thanks." He held up the flowers grasped in his other hand.

"Nell didn't mention you were so good-looking. I swear that woman needs to get…" She stopped, sparing a sideways glance at the little girl. "Lacey, entertain the gentleman. And take off that wet coat. Nell will kill me if you catch a cold. I'll be right back." When the redheaded vision whirled out of the room, Jordan stared at the child who looked small enough to fold up and put in his pocket. She had her mother's big green eyes, but her curls were fair instead of Nell's dark hair.

Lacey took off her wet raincoat and carefully hung it over the back of a chair. Looking like a little pink puff ball, topped with frothy blond curls, she smoothed her hands over her pink leotard and adjusted the feathery thing around her neck.

"Hello, Mr. Jordan. It's nice to meet you." Jordan couldn't help smiling as he shook her tiny hand.

"It's nice to meet you, too, Lacey. Are you a ballerina?"

"Yes. Would you like me to dance?"

"Maybe we should go find Melody first." He knew squat about kids except they came with a ton of rules. What he did know was Nell had almost killed him yesterday when he'd tried to talk to Jacob. No doubt she'd go ballistic if she found him alone with her precious Lacey.

"Melody will be right back. She's on the phone." Lacey dropped a deep curtsy.

"How do you know that?"

When Lacey pointed at the ceiling, Jordan grimaced at the low murmur of someone talking upstairs. Another wave of wet wool, and—what was that smell, mold?—hit him. It felt as though he were light-years, not mere miles, from his condo.

"Look, I'm a kitty cat."

Lacey hopped and twirled around the room. She didn't remotely remind him of a cat, but she looked so earnest and serious, he smiled encouragement whenever she glanced his way. Which was often. After a few minutes of watching her twirl on one spot, Jordan started to worry. If memory served him right, kids spewed from far less agitation.

"Lacey? Maybe you better—"

Lacey came to an abrupt halt and flung herself into a heap on the floor. Her head drooped down to her chest. She didn't make a sound.

"Um...that was an incredible dance. Thank you." He clapped, hoping the blond curls would stir.

After waiting for a couple of minutes, he reached down to her limp body and wrapped his hand around her amazingly tiny arm. "Are you all right? Did you hurt yourself?"

Like a firecracker, she crackled and fizzed to life as she shot to her feet. "Did I scare ya?" Winding her tiny body around one of his legs, she beamed up at him. Her damp curls framed her sweet, round baby face. Her eyes were so alive with childish delight, Jordan felt a twinge. A twinge of what, he wasn't sure. Maybe a long forgotten memory from his own childhood. Surely there had been good days before he understood his life was never going to be like the other kids. He shoved the past down, out of sight where it belonged.

He smiled at Lacey, gently tried to shake her off. She giggled and wound her arms tighter around his leg. He started to shove his hands in his jean pockets but ended up sticking them under his armpits.

"Maybe you want to let go of my leg."

She continued to beam at him as if he'd invented the sun. "Why?"

"Well." He cleared his throat. "We just met, and it's not a good idea to...with people you've just met it's maybe better…" He had no idea where he was going with the sentence. Lacey twinkled up at him.

"I have to go to the washroom." Genius solution. As they grinned at each other, the door banged open.

Nell stood in the doorway, hands on her hips. "What's going on here?"

Lacey let go of his leg and ran over to wrap herself around Nell's legs instead. Feeling as if he'd been caught doing something he shouldn't have, Jordan scowled at the twin sets of green eyes staring at him. The indomitable duo. Man, if those two sunk their hooks into some poor, clueless guy, he'd be a goner. Thank God he wasn't susceptible to that kind of thing.

"I was dancing for Mr. Jordan," Lacey explained.

"The bunny dance," Jordan added. "It's fascinating. Have you seen it?"

A smile slowly spread over Nell's face. As he watched her body relax against Lacey, he felt as if he'd passed some kind of test. "I think you mean the kitty cat dance. Where's Melody, Lacey?"

"Here," Melody called from the doorway. "I got caught on the phone." She turned to Nell. "I have a four-thirty appointment. I'll have to take a rain check for dinner. Sorry. Nice to meet you, Jason."

"Jordan," he murmured.

She turned back from the door and smiled at him. "I knew that. Oh, here's the vase. You know, if you're really nice to these two ladies, maybe they'll invite you to dinner. I hear their exalted dinner guest bailed."

A bell rang in the deep recesses of the house. "That's

my four-thirty already. Damn that man, he's always so needy. Later, all." Melody slammed out of the room. A moment later, Jordan heard her talking to a man as they ascended the stairs.

He turned to Nell and raised his eyebrows. "Is this something I should be worried about?" If Melody was a call girl he needed to know. That was the kind of thing that could easily scare off potential buyers. He watched Nell closely, waiting for her reply. He didn't think she'd outright lie to him, but neither would she hesitate to protect her friend by not telling the entire truth.

"Do you like curry?" Lacey had crept back to his side and slid her hand into his.

"Um…" He shot a look at Nell, but her face was blank. No help there. "Sure. What kind of curry?"

"Chicken."

"Did someone say curry? I adore curry, especially, chicken curry." Mrs. Trembley stumped into the room on short thick legs that, unfortunately, her bright blue-and-red-plaid shorts didn't cover. She was followed by a frail-looking older man. Had Nell mentioned anything about Mrs. Trembley having a husband?

Nell's shoulders drooped for a second before she pasted a smile on and turned to Mrs. Trembley.

"Rodney! You're here, too. Jordan, this is Rodney. He's a friend of Mrs. Trembley's."

"He's staying with me for a while. Just until he's feeling better. Isn't that right, Rodney?" Jordan winced when Mrs. Trembley poked Rodney in his painfully thin ribs.

Rodney nodded in Jordan's direction but avoided eye contact. He looked as though he was about to pull his forelock and bend a knee. Jordan looked around the crowded room. His crowded room. He already had tenants of every possible description. Why not throw an English servant into the mix?

"I'm hungry." Lacey tugged on his hand.

Nell headed for the door. "I'll have to cook more rice and see what else I have on hand. Come on, Lacey. Jacob's waiting upstairs."

It didn't even occur to her to say no. Amazing. Jordan stepped sideways to block her exit. "Ever hear about takeout?"

"Takeout?" Nell repeated. The room grew suspiciously quiet. "It costs too much. I mean, there're four of us, two of them. Melody will want to eat once she smells the food, even though she claims she's bailed. No, it's okay. I'll cook more rice, and see what else I can throw together."

He felt a jolt as he caught her arm just above her wrist to stop her. Their eyes connected for a second, a look of surprise and cautious curiosity passing between them before she pulled away. "I saw an Indian restaurant a few blocks over when I was driving here. I'll order some food and pick it up while you cook the rice. It'll be my treat. Sort of a new-landlord get-to-know-you meal. Anything I shouldn't get?"

"Just make sure all the sauces are mild," Mrs. Trembley piped up. "Too much spice gives me gas."

That was a detail he could have done without. When

no one else offered any objections to him buying dinner, Jordan shoved the flowers in the vase and splashed some water in it, then snagged his jacket and went outside. He was about to dash to his car when he realized he'd left most of his tenants in his apartment. He turned back, held the door open. "If everyone's finished in here?"

Mrs. Trembley shuffled out with Rodney following like a faithful dog. Lacey skipped after them, her raincoat draped over her head. Nell stopped at the door, a crease forming between her eyebrows as she frowned up at him.

"I'm sorry you got pulled into this dinner thing. If you want to bail, I'll tell the crew you had a former engagement. I can scrounge together enough food for everyone. It's not a problem."

His tough little caretaker was trying to protect him from his tenants. Unbelievable. Or, he narrowed his eyes, she didn't want him talking to them for some reason. She'd said it herself, Aunt Beulah hadn't paid attention to anything unless it directly affected her. God knows what Nell had been up to the past two years; charging for repairs that hadn't been done. Or for building materials never used, then refunded. There were a number of ways for her to skim extra money off the top. Miss Nellie had been running things her way for too long. She was about to discover what it was like to have someone else in charge.

"As I said, it'll give me a chance to get to know everyone better. Unless, of course, it's too much work for you. You didn't plan on having so many people for supper." He smiled, waiting to see if she would take the bait and wiggle out of the invitation.

"I can handle it if you can." She gave him a quick two-finger salute and scooted out the door.

She'd passed with flying colors. He didn't know whether to be reassured or not as he flipped up his collar against the rain and ran for his car. Dinner at Dunstan Lane. Not what he'd call a hot Saturday-night date, but it was a necessary one. He needed to find out if Miss Nellie was as sweet as she seemed or if she'd been lining her pockets with the monthly operating budget. If there even was a monthly budget. What if Beulah had left Nell a pot of money to use at her discretion? Could she have been that batty?

He climbed into his car and with an unfamiliar weariness, wiped the rain from his face. He also needed to know more about his tenants so he wouldn't be blindsided by any unsavory details, like an illegal prostitution ring or…at this point, the imagination was the limit.

As a business consultant he was used to not only assessing tangible assets but personalities, as well. He'd have the tenants of Dunstan Lane categorized, lined up and flying straight before the week was over. Buying dinner was a good place to start.

SWEAT TRICKLED DOWN THE MIDDLE of Nell's back as she whipped around her small kitchen. She'd planned to have a long, hot soak in the bath tonight while Jacob and Lacey watched the movie she'd rented for them, not prepare and serve a meal for six—or seven if Melody showed up. And especially not for Jordan Tanner. She grabbed a stack of plates out of the cupboard and placed them on the small table along with the cutlery and napkins. Water, tea or coffee would have to suffice. She could barely afford to buy juice for the kids let alone wine or beer for guests. She placed the coffeepot under the tap and turned on the water.

For the life of her, she couldn't understand why she was so stressed about having everyone over for dinner. Mrs. T. had a habit of popping up close to supper time once or twice a week, and Rodney... Nell sighed. Taking on two small children should have been enough for anyone. Melody liked to tease her that she'd taken the role of caretaker to heart. She had to learn how to say no more often.

And now she had Tanner to deal with. Not that he needed her help, but he was a man who had a certain presence. A man who would take up way too much space in her already crowded life.

And wasn't that a shame?

Three years ago, it might have been a different story. Yeah, right. Who was she kidding? She'd never circulated with the yuppie crowd. She'd always had her hands stuck in the soil or had been cramming in as many lectures as she could after work on landscape design or plant propagation.

Not that she didn't still have aspirations. She lingered over the word for a minute; it had such a hopeful sound.

But Jacob and Lacey's welfare came first now, which meant her dreams would have to wait. Anyone with half a brain could see Tanner was going places, expensive places. Dunstan Lane was a means to an end for him. For Nell, Dunstan Lane was familiar and secure, a home for her and the kids.

"I think you've got enough water, Nell," Jacob commented from his station by the kitchen doorway.

Startled, Nell pulled the coffeepot from under the stream of water. "Did you make your bed?"

"Yeah. I don't know why I can't have a lock on my door. Mrs. T. always snoops around."

She dumped coffee grinds into the machine and turned it on, the muscles in her neck cranking tighter. "We've been over this, Jacob. I need to know I can get into your room in case you hurt yourself."

"If we bought a lock with two keys, you could have one and go into my room when you want."

The child drove her nuts with his logic. In the beginning, she'd tried reasoning with him when they disagreed. But she'd soon learned Jacob could outreason anyone, and much to her chagrin, she resorted more often than not to the dreaded because-I-said-so refrain.

"That's a good point. I'll think about it." Another empty phrase that didn't fool either of them. From the corner of her eye, she watched Jacob drum his fist against the doorjamb.

"Are you upset people are coming for dinner?"

"No." *Rap, rap.*

"Do you like Mr. Tanner?"

He rounded one shoulder. "I guess. Do you?"

Nell blew out her breath and leaned against the counter. "I haven't made up my mind yet." Truth was there was way too much to like about him. Other than trying to bribe Jacob, he'd been unfailingly kind and courteous. When everyone else had heard the mention of food, they'd lined up at the trough. Tanner, on the other hand, had offered to help by paying for the meal. A meal she wouldn't have to prepare other than dumping it into serving dishes. Imagine having someone like that to lean on once in a while.

She straightened her spine. No need to get carried away. Tanner was taking advantage of the opportunity to check them out. How long would it take for Mrs. T. to insult him or Rodney to let slip that he'd been staying in the bedsit rent-free? Now that he'd moved in, she'd have to be on guard all the time, and the only way to get rid of him was if the house sold. Lord, she wasn't ready for any of this. "We probably won't see too much of him," she said to Jacob. "He's a busy man."

"Yeah." Jacob started to leave the room but turned back. "Nell?"

Finally they were going to get down to what was bothering her little man. "What is it, sweetie?"

"Dad called. You said to tell you if he did."

Nell stopped short of slamming the cupboard door shut. The closer Tony got to his parole hearing the more often he phoned. She tried to intercept his calls, but he was their father and her lawyer had cautioned her to treat him with kid gloves until the adoption went through. Especially now, because of the complaints he'd lodged with Child Welfare.

Nell had never understood what her sister had seen in him. Tony had the uncanny ability to know within minutes of meeting someone exactly how to hurt that person the most. But he was careful whom he chose to abuse.

Jacob and Lacey were often sullen and withdrawn after talking to him, and no wonder. The man was poison. The day her sister died, she promised herself she would do whatever was necessary to keep her niece and nephew in her custody. That promise was turning out to be a lot harder to keep than she'd anticipated.

Nell threaded her fingers together as she prepared to pick through the minefield that existed between Jacob and Tony. "How is he?"

Her question was met with a shrug. "He said he wants to see Lacey and me."

Why? She bit back the word before it popped out. "What did you say?"

"That I'd ask you." His eyes grew red.

"Oh, honey." She moved to hug him, but he jerked out of reach. Having been on the receiving end of Tony's vindictive tirades many times, she knew how deep his words could cut. It hurt that there was nothing she could say to ease Jacob's pain.

A knock at the door interrupted their conversation. Later, after everyone was gone, she'd try to get Jacob to talk about his father. She grabbed him, gave him a quick hug and a whispered "I love you," then let him escape into his room while she answered the door.

JORDAN DELIVERED THE CARTONS of food to the kitchen and retreated to the living room when Melody elbowed him out of the way. Guess the smell of food had reached all the way down to her apartment. Whatever her "client" had needed, it hadn't taken long to satisfy. Jacob had disappeared somewhere, smart fellow, and Lacey was serving Mrs. Trembley watered-down tea in teacups the size of his thumb.

He sat on the opposite end of the couch from Rodney and accepted a thimbleful of tea from Lacey. He'd anticipated this dinner to be more like a meeting, but everything felt way too cozy for his comfort. How was he supposed to calculate assets and ulterior motives when a little girl was serving him tea, for Pete's sake?

Although Nell's apparent fatigue had prompted him to offer to buy takeout, he'd realized on the way to the restaurant, it would also earn him brownie points with Nell and get supper over more quickly. He needed to see the books, ask her what the profit margin was, what kind of budget she worked with, and what shape the old house was in.

He wrinkled his nose and studied Rodney. The old man smelled musty, the same moth-eaten stink that was in Jordan's room. As Jordan started to smile, Rodney smiled in return, giving him a glimpse of the man he used to be. That was why Nell refused to show him the room yesterday; Rodney had been living there. It also explained why he was staying with Mrs. Trembley. With his new insight, Jordan's mind raced over everything that had happened in the past two days. He'd assumed these were normal people, but he should have known better; normal wasn't Aunt Beulah's style. He'd better check the basement and any outbuildings in case Miss Nellie had a whole colony of misfits squirreled away.

Nell peeked into the room. There were dark circles under her eyes, but she kept her tone upbeat. "Dinner is ready. It's self-serve."

Jordan's appetite suddenly disappeared. Nell shouldn't let people take advantage of her, bringing up two children alone was more than enough responsibility. He could help with that. Not the kids, but the taking advantage part. He was good at maneuvering people around to his point of view. Mrs. Trembley and Rodney wouldn't know what hit them. As for Melody...

What was he thinking? He was the worst culprit of all. If Alex found a buyer tomorrow, Nell and the kids would have to go or start paying a much higher rent. He'd been working his butt off, hoping for a break since he was fifteen, and inheriting this house was as close as he was going to get.

Okay, maybe his mom's life would have been better if someone had held out a helping hand. But no one had, at least not in time to save her, and he'd survived. Hell, he'd thrived. Nell and her children would, too. That didn't mean he wouldn't try to find a way around the whole mess.

He stood, rolled his head back and forth to ease his aching neck muscles. There was a solution to every problem. He just had to find it.

NELL WEARILY LIFTED HER HEAD from the couch when the door to the apartment creaked open. Tanner had left in his sparkly, expensive car two hours ago. Hopefully, he hadn't returned already with more questions. She didn't think he bought the story about Rodney staying with Mrs. T.

Melody slipped into the living room and beamed at her, her hands behind her back. "Guess what I have."

Nell pulled herself upright. "A magic wand to make Tanner go away?"

"They do sell wands at work. And there's this guy who comes into the store who's into magic. I wonder if I—"

"Is that a cold beer?"

"Voilà." Melody brandished a beer in her direction. "One for both of us. I thought you'd appreciate it after that excruciating supper. I was sitting on pins and needles waiting for Mrs. T. to start one of her tirades. And Jordan is so intense. Amazingly good-looking, but wow, the waves of energy he gives off." She sat on a padded stool and opened her beer.

Nell took a long, appreciative swallow of hers. "Intense. That's one way to describe him."

"And hot," Melody added.

"I wish he'd go be hot somewhere else."

Melody wiggled her eyebrows. "He got to you, did he?"

"I'm tired, not dead. I think he even got Mrs. T. worked up. Did you see how much lipstick she layered on? How about you? Tanner do anything for you?" She held her breath, as if Melody's answer were important. Which was silly, if Melody wanted to dally with Tanner, it wasn't any of her business.

"He's not my type."

"Not mine, either." Nell took another drink and put the bottle on the coffee table in front of her.

"Things are going to change, Nell. We knew that when Beulah died."

"I know. I just didn't expect…Tanner. He's so take-charge. So focused."

Melody smiled. "Kind of like the pot calling the kettle black, isn't it?"

"You think I'm bossy?"

Melody's smile disappeared. "I've watched you fight hard to keep everything on an even keel the past two years. Which is understandable, considering what you and the kids have been through. But you can't control the entire world. Sometimes you have to go with the flow."

Nell pleated the bottom edge of her cotton blouse. "You think I should give up without a fight?"

"I think you should give Jordan a chance. Who knows, maybe something good could come out of this."

"You're trying to set me up with him." Nell laughed at the absurd idea.

"All I'm saying is, why does change always have to be a bad thing? Why can't you have fun with it?"

Nell smiled. Melody was a good-time girl who reminded Nell to laugh when life turned weird. She did silly things like buy them secondhand cocktail dresses and insist they dress up and go out for a drink, if only for an hour. Or slip her delicious romance novels that Nell read late at night instead of how-to books. She discussed Harry Potter for hours with Jacob and bought Lacey's pink ballet outfit. Over the past two years, she'd slowly filled the hole left from the death of Nell's sister. She liked that Melody made her look at things differently. Not that she was right about Tanner. Nothing was going to happen there.

"You're one to talk," Nell countered. "I have the kids. What's your excuse for hanging around here instead of going out and having fun?"

"I'm still recovering from Peter What's-his-name. Talk about a total lack of judgment. I'm not looking at another man until I know for certain he's the one."

Nell leaned her chin on her hand. "You think there's The One for everyone?"

"There is for you."

She let the comment pass. She didn't want her fortune told tonight, or any other night. "I think Tanner plans to sell the house."

"I was afraid of that. Has he said anything definite?"

"No, but he almost had a heart attack when I told him what I was paying for rent. I don't know what I'm going to do if he raises it. Any other time, I'd suck it up and look for a cheaper apartment, but right now... Tony's been phoning the kids again. I know he's up to something. He's not getting those kids. I don't care if he is their father. He's an abusive alcoholic, and Jacob and Lacey are not living with him. Ever." She gulped back the fear in her throat.

Melody sat beside her and slipped her arm around Nell's shoulders. "It's going to be okay. There are far worse things than looking for new digs. And Tanner, sure he's focused, but I think underneath that polished exterior lives a good man. Tell him about the adoption. A few weeks one way or the other, what difference does it make to him for selling the house? He'll understand." She smiled. "After the adoption, we'll look for a new apartment together. No way am I staying here without you and the kids."

Nell leaned against her friend for a second before pulling away. Melody was right. They'd survive moving, could maybe even afford a nicer place with Melody sharing the rent. But not until the children were legally hers. The social worker had emphasized over and over the need to provide a stable home atmosphere. Jacob and Lacey had been in this apartment for two years now, half of Lacey's life. Moving was bound to stir up some of the anxieties they'd worked hard to leave behind. Jacob had already reverted to hiding in his tent, although he'd dismantled it before people came for dinner.

She picked up her bottle and drank the last of her beer. At the very least, she'd try to convince Tanner to delay the sale of the house. Maybe Melody was right. Maybe he'd understand.

CHAPTER THREE

A SCREECH JERKED JORDAN out of a deep sleep the next morning. He blinked at the alarm clock. Eight o'clock. It was the weekend, wasn't it? Forty miles and a universe away, his condo would be quieter than a church.

Another screech ripped through his open window, followed by a full belly laugh. "You're it."

Jordan groaned as he burrowed into his pillow. That would be Jacob. The laugh, no doubt, was Nell's.

"Am not. You didn't touch me." Lacey, his little kitty cat.

Jordan catapulted out of bed, pulled on a pair of jeans and stalked to the window. *His* kitty cat? Man, one day and the place was driving him nuts already.

A reluctant smile spread over his face as he watched Nell let Lacey tackle her to the ground. Jacob piled on top of them with a whoop. All he could see of Nell was one hand waving in the air, and her overalls-clad legs.

A memory of his mom playing tag with him in a park blindsided him. She'd take him to the park down the street early on Saturday mornings before whatever lout she'd hauled home the previous night woke up. He lived for those mornings with his mom. How could he have forgotten them? He snapped the blind closed.

He hoped Nell changed her clothes after breakfast. He needed to talk to her this morning, and he didn't want any distractions.

A giggle from outside followed him as he wandered over to the kitchen corner and dug his espresso machine out of a box. As soon as he talked to Nell, he was out of here. He didn't know where he was going, just that he was. A solid twenty-four-hour stint at Dunstan Lane was more than enough; the walls were closing in on him. He already knew way more than he wanted to about his tenants, and yet he knew next to nothing about Nell. He'd hoped to talk to her last night, but after supper she'd explained she and the children had a winding-down-the-day routine that was important to adhere to. She didn't have time for him. Well she'd better *make* time this morning or he'd have to let her know who was boss. He dumped water and coffee into the machine, turned it on and headed for the shower.

A lukewarm trickle of water dripped down on him. "Oh, come on." He thumped on the side of the showerhead, regretting his action as the sound of cheap metal reverberated through his head. Hell. He peered at the taps. Yup, that was supposed to be hot water. He turned the tap off and tried the other one. An even smaller trickle of cold water eked out.

Starting the day without a shower was not acceptable. But it was his first morning, and obviously there were a few kinks that had to be worked out. He splashed cold water on his face and reached for a towel that wasn't there. Okay, maybe he needed to unpack before heading out. He'd have a coffee, then corner Nell and find out what the problem was with the water. At least he'd had enough water for coffee.

But no milk. Jordan slammed the refrigerator door closed. He took a sip of black coffee and spit it out. He could throw back shots of Scotch, bourbon and tequila, but he could not drink his coffee without milk. Without thinking, he strode to the door and threw it open.

"Nell!" he bellowed.

The three of them froze midchase. Nell's eyes were as round as saucers as she swiveled toward him. For God's sake, the overalls were bad enough, did she have to wear another damned cropped shirt?

She rushed toward him. "Are you okay?"

And suddenly, just like that, he was.

NELL STOPPED A FEW FEET short of Jordan. *Wowzers!* Her lungs collapsed, devoid of oxygen. Of course she'd seen half-naked men before. But this…Jordan's chest…. She bent over at the waist and tried to catch her breath. Hopefully, he'd think she was winded from playing with the kids, not overwhelmed by the sight of his magnificent torso. She slowly straightened and just as slowly, sucked in some air. His shoulders were wide, his chest broad with a sprinkling of dark hair that very nicely arrowed down over a flat tummy and disappeared into his low-riding jeans.

She peeled her tongue off the top of her mouth and managed to tear her gaze away from all that manly muscle and skin. She raised her eyebrows. "Problems?"

"You do know it's the weekend, don't you? Some people like to sleep in. It's not even nine o'clock."

Nell tried to hide her smile. It looked like someone had the grouchies. "Children don't sleep in. Ever. But—" she held up her hand to halt his protest "—because this is your first day, we'll be nice and move our games elsewhere. Okay?"

His scowl deepened. "I'm sorry for grumbling, but I got off to a bad start. There's no water and I don't have any milk for my coffee."

She swallowed a curse. How many times had she asked Mrs. T. to wait to do her laundry until midafternoon when most of them were out of the house? Maybe she should send Tanner up there to chew her out.

"Jacob." She twisted round and beckoned him over.

Jacob smiled shyly at their new landlord. "Hey, Mr. Tanner. Look, the sun's out finally."

Tanner looked around the side yard as if seeing it for the first time. "Yeah, nice day." He turned to Nell. "Is this a double lot? Can you subdivide here?"

Unbelievable. The guy probably never switched off. "Jacob, would you run upstairs and get Mr. Tanner the milk? Lacey?" She curled her arm around the sweaty little girl when she ran to Nell's side. "I have to go down to the basement to fix the pump. You can stay outside, but you have to play in the backyard. Okay?"

Lacey nodded, her eyes glued to Tanner's chest. "Is he naked, Nell?"

Nell choked back a laugh as red stained Tanner's cheeks. "No, sweetpea. Naked is when you're not wearing anything. Like when you get out of the bath." Or make love. She felt her own cheeks flush at the thought.

She ruffled Lacey's hair. "Okay, backyard for you, little one, while I see what I can do about the water."

"Hang on. Let me grab a shirt and some shoes. I wanted to look at the basement today, anyway."

Nell fidgeted as she waited for Tanner to get dressed. She hoped he was more interested in looking around the basement than helping her, because it was a tight squeeze in the corner where the pump was. And a tight squeeze was exactly what she needed to avoid when it came to her landlord. She had a long list of reasons for keeping him at a distance, and right at the top were the children and not giving Tony any reason to interfere with the adoption. It would be just like the rat to send a couple of his friends to sniff around her life to see if they could find any weakness.

When Tony had first gone to jail he'd been so full of remorse for killing Mary, he'd signed over legal guardianship of the children to Nell. But with his first chance for parole coming up, he was looking for ways to get them back. Nell had no illusions as to why Tony wanted Jacob and Lacey. He thought he had a better chance for parole if he could say they were waiting for their daddy. Even though drinking with his buddies had always held more interest for him than spending time with his kids. To top it off, he was a mean drunk. Despite the warm morning air, Nell shivered. Rescuing Mary and the kids when Tony was on the rampage had increased in frequency the last year of her sister's life.

But when Mary had sworn things were going better with her marriage, Nell let herself be convinced and had agreed to go away for that long-delayed weekend with her boyfriend, Barry. She hadn't been there when Mary needed her the most, and her sister had died. Nell intended to make up for that mistake until her last breath, but she still didn't think it would be enough.

Strike two. It had happened before. People she loved had died because she'd let them down. It was never going to happen again.

She stuck her hands in her pockets and rolled back on her heels. Her life was one big complicated mess. And getting worse by the minute.

Tanner strode out of his apartment at the same time Jacob returned with the milk. His "Thanks, man," earned him a big grin from her little boy.

Jacob hitched up his jeans. "Need any help, Nell?"

Her heart softened at his manly offer. "I'll manage. Thanks. Can you keep an eye on Lacey for a few minutes?"

"Sure thing. See ya, Mr. Tanner."

"Jacob?" Jacob turned back to Tanner.

"Yeah?"

"Call me Jordan, okay, pal?"

If his grin got any wider, Jacob's face would split. "Sure thing, Mr.—Jordan."

Nell watched with envy as the two males exchanged a look. She'd spent the past two years trying to coax Jacob out of his shell. She knew he loved her and had learned to trust her, but what had just passed between

Jordan and Jacob was different. Obviously, she hadn't been born with the right equipment to earn that kind of connection. While it wasn't fair, it was also worrisome. Tanner was looking to make a fast buck, not lifelong friends.

"Sorry to keep you waiting." Wearing a white T-shirt that clung to well-defined muscles, Tanner smiled down at her. Hard to tell the man made a living behind a desk. Why couldn't he have been fat and balding? Have bad teeth, bad breath? Anything. He was too perfect for his own good.

Nell sighed in defeat, led the way to the front door of the house and pulled a key ring from her pockets.

"The house has its own well," she explained as she unlocked the door. "We're just outside village limits. If the tenants take everyone's needs into consideration, it works out okay." She switched on the basement light and started down the stairs, Tanner so close on her heels, she felt heat from his body.

"What does that mean?"

"It means if you want to do laundry, it's better to wait until the middle of the day when most of us are gone."

"Let me guess, Mrs. Trembley."

Oh, no, she wasn't giving Tanner any ammo to evict the old gal. Mrs. T. barely got by as it was. She'd never find another apartment for four hundred a month. Ignoring him as best she could, Nell switched on the light in the dark corner where the pump was installed.

"This will only take a minute. Why don't you look

around? The foundation's not bad for being over a hundred years old."

"I want to see what you're doing in case I ever have to fix the pump."

Nell swore under her breath as he crowded in after her. "You open this valve and let the air escape for a few minutes. Once the water starts coming out, you close the valve and hope there's enough in the well to bring the pressure up."

Tanner stood at least a foot above her, his broad shoulders blocking most of the light. If he'd been anyone else, she'd have elbowed him to get him to back off. But he was her landlord and part-time employer. And yeah, his heat warmed her in places she'd been cold for what felt like forever. He smelled good, too. Damn it.

She closed the valve when the water spurted into the bucket she'd left the last time she'd had trouble. "Okay, show's over. Can you back up? I'm suffocating in here."

In the dim light she saw him grin. "Is that what you call it?"

She followed as he squeezed out of the narrow space, tension stiffening her spine. She needed to set Tanner straight right now. She took care of the building. That was it. Being the landlord did not come with fringe benefits. "In case you haven't noticed, I've got kids. I can't afford to fool around."

His gray eyes darkened, his gaze straying to her midsection and staying there. She tried not to squirm as heat coiled in her belly. She was wearing overalls, for heaven's sake. *Overalls.* Was the man sex deprived?

"I didn't figure you for a coward." As his voice slid over her, she dug her fingernails into the palms of her hands. They were so not going to happen.

"Listen, Tanner. You seem like a nice man, but you're not getting it. Jacob and Lacey have had a rough life. I know you're not planning on being around for long, and I'm asking you to not get too close to them. Or me. You'll only end up hurting them if you do."

JORDAN'S HEAD JERKED BACK as if she'd slapped him. Man, Miss Nellie didn't believe in dressing up her message. Which could be an asset in certain situations. But not when he'd been about to make a move on her. First it was the glimpses of her smooth, flat belly that had him salivating, then he'd fixated on her ears. They were tiny and pink and damned near perfect. He wanted to explore…everything about her. She fascinated him.

Thank goodness one of them was thinking straight. She had kids. Period. He was out of here as soon as the house sold, and he wasn't looking for a ready-made family. Not that Lacey and Jacob weren't nice kids. Having only known them a day, it surprised him how often they popped into his head. He thought about their mother more, especially about what she wore under her overalls. Each time he caught himself thinking about Nell, he tried to turn it off, but there was something about her that made him a little crazy. He needed to get his priorities straight; he'd never had trouble focusing on his goals before. He'd clawed his way out of his childhood, and he planned to keep on climbing until... well, he'd know when he'd arrived.

Jordan put his hands up in surrender. "Message coming through loud and clear. You're right. They're good kids, and I don't want to hurt them. Or you."

He pivoted away and studied the rock walls of the basement. It was one thing to lust after Miss Nellie, another thing entirely to get caught up in her problems.

"Good to know you don't have anyone stashed down here," he said in an attempt to lighten the mood. When she chuckled, he felt a spurt of pride, as if he'd accomplished something important.

"I'd like to have my own set of keys to the house," he added as he followed her up the stairs a few minutes later.

She hesitated for a brief second before continuing on. "Of course. I think I still have Beulah's set somewhere."

"I'd also like to have a look at the books."

She came to a dead stop and turned around. "What books?"

"Your operating budget. You know, expenses, the rent collected."

"Oh, that. Terry Folger takes care of the rent money, and when I need cash to fix something, he gives it to me. I'll give you his number."

Of course Beulah wouldn't let just anyone handle the money. What had he been thinking? She may have been eccentric, but according to his mother, Beulah had been canny about money. If Folger measured up to his standards, all he had to worry about was the non-paying tenants, the low rents. Repairs. Might as well find out exactly what he was up against right away.

"I haven't had a chance to look around outside. Are there any outbuildings?"

"An old garage in the backyard. I store the lawn mower and yard tools in it. Oh, and the occasional alien. Would you like to see it?"

He laughed and opened the door for her. There were three vehicles in the driveway on this side of the house; a red Toyota Yaris, a gray Ford sedan and a battered old quarter-ton pickup truck. Not hard to guess who drove the truck.

"Yours?" He kicked the front tire as they walked past.

"Bought and paid for." She hesitated at the corner of the house. "I, uh, dug up the backyard when I first moved in. Beulah didn't mind."

Jordan was struck speechless when he rounded the corner of the house. Nell had turned the yard into a paradise. He didn't know much about flowers, but even he recognized a marigold when he saw one. Bright yellow and orange marigolds rimmed a tomato patch. When he bent down, he saw several ripe tomatoes peeking out from under dark green leaves. Lacey waved to him from a swing that hung from an old oak in the far corner. Beside her, water trickled over a small man-made—or woman-made—waterfall. Sitting on a wood bench beside the waterfall, Rodney stopped cleaning his fingernails with his jackknife to nod at Jordan. Sunflowers lined the back wall of the house.

The sun warmed his back, and tension he hadn't realized he was carrying slid off his shoulders.

"You did all this?" Miss Nellie was an artist in her own right.

She nudged the loose soil with the toe of her sneaker. "It took me two years. Rodney's been helping lately. He used to be a farmer. "

"Hey, Jordan."

Jordan looked up into the canopy of green oak leaves. Jacob was lying on what appeared to be a small front porch of a half-built tree house.

Nell had built a paradise for her kids. And she was willing to share it with a man like Rodney? The hair on the back of his neck rose. What did she know about the guy? He looked like he belonged in a hospital, or, God forbid, that street corner in Seabend where all the winos hung out. The more Jordan looked at him, the more he was convinced he recognized him. He passed that corner several times a week when he was jogging.

He grabbed Nell's elbow and propelled her toward the garage, a generous name for the decrepit structure. "Let's check out those aliens."

"No problem." She pulled the keys out again and unlocked the side door. The garage was dim with light trickling in from one dusty window and the open door behind him. Crammed full with bits and pieces of everyone's lives, plus the requisite lawn mower and tools, there was barely enough room for him and Nell to stand inside.

"What's the story on Rodney?" he asked.

"Oh." Nell plucked a rag from a basket beside her and started wiping down an old dresser that was missing one drawer. "He's been sick, but he's getting stronger every day."

"I can see he's ill. Where does he live?"

She chucked the rag back into the basket and met his glare straight on. "He was living on the streets in Seabend, but he was sick. So I brought him home and let him stay in your room for a few days. Like I said, he's getting better. He'll move on soon. He's not one to accept charity lightly."

Jordan suppressed the urge to shake some sense into her. Didn't she know what kind of people lived on the streets? "You brought a bum home and let him stay? Are you crazy? He could be a serial killer for all you know."

"He's a sweet man who recently lost his wife of forty years and can't stand to go home."

"You knew this before you brought him here?"

"Some of it. I knew him years ago. My parents had a convenience store, and he used to sell eggs to them."

A tenuous connection at best. "He has to go, Nell."

Nell leaned forward and pushed the door shut. "Let him stay for a couple more weeks, just until he's stronger. I'll…I'll make it up to you."

Jordan's black mood lifted. Negotiations. Home ground for him. Once he finished with Nell, he'd drill

Rodney about who he was and why he was hanging around Dunstan Lane. "How?"

Nell's eyes went a little wild, then she settled. "I'll cook you supper for the next two weeks. I'm a good cook."

He folded his arms over his chest and tried his best not to smile. Nothing sweeter than having the upper hand. "Not good enough. What else?"

"I'll do your laundry. And clean your room." She murmured the last under her breath.

"Deal." He stuck out his hand and shook hers. He knew when not to push too hard and by the murderous look in her eye, he'd reached her limit. "You can start today. My room stinks."

"I can't. I have to go to work."

"I thought you were at work."

"I have another job at a garden center. I try not to work weekends, but I couldn't get out of it this time. They close at seven on Saturdays, but maybe I can clean your room after the kids are in bed."

Jordan bit back a curse. He hadn't realized Nell worked another job. He'd thought…he hadn't thought, had he? He didn't know the first thing about her. "Forget the room and laundry. But just so we understand each other, no more strays. This is not a charitable enterprise."

"Gotcha." She looked so downcast, he wondered who else she'd planned to drag home. Taking advantage of an absent landlord was no laughing matter, especially if you were the landlord. So why did he feel like laughing? It was going to be a challenge keeping up with Nell. Good thing he thrived on challenges.

"How many jobs do you have?"

"Just the garden center and here."

Neither of which put much money in her pocket. This was the perfect opportunity to see how he could help her move on to something new. "If you had your pick, what would your dream job be?"

Nell leaned against the dresser and hooked her thumbs inside her overalls. "That's easy. Farmer."

"Farmer?" Of course he knew somewhere out there farmers were hard at work, but it had never occurred to him anyone actually aspired to be one.

"I'm hoping once the kids get a bit older, I can rent an old farm and start growing herbs. I want to make tinctures and essential oils and dried herbs. Teas, too." She glowed as she listed the products.

"Herbs," he repeated.

"Like oregano and sage. You do know what herbs are, don't you?"

"Of course. I just... Is there a market for those products? Can you make a living growing that sh...stuff?"

She shot him an incredulous look. "Where have you been, Tanner? People are crazy about them."

In whose universe? Certainly not his. Why did people always think starting a business was easy? "Have you thought about the business side of this venture? How much land would you need? How would you get your product to market? Who's your target group?"

She beamed up at him. "I have a business plan.

Maybe you could look at it. You'd probably have some great ideas. This is wonderful. Rodney's going to make me a still, and you can iron out the wrinkles in my business plan. I knew it was all going to come together for me. I just didn't think—"

"Hold on. Back up a minute. What's this about a still? Isn't that illegal?"

"I don't think so." She dug a small notebook out of her back pocket and jotted something down. "I'll have to check on that, but I think it's more what you make with the still than the actual equipment. Like hemp oil. That would probably be illegal."

Jordan swallowed a surge of panic. "Please tell me you're not growing that stuff here."

She glanced up from her notes. "What stuff?"

"Marijuana."

"Of course not. I wouldn't do anything to jeopardize the adoption."

"Adoption?"

She stared at him for a minute, looking as confused as he felt. "I forgot you don't know about that. Lacey and Jacob are my sister's children. She died in a car accident two years ago, and they've been living with me ever since. The adoption is all set to go through. Their father, Tony, he's making a few waves, but I think it's going to be okay. We just have to get through the next few weeks without any big upsets. It's going to be okay," she repeated.

Okay for who? Jordan staggered from one dizzying thought to another. He'd assumed Nell was their mother.

Anyone could see she loved the kids. But she wasn't; she was adopting them. And it all came down to the next few weeks. He got a bad taste in the back of his throat like he did every time a deal started going sour on him. When had the government ever accomplished anything on time? "Exactly when is the adoption set to go through?"

"The social worker said it would be soon. Maybe a month at the most. And then, you know, Tony. I think he's changing his mind about letting me adopt the kids." She huddled down into herself. Obviously, things weren't as okay as she wanted to believe.

"Tony's the dad?"

"Yeah. Tony Bleecher."

"Where is he?"

"Jail." She tried to smile, but failed miserably. "He was drunk, and my sister… I don't know what happened. She got in the car with him, and they…he… there was an accident. She died. He's serving five years for drinking and driving causing death, but he's up for parole soon."

Getting details from her was like pulling nails out of concrete. "And the kids won't live with him when he gets out because…?"

She wrapped her arms around her waist. "Tony's… different. To meet him you'd think he was a nice guy. He comes from a rich family and is well-educated. But he's mean beneath the nice-guy act. He'd pinch my sister so hard she'd have a bruise for weeks, but only where no one would see. And if he thought you weren't important, he'd say things to you, especially if he was drinking. Stuff that would make you feel lousy about yourself even though you knew it wasn't true. Lacey and Jacob are scared of him. He's a mean drunk."

Bile burned Jordan's throat as he forced his clenched fists open. He hated the thought that anyone, but especially their father, would hurt Jacob and Lacey.

An endless procession of his mother's boyfriends had tromped through his life, dispensing slaps, punches and toxic comments in their wake. Even now, he could coast along for the longest time, think he'd forgotten the abuse, but the slightest trigger, such as what Nell had just told him, would bring back the appalling helplessness he'd felt as a child.

He took a minute before he spoke; the last thing Nell needed was another angry guy. "So you're going to adopt them," he said in a mild voice.

"Yeah. But I love them, too. I *want* to adopt them."

How could he possibly sell the house until the adoption went through, and Nell and the kids were safe? Jordan closed his eyes, hoping the whole situation would magically disappear. But a minute later, when he opened his eyes, Nell still looked as though she was expecting her world to bottom out. Damn it. There had to be another way out of the mess.

"What about your parents? Do they support your decision?"

"My parents died when I was twelve. I've been pretty much on my own since then."

"No one lets a twelve-year-old run around on their own. Were you in foster care?"

"My aunt took us in."

"And?"

She shrugged. "Aunt May already had five kids. I was the oldest of the whole brood, so I became chief cook and bottle washer. No big deal."

And she'd been taking care of people since. Just his luck that Nell Hart was an incredibly giving, sexy, smart woman. And she was standing between him and everything he'd ever wanted. "So, bottom line, you need to maintain the status quo until after the adoption. There's nothing else you can do to guarantee it'll go through?"

A flicker of amusement lit her eyes. "I could get married."

Jordan choked. "Good luck with that one. For the record, I'm not looking to get married anytime soon."

Nell reached past him to shove the door open. "Relax, big guy. I hadn't even considered you."

"Was that an insult?"

She laughed a warm throaty chuckle. He liked the sound. It made him want to do something goofy to hear it again. Man, he had to get out of the shed and away from her. But first he had to let Nell know he understood how important it was for her to adopt Jacob and Lacey. Maybe it was time to do something for someone else, for a change.

"Okay, I'm not on board with the marriage bit, but

anything else I can do to help make the adoption go smoothly, you've got it. Let's make this happen."

NELL KNEW WHAT TANNER was saying was important, and in a minute she'd nail down exactly what he meant. She just needed a second to settle. Her brain had heard the supportive message, but her body had shifted into flight mode—drumming heartbeat, energy skimming along her veins. It was the way he'd said "we" that had thrown her. Stupid, but automatic. She didn't do "we" these days. And she certainly didn't do it with Tanner. He was the kind of man a woman like her could really fall for. But he wasn't staying, and she wasn't going anywhere. End of story.

She settled her hands on her hips and called up her best don't-mess-with-me attitude. "What are we talking about here, Tanner?"

She hardened her gaze when his mouth twitched at the corners. He better not be messing with her.

The angles of his face softened. "Save some of that energy for fighting the bad guys, Nell. You're aware I'm planning on selling the house?"

Watching him closely, she nodded. Last night Melody had warned her he wasn't stupid, that he'd do everything he could to make the house look like a good deal. Not that she needed Melody to tell her that. Beulah Winer may have needed her, but Tanner didn't. And her job as caretaker was tied to her low rent. No job, no more low rent. Under different circumstances, she'd admire him for his tenacity. He knew what he wanted, and he was going after it. Just as she was.

He held her gaze. She'd never thought of gray as a warm color before. "Good. I meant to discuss the situation with you right away, but it's been busy."

"Discuss what? My job?" She barely managed to get the words past her tight throat.

"A live-in caretaker makes the house almost impossible to sell. Not many people are going to be interested in keeping you on. So, considering the circumstances... I promise I won't put the house up for sale until the adoption goes through." He said the last bit in a hurry, probably already regretting his offer.

What a relief. She closed her eyes for a second, swallowed her tears. As much as she hated accepting help from people, especially such reluctant help, she wasn't in the position to turn it down.

"Thank you," she said. "I appreciate it." She wanted to ask him why he was being so kind, but she refrained. With Tanner, the less she knew about him, the safer she was.

"Good. If there's anything else...I don't know what adoptions entail."

Without her noticing, he'd somehow shifted closer to her. She smelled his lovely spicy scent. Not as strong as an aftershave, more like a faint trace of soap. Just enough to make her want to lean in.

"I do have one favor to ask, though," he continued.

Nell straightened. Of course he did. Nothing came free. "I'm not cleaning your room."

He laughed, a beautiful masculine sound that wound around her. "That's not it. But I'm not letting you off the hook on the dinners. I'd like you to call me Jordan."

She hadn't realized she'd been using his last name. *Jordan* seemed so intimate to her. Which was silly, really. It was just a name; no need to hit the panic button. Jordan looked more amused than anything else. So why did it feel as though he'd asked for something more?

"Jordan it is." She grasped the handle of the lawn mower and maneuvered it between them. "I need to mow the front lawn before I go to work. You're in my way."

His smile dimmed. "God forbid I should ever get in your way."

Pushing the lawn mower in front of her, she followed him outside. She checked that Lacey and Jacob were still busy in the backyard, then trudged around to the front and started the mower. The angry sound of the motor corresponded perfectly with the grinding feeling in her gut. She was attracted to Tanner—Jordan. Attracted? Hell, she wanted to jump his bones and not come up for air for a few days. Worse, she liked him. A lot. He couldn't have come along at a worse time in her life. And he lived here.

She marched up and down the length of the lawn, her mind performing mental gymnastics to find a solution to her problem. She could try to ignore him when he was around, except he wasn't easily ignored. What she needed was to focus on Lacey and Jacob. And while she was focusing, she'd make sure one of them was with her at all times when Tanner was around. At the very least, that would ensure nothing would happen between them.

CHAPTER FOUR

"You did what?"

Jordan digested Alex's alarmed expression before turning his attention back to the ocean view from his fifth-floor condo.

"I promised Nell I wouldn't put the house up for sale until the adoption went through." The more he repeated the promise, the harder it was to believe he'd made it. Standing in the old garage, gazing into Nell's eyes, it had seemed like the only thing he could do. But now, back at his condo, surrounded by his belongings and the evidence of how far he'd come in the past ten years, his promise seemed outrageous.

"Have you lost your mind?" Alex pulled Jordan round to face him. "I told you I was lining up clients to look at the house. You get one shot at these people, then they move on."

"There'll be more where they came from. You don't understand. There's more at stake than what we want. Come with me." He scooped up his keys and headed for the door before Alex could launch a counterattack.

"Where?"

"I want to show you the house and introduce you to

the tenants. This isn't one of our hypothetical situations. We're talking about real people and real consequences."

Alex grabbed his black leather jacket from the closet and followed close on Jordan's heels. "You can explain to me on the way what people we're talking about, and why you're suddenly willing to put our plans on hold when we're so damned close."

Jordan wondered what tactic Alex planned to execute on the drive over. They thought they knew each other so well. But he'd told Alex just enough about his childhood to give him a general idea of his background—nothing more. He'd thrown his friend for a loop with this sudden change of plans. The only way to explain why he'd slowed things down was to show him. Jordan hoped it would make more sense to himself, as well. He never made impulsive decisions, especially one that could jeopardize his future.

He'd be kidding himself if he didn't admit that offering to delay the sale of the house troubled him. Security came in all sorts of packages; his came with a big fat bank account and the freedom to choose. Having put in his time working lousy jobs around the clock to make enough to get by, he was never again going to have to go without or be at the mercy of small-minded, mean-spirited people. So yes, he understood Alex's objections. But there were some things you couldn't change.

His mother had died over twenty years ago when he was fifteen. Despite having to strain to remember what she looked like, he'd never forgotten her credo of common decency. When he used to rant about not letting people walk all over her, she'd smile sweetly and insist that kindness was a virtue, not a weakness. That was his inheritance from his mother, and no matter how hard he tried to push that line, there was a limit to what he would do to succeed.

He arrived at the car, got in and waited for Alex. When they'd first met, Alex was taking pre-law, and Jordan was sitting in on any university class he could where he wouldn't be noticed. He made enough money to pay his rent and eat, but the dream of getting a real education was out of his reach. He didn't even have a high school diploma. Alex had noticed him after a couple of months, and they struck up a friendship that had lasted to this day. It was Alex who walked him through getting his GED and helped him to fill out the forms for a student loan.

His friend had helped get him this far, and now with the money from the sale of the house, Jordan hoped to take them to the next step—their own business. It didn't matter what business it was as long as it was viable and lucrative. Good deals crossed his desk monthly, great deals rarely. They needed to be ready for the elusive great deal. If the Big One came along before they had the capital, it could be another year or two before another appeared. Jordan drummed his fingers on the steering wheel. Alex was right, he was crazy.

Alex climbed into the car and slammed the door. "Start talking," he demanded as they pulled out into traffic.

Forty minutes later, Jordan exhaled wearily as they

turned onto Dunstan Lane. Alex had gone the spill-your-guts-and-spot-the-weak-link route; Jordan's reasoning to delay the sale of the house had holes the size of the old Victorian through it. Okay, so he wasn't making economic sense, but Alex hadn't met Lacey and Jacob yet, not to mention Nell.

He tried to see Dunstan Lane through his friend's eyes. It was an old neighborhood, way past its due date, but you didn't get big, old trees like that in just any neighborhood. The street was wide, and the houses—some huge rooming houses like his, others smaller family dwellings—sat far back from the street. People had yards big enough for kids to play in.

"Which one's yours?" Alex asked.

"It's up ahead on the right. The one with the—" Police car in front? Jordan stepped on the gas and roared up to the house. Nell, Melody and Lacey were standing by the curb talking to a policeman. The only thing good about the scene in front of him was that Nell wore beige slacks and a brown T-shirt, not her overalls. If he'd had X-rated thoughts about the damned things, chances were so did other guys.

"What's going on?" Jordan demanded, jumping out of the car.

The group turned as one toward him. He zeroed in on Nell. She looked more miffed than worried.

The cop straightened away from his patrol car. "And you are?"

"Jordan Tanner. I own this house. Is there a problem?"

Nell shifted closer to the cop and laid her hand on his arm. "Jordan, this is a friend of mine, Perry Conroy. He stopped by to say hello. We were just talking about you."

She started to turn to her cop friend, who looked like a freaking Greek god, when a smile lit her face. Jordan grinned through clenched teeth. *Alex.* With his blond hair and hazel eyes, Alex had that effect on women. He didn't have the cop's model looks, but for some reason, women couldn't resist him. He'd have thought Nell was above Alex's come-hither charm.

Nell made a beeline for Alex. "I don't believe we've met."

Alex took her hand in both of his. "You must be the enchanting caretaker Jordan told me about. I'm Alex, Jordan's business partner."

Nell darted a sardonic look at Jordan before pulling her hand away. "Nell Hart, and yes, I'm the caretaker, but hardly enchanting. This is my niece, Lacey, and my friend Melody. Oh, and Perry, of course."

Jordan felt a smidgeon of satisfaction that Nell hadn't sounded too interested in Perry, but did she have to stare at Alex with that dreamy look on her face? Okay, so he had the Brad Pitt look-alike thing going on, but what was so great about Brad Pitt, anyway? Melody, smart woman, didn't look the least bit interested. Of course, she'd forgotten Jordan's name, as well. She nodded vaguely in their direction, her attention drifting to something across the street.

Lacey tugged on Nell's hand while pointing at Alex. "He's pretty, Nell."

"Sweetie, it's not polite to talk about people like they're not there." Nell ruffled Lacey's curls.

"Oh." Lacey frowned and turned to Melody, who was still busy studying the empty yard across the street. "Melody, don't you think Mr. Alex is pretty?"

Melody blushed, glanced at Alex and smiled vaguely at the rest of them. Before she could answer, Perry snorted his disgust. "I got better things to do than stand around talking with pretty boys. I'll call you later about going out Saturday night, Nell."

A minute later, Jordan watched as the police car disappeared around the corner. The cop was dreaming if he thought he had a chance of dating Nell. With two part-time jobs and the kids, she'd never make time for a date. Unless they had a thing going. Which made sense. Of course a beautiful woman like Nell would have a boyfriend; Child Welfare probably loved that he was a cop. Perry was a good-looking dude, and he was in great shape. He probably spent a lot of time at the gym. Unlike him. If he got in three, four runs in a week, he was doing good.

"Where's Jacob?" he asked.

"He's hiding," Lacey said, tilting her head back to look up at him. "He doesn't like Perry." She slipped her tiny hand into his. Her hand felt sticky and sweaty, and for a second he thought about the new, expensive shirt he was wearing, then shrugged and swung her up into his arms. He wasn't all that fond of Perry himself. "I wanted to show Alex around," he said to Nell. "I've been trying to explain about the house and... everything. It seemed easier to bring him over and show him."

Nell eyed Alex. "You two work together? You're both business consultants?"

Nell sounded as enthused about his job as he felt about her being a farmer.

"Jordan's the consultant—I'm a lawyer. We work for the same firm." Alex had somehow worked his way around to stand beside Melody. He turned to her. "What do you do?"

Jordan didn't like Nell's grin or Melody's secretive little smile. If she was a call girl he had no idea what he was going to do. Of course, if he evicted Melody, chances were everyone would be so angry they'd leave, too. It would solve a lot of his problems. But then he'd have an empty house with no one paying rent. Not very attractive to buyers looking for an investment property. Maybe he'd better not be too hasty on evicting anyone just yet.

"Oh—" Melody swept her hand through the air "—I do this and that. You'd better get ready for work," she said to Nell. "Come on, Lacey. Let's get Jacob and make those gingerbread men I promised you."

Alex laughed. "Gingerbread men? It's August. I thought they were more a Christmas thing."

"You thought wrong." Melody took Lacey out of Jordan's arms, set her down and headed for the house.

Jordan scratched his head as Melody walked away. She'd been so open and friendly yesterday.

"I have to run into work for a couple hours, and the new couple renting 1A are coming soon," Nell addressed him. "If you want to show Alex that apartment, you should do it now." Her smile didn't make it to her eyes. "You're welcome to look at my apartment if you like. Sorry it's not all that tidy today. But if you want to look at Melody's and Mrs. Trembley's, I think it would be a good idea to ask them first." She glanced at the man-size watch on her wrist. "Gotta go."

"Hang on a sec." He sounded almost desperate, for Pete's sake. Nell, Melody and Lacey all stopped their hasty retreat.

"I need to talk to you." He didn't like being dismissed or told what to do. Okay, he just moved here, and he was an outsider, but damn it, that didn't mean—a light went on in his thick skull. They didn't want him tromping through their homes. He was such an idiot.

He braved Nell's glacial glare. "Go get ready. I'll drive you to work and pick you up later. We can talk in the car." He was pushing his luck, but sometimes the take-charge routine worked.

He should have known better. Melody snickered as Nell's green eyes blazed. "I think not." She spun on her heel and marched toward the front door.

He laughed before he could stop himself. There was nothing he loved more than the thrill of the chase. Miss Nellie had just found herself a sparring partner.

Melody shot him a speculative look as she reached out and grabbed Nell's arm. She stepped in front of Nell and spoke to her quietly for a minute. Nell hung her head as she listened to her friend. Her shoulders sagged. All he'd wanted to do was apologize without the entire neighborhood watching.

"Forget it," he said. "We can talk later."

"I'll be down in ten minutes, Tanner," she said without turning around. "You'd better be waiting."

"Lacey and I can show you around while Jordan's gone, if you like," Melody said to Alex without looking him in the eye.

Alex hustled over to Melody and Lacey. "When I woke up this morning," he said as he took Lacey's hand and placed a hand on the middle of Melody's back, "I wished for two beautiful women to spend the day with. And here I am."

Jordan watched the three climb the stairs to the front door of the house. He didn't have a clue what was up with the girls, but Alex's behavior he understood. The only time Alex laid it on this thick was when he felt unsure of himself. Jordan chuckled as he went to his car to wait for Nell. His friend had his work cut out for him if he thought Melody was going to be an easy catch. Unless, of course, she was a pro. Oh, to be a fly on the wall for that conversation. Jordan started whistling as he rubbed at the grubby fingerprints Lacey had left on his shirt.

He'd be happier if he could get Nell's help to formulate a strategy for selling the house, and he wanted her opinion on a couple of things that he'd been thinking about. Best of all, though, he got to have Nell to himself for a while. Not that it was a big deal. This was business. So why did he feel like a kid going out on a date?

NELL STARED STRAIGHT ahead after giving Tanner directions to the garden center. Surreptitiously, she massaged the soft leather of the seat. The car didn't roll as much as drift along the street, unlike her old truck that creaked and groaned its way over the roads. She consoled herself by thinking of the astronomical monthly payments he had to come up with. She wouldn't be sitting here at all if Melody hadn't insisted she let Tanner drive her to work. Melody had played the sacrifice-for-the-greater-good card. Apparently, making peace with the new landlord had become Nell's responsibility. She couldn't help feeling a tiny bit betrayed, as if she'd been thrown to the wolves—or wolf—by her best friend.

"I thought you didn't like to work weekends," Tanner asked as he turned out of the neighborhood.

"I don't."

"So why are you?"

She glanced at his profile. He had a stubborn chin and thick, wavy hair, dark enough to be called black. And, oh, those eyes. She forced herself to look away and stare out the side window. Gray, with a tinge of blue, framed by black lashes. Irish eyes. Poet's eyes.

"Hey, you fall asleep?" Jordan elbowed her.

No, but if she was thinking Tanner had poet's eyes she was definitely in trouble. Or crazy. "Just enjoying the scenery." She kept her nose glued to the passenger window.

"So, about work," he prompted.

"You can't pop in and out of people's apartments whenever one of your buddies wants to see your new toy, Tanner." Might as well get that one out of the way right off.

He ran a hand through his hair. She watched it slide silkily onto his forehead again. "You're right. Not about the toy part." He glanced at her. "Owning the house is a big deal for me. But I should have asked you first about offering to show it to Alex. I apologize."

She straightened out of her slump. "It's your house. You don't have to ask my permission. I'm mad because..." Because she suspected he thought they were a houseful of freaks. Who could blame him? She wanted to be a farmer in a time when people didn't know where their food came from or how it was grown. Rodney was next to homeless. Mrs. T. was a caricature of a desperate, lonely old woman. And Melody... Tanner was going to have field day when he found out what she did for a living. So, yeah, maybe they did qualify as a bunch of misfits, but they were all good people in their own way. Nell rubbed her forehead, wondering how she'd arrived at this point of her life, defending the inhabitants of Dunstan Lane.

She grabbed the door handle as Jordan pulled into the empty parking lot of the garden center.

"You don't answer questions very well, do you?" He turned off the engine.

Nell opened her door. "It doesn't matter why I'm mad. I'm not even mad anymore. See?" She bared her teeth and grinned. "I have to go to work. Thanks for the drive."

She hopped out and headed for the employee entrance at the side of the main building that fronted the greenhouses, but stopped halfway when she heard footsteps behind her.

"What are you doing?" Her voice squeaked with frustration.

"Coming with you. We haven't finished our conversation."

"I have to work, Tanner."

He looked around the empty parking lot and raised his eyebrows. "I don't see any customers. And the name's Jordan, remember?"

She continued on her way. "I do a lot of other things besides waiting on customers."

"I won't take much of your time."

As she walked through the sales center, saying a silent good morning to all the plants, she pretended not to notice Tanner's interest. He had an intent look on his face, as if he was calculating the fiscal value of his surroundings.

Flaming red-and-orange canna lilies were arranged in different groupings. At this time of year, those needed to move quickly. There were a couple of cash registers on the counter, a rack of gardening books and pamphlets and a variety of large decorative pots on the floor where customers would be sure to notice them while waiting to pay for a purchase. Regardless of what the new owners thought, she'd done a good job of maximizing the space.

"Who owns this place?" Tanner—Jordan—asked from behind her.

"The Fitzgeralds. They just bought it last month." She propped open the front door and started to push a cart full of miniature sunflower plants outside, the morning souring at the thought of her new employers.

"It's okay, I've got it," Nell protested when he tried to take the cart handle away from her.

He followed her outside. "They have you working weekends?"

"That's right." She suspected they'd be happy if she didn't work at all, but if they fired her, most of the staff would quit. She'd tried to encourage everyone to defer to them, but people got used to doing things a certain way, and change didn't happen overnight. Nell had been the manager for the past four years. Mr. Fitzgerald— as he insisted everyone call him—was young, had just graduated from university and had an ego the size of the Atlantic Ocean. To make matters worse, his in-laws had invested heavily in the garden center, and he was anxious to prove to them that he could handle the job. He knew his plants, but lacked the people skills necessary to run a garden center. People didn't come just to buy plants; they wanted to talk about their gardens this year and next. She'd tried explaining to Mr. Fitzgerald that a few minutes spent chatting with a customer often translated into a bigger sale. He didn't get it.

She couldn't help it that not only the staff, but the customers as well, preferred doing business with her. If only young Fitzgerald would take the time to listen. But he was too busy proving himself.

His way of dealing with the dilemma was to ask her to work odd hours, knowing it was often difficult for her to find a babysitter. Maybe he wasn't smart enough to realize what losing her would do to the center or maybe he really believed he could do better. He could be right for all she knew. Either way, he was hoping she would quit.

Nell strode inside and continued on to the two sets of patio doors along the back of the building. She needed to hang on for another two months to finish off the season. Next spring, she'd find a job at another garden center. She pushed the doors open, and the sweet, moist smell of plants growing, along with the whirr of fans, slid into the sales center. She inhaled deeply and relaxed. It was impossible to sustain a bad mood surrounded by so many plants.

Jordan arrived on her heels and caught her arm before she could escape into the greenhouses. "I'm not running after you to get advice. Five, ten minutes, that's all I need."

She rubbed the spot where he'd touched her elbow. Against her will, she felt her curiosity hitch. He didn't strike her as the kind of man to ask for advice often. "What do you need?"

"It was stupid of me to show up with Alex unannounced and expect to show him the house."

"Yes, it was. You need to give people notice before going into their homes." She toed the tall cactus beside her a few inches to the left.

"So how are we going to do this? Potential buyers need to view the house."

She narrowed her eyes. "You're not trying to suck up to me, are you?"

Jordan's lips twitched. "And why would I do that?"

"The old rah-rah, we're a team thing. So I'll keep the local zanies under control while these potential buyers of yours look around."

Jordan burst out laughing. She couldn't look away from him to save her life.

"Trust me, I don't need your help handling people."

No kidding. If he so much as crooked his finger, she'd jump into his arms without a second thought. "I bet you don't." She grabbed a hose and started watering the plants on the bench. She had to do something to cool things off.

Still smiling, he cocked his head to one side and considered her. "You're a cautious little lady, aren't you?"

Not as cautious as she should be. While her brain was busy lecturing her on all the reasons why she should stay away from Tanner, her body hummed with anticipation of all the delicious things they could do together—if only.

She forced her thoughts back to his question. Potential buyers. Right. "I think it would be a good idea to sit down with us as a group and tell us what your plans are. Everyone understands you want to sell, but they need to know if you plan to raise their rent, and if you do, when. Not knowing is always the worst." She moved slowly and methodically along the rows of rosemary plants, lightly sprinkling them. Their clean, resinous smell tickled her nose and cleared her head. "Was there anything else you needed to talk about, because I really am busy."

"What's the story on the cop? Is he your boyfriend?"

She glanced over her shoulder. "Why?"

He shrugged. "I'm not crazy about having a cop car in front of the house all the time."

"Fair enough. I'll tell him to park down the street. Next question."

He chuckled. "You haven't answered that one yet."

"I'll let you know when I've made up my mind." Nell turned off the hose and put it down. Feeling almost giddy, she picked up a rosemary plant and smiled into it as she studied it closely, supposedly for aphids. Talking to Tanner was far more enjoyable than she'd expected. They both knew this wasn't going anywhere, but what the heck, what was the harm of enjoying a little verbal foreplay? But, at the same time, what was the point? She inhaled the aroma of the plant and placed it back on the bench. As if someone had pulled a plug, her giddiness drained away, leaving her tired and disheartened.

"If that's all, I have to get back out front in case someone comes in."

"What does Melody do for a living?"

She knew he thought Melody was a call girl, and if she could figure out a way to torment him a bit longer, she would. Unfortunately, she'd never been good at stringing people along. "She's a fortune-teller."

Tanner's face went blank. "Excuse me?"

"She tells fortunes. She's good at it, too." That's why Melody's reaction to Alex had been so interesting. One glance at Alex, and Melody had looked as if she wanted to run far and fast. Nell couldn't wait to pry out of her friend what her reaction was all about.

Tanner followed Nell back to the store front. "What does she do? Reads tea leaves or...what?"

"Sometimes she reads palms, but mostly she asks for a personal belonging of a client." She opened one of the cash registers and prepared to count the float.

Tanner leaned on the counter across from her. "Is she any good?"

"She has a lot of customers." She wished he wouldn't lean quite so close. His scent, and what Melody would call his aura, made it hard for her to concentrate.

"She makes a living from telling fortunes?"

"She works at Stargazer as a clerk and tells fortunes on the side." She slid the twenties back in their slot, having no idea of how many she'd just counted.

"Stargazer. What is that, some kind of new age shop?"

"They sell tarot cards, stuff like that." If he was so darned interested in Melody, why didn't he just talk to her?

"Has she ever told your fortune?"

Nell slammed the cash drawer shut. "Once."

She watched him turn that over in his mind. "Only once?"

"Yeah." She gave up the pretense of work and waited for the question.

"What did she tell you?"

Nell wrapped her arms around her waist. "That I would suffer a terrible loss. Two weeks later my sister was killed."

They'd both learned an important lesson. Melody no longer paid heed to the occasional gloomy premonitions she received about her clients; she concentrated only on the positive. And after a great struggle, Nell had finally learned there was always the light side of dark if she looked hard enough. Lacey and Jacob were the light she had found in the darkest part of her life. She would do everything necessary to keep that light alive.

It had been a balancing act from day one. Of finding a job that would make enough money, but allow her to be home for part of the day. Of meeting Jacob and Lacey's emotional and physical needs. Of hanging on to her own sanity throughout it all. She thought she had her life under control. She'd even believed she could ride out the storm Tony's complaining had stirred up. But Jordan's arrival was one too many things to handle. Maybe even in the best of times, he'd still affect her equilibrium. All she knew now was, she was off balance, and everything felt out of control.

CHAPTER FIVE

AT THE END OF THE WEEK, Jordan strode into his cramped room—had he really thought the first day at Dunstan Lane that the bedsit would be big enough?—and tossed his briefcase on the rickety coffee table. Even after the cleaning lady he'd hired—not Nell, for all he'd teased her—had scrubbed the room and the windows had been left open for most of the week, the smell of decay still assaulted him every evening. He uttered his daily curse to Great-aunt Beulah. The one time he'd met her, she'd told him he'd come from trash and would always be trash. Jordan's jaw hardened at the memory. He'd been fifteen, his mother dead only a week, and he'd made the mistake of asking for help. He hadn't understood then, but Beulah had done him a favor by refusing to support him in any way. He'd learned to claw his way out of the muck on his own. And he planned to keep on climbing.

Jordan clenched his teeth when a rhythmic banging came from the other side of the wall. The new tenants were going at it again. Okay, so they were newlyweds, but man, they'd been at it until three last night. Couldn't they give it a frigging break? There should be a course available, Landlord 101, and the first thing should be how to diplomatically tell your tenants the boisterous sounds of their endless lovemaking was keeping said landlord up at night. Every night. Not only that, the intimate sounds coming through the wall underscored his total lack of a love life.

He shucked his office clothes, pulled on a pair of jeans and a white T-shirt, grabbed the bag of groceries he'd picked up on the way home and slammed out of the room. He took the stairs two at a time, heading for Nell's as he had every evening this past week. He hadn't found a way to tell her about his noise problem; she thought he was starving and could hardly wait for supper. After one night of fish sticks and another of macaroni and cheese, he offered to give her money for food. He knew she operated on a tight budget, but she'd looked so horrified at accepting money from him, he'd changed tactics. Instead of asking, he bought food on the way home from work and presented it to her. Tonight was salmon steaks, a red onion and a bottle of balsamic vinegar to accompany the salads she put together from her garden.

When he'd made the deal with Nell to cook supper, he'd thought he might drop by two, three evenings a week. But it was surprisingly entertaining to talk to Jacob about the neighborhood kids he hung out with and what they did with their last days of summer freedom. And Lacey's futile attempts to bully Jacob and him into playing her girlie games amused him. He was in awe of Jacob's patience and his courtesy toward his sister.

He'd never been privy to the delicate mechanics of

a family. He didn't have siblings as far as he knew. His father had remained nameless and his mother had been only sixteen when she'd had him. Without any support from her family, she'd done the best she could, but looking back, he realized she'd just been a kid herself with no idea of how to be a mother. He'd started cooking meals of a sort—peanut butter and banana sandwiches, canned tomato soup—by the time he'd started school. These days he ate in restaurants more often than not. Yet it felt almost luxurious to return after work to the cozy smell of food cooking along with the sound of Nell humming in the kitchen and the children playing. He couldn't seem to get enough of it, even with Nell kicking him out as soon as supper was over.

He knew he had to cut back on the number of nights he shared supper with them. Like Nell said, he was going places. Alone. But he'd had a hard day at the office, due mostly to his lack of sleep. All day he'd looked forward to putting his feet up and letting the kids' chatter wash over him as he listened to the sounds of Nell cooking. It was one of life's ironies to have found a measure of peace in a transient situation.

He tried the door, but for the first time it didn't swing open. Had Nell mentioned she wouldn't be home this evening? He leaned against the door and tried to identify the empty feeling in his gut. He was hungry, but that wasn't it. No, this was disappointment. Which was ridiculous because he'd only known these people for a week. Of course they had things going on in their lives he didn't know about. Just as he did. He had his job and friends like Sandra, who, for some reason he didn't care to examine, he'd been avoiding all week. Maybe this would be a good night to call her, see if she wanted to meet for a drink. The last thing he needed to do was stand around waiting for Nell to show up when she hadn't even had the courtesy to let him know they were going out.

Jordan started back down the stairs. He could go to his condo, have a drink and listen to some tunes. Alex had mentioned having a hot date, but he'd feel like he was visiting in his own home, and that sucked. Plus he'd have to drive all the way back out here later.

He should call Sandra. She'd left a couple of messages that he hadn't returned. Even if he didn't want to take their relationship to the next stage, she was still good company. He'd been spending way too much time with Nell and the kids. He needed to get dressed up and go out to a restaurant, remind himself exactly where he was headed. Except Sandra wasn't the kind of woman you phoned at the last minute.

The red onion he'd bought to add to the salad fell out of the bag as he reached the second-floor landing. Absently, he watched it roll over to rest in front of Melody's door. If he were being honest, he preferred to help Nell grill salmon steaks than drag himself back to town to eat an artistically arranged tablespoon of food for a hundred bucks at an upscale restaurant.

He scooped up the onion, tossed it in the bag and eyed Melody's door. What were the chances she didn't have plans on a Friday night?

His knuckles barely hit the door when it flew open, as if Melody had been standing on the other side waiting for him.

"Oh, it's you," she said.

That was the kind of welcome a guy waited for. "Where's Nell?" he blurted out. He'd meant to ask if there was a local bar around and would she like to go for a drink. Not that he was attracted to Melody. She was very attractive, but too airy-fairy for him.

She peered out into the hallway, then dragged him into the apartment by the front of his shirt. "Do you know how to cook rack of lamb?"

"No." He looked around the apartment. The small dining table in the corner, covered with a white linen cloth, had been set for two. A graceful glass vase of roses sat in the middle of the table, and a bottle of wine was breathing on the kitchen counter. Looking gorgeous in a green silk sheath, Melody stood in the kitchen, wringing her hands.

He wandered over to the counter and turned the wine bottle around so he could read the label. A very nice Cabernet. "Let me guess, it's a first date and you're trying to impress the guy."

"Is it that obvious? Why do I do these things to myself? I don't even know how to cook, and Nell had to go to jail, so she's not around to help. The recipe didn't say you had to defrost the lamb before cooking. I've had it in the oven for thirty minutes and it's still bleeding, and it's six-thirty, and I said come at seven, and—"

"Whoa." Jordan grabbed her shoulders and forced her to look at him. "Nell's in jail?"

A look of horror passed over Melody's face. "She is? Oh, my God. I knew Tony would drive her over the edge. Did she kill him?"

Jordan reined in his panic and dropped his hands, afraid he'd shake the dickens out of her if he didn't. "Let's start again. Where's Nell?"

"Oh." She shot him a sheepish grin. "Tony called and insisted on seeing Lacey and Jacob this afternoon. Nell had to drop everything and rearrange her work schedule because he said 'jump.' If she doesn't kill him, I might."

He relaxed enough to breathe. "Which jail?"

"Galsworth. They left about an hour ago on the bus. She didn't trust her truck to make the trip, and I forgot to renew my registration."

Galsworth was at least a half-hour drive. If he left now, he'd get there in time to give them a lift home, which would be a lot more pleasant than riding a bus on a Friday night. "Does Nell have a cell phone?"

"No. Are you thinking of picking them up? I think that's a wonderful idea. Tony can be pretty rough on Nell and the kids."

An image of Jacob's pale face flashed in his mind. The kid always looked so damned defenseless. At least Nell was with him. "That's my plan, but I better get going. I'll have to find the bus stop and wait there, so I don't miss them." He started for the door, but swung back. "Here. Salmon steaks. Squeeze half a lemon over them with a pinch of dill, if you have it, and put them under the grill for fifteen minutes tops."

Melody threw her arms around him. "Thank you. I knew the storm that was brewing the first day you came here was a good omen."

Jordan peeled her arms away from his neck. "Can you really tell fortunes?"

Melody's enigmatic smile appeared. "I can make a prediction right now. If you don't hurry, you'll miss Nell and the kids, and they'll have to ride the bus home."

Jordan laughed and left it at that. As he pulled out of Dunstan Lane, he thought he recognized Alex's SUV turn onto the street. Couldn't be. He was sure Alex had said he had a date tonight. Unless—Jordan started to smile—he was taking a special interest in one of the tenants. Too bad his old buddy was allergic to fish.

His light mood didn't last as the car ate up the miles to Galsworth. He gnawed on the idea that Tony could call Nell and disrupt her world any time he wanted to. That didn't seem right to him, but what did he know? The guy was the kids' dad. Jacob and Lacey were good kids, and funny, too. He could hardly stand the thought that their father would deliberately hurt them. Surely Tony could see they were better off living with Nell.

He shook his head to clear his thoughts. What he should be thinking about was why he was so eager to rescue them. Not that it was a big deal. He didn't have anything else planned. Kind of odd, now that he thought about it. His weekends were usually completely booked. A lot of deals were finalized over a beer, just as a lot of information was exchanged. It hadn't even occurred to him to stop by the bar closest to his work for his usual Friday evening drink.

Instead, he was driving miles out of his way to pick up Nell and the kids. Okay, he was attracted to her. And not just physically. He loved how feisty she was, that she didn't let him get away with anything. Jordan shifted in his seat. He *admired* how feisty she was.

What was he doing? They'd survived without him just fine up to this point. It was arrogant to think they needed him now. But the idea that they were wandering around the tough neighborhood that surrounded the jail... And don't forget the bus. God knows who would be riding the bus out there at this time of night. Any half-decent person with a bit of spare time on his hands would do the same. That's the kind of thing good neighbors did for each other. And in a way, he was protecting his interests. If anything happened to Nell, who would take care of everyone at Dunstan Lane? He had to look after his investment. Yeah, that was it.

NELL WANTED TO SCOOP both Jacob and Lacey into her arms and run as fast and far from the prison as was humanly possible. But she wasn't big enough, strong enough or fast enough. She caught her breath on a sob. They would never be free of Tony. He would always drag them down into his subterranean slime. A burst of rage spurred her on to the last gate before freedom. She clutched Lacey's and Jacob's hands and practically ran the last few yards. If only he wasn't such a conniving, two-faced son of a—

"You're hurting me," Lacey whined, tugging her hand out of Nell's death grip.

"I'm sorry, baby." Keeping her hand on Lacey's shoulder, Nell didn't slow her pace until she heard the metal clang of the gate closing behind them. She came to an abrupt halt and swayed back and forth, her shoulders drooping with relief. Another visit over and done with.

"Are you okay, Nell?" Jacob's voice was barely above a whisper. Tony had chosen to go after his son this time. Why wasn't Jacob more interested in sports? Was he a pansy? Tony's words, not hers. She'd had to stand by silently and watch Tony berate her sensitive little nephew. Other times, when she'd tried inserting herself between them, Tony had been swift to retaliate. Maybe she wasn't a good enough mother for his children. Maybe he wouldn't let her adopt them.

What had her sister ever seen in him? Even if he'd fooled Mary in the beginning, the last few years had been rough. Nell knew—she'd been on call as the rescue squad. No matter how hard she'd tried, she hadn't been able to stop Mary from going back to the dick-wad time after time.

Nell forced a smile, squeezed Jacob's hand and let go. "I'm okay, just hungry, I guess. How about you?"

"I want a hamburger." Lacey leaned heavily against Nell's leg and stuck her thumb in her mouth. Oh, Tony. Did he have any idea of the damage he was causing his children? Not that he cared. Pushing away the depressing thought, Nell shepherded her wounded family toward the bus stop.

"We can't miss this bus. The next one doesn't come for another hour. Maybe I can make hamburgers when we get home." She tried to infuse a note of enthusiasm into her voice, but the thought of having to cook made her tired.

Would Jordan be waiting for his supper when they got back? She hadn't known how to contact him to let him know they wouldn't be there, but it was Friday—chances were he had plans anyway. No matter how often she told herself he wasn't her responsibility, she still felt bad she hadn't been able to warn him they wouldn't be home. It surprised her that he seemed to enjoy his nightly visits. All they did was eat supper, but he got this look on his face when he came through the door every evening. It was almost as if he was shedding a skin, becoming someone younger and softer. She'd made enough mistakes in her life to know when she was making another one, but she loved that minute when Jordan walked in all smiles and eager to ask the kids how their day had been. Like it mattered to him.

She was kidding herself if she thought pushing him out the door as soon as supper was over was helping. His name continually cropped up in the children's conversation. As for her, the nights had become torturous, filled with dreams that left her yearning. Incomplete. She supposed in a way she was; what adult didn't wish for a partner to share their life with? But that didn't explain why it was Jordan who inspired her restlessness. Why couldn't it have been Perry, uncomplicated Perry who made no secret of his interest? And why now?

"I want a real hamburger." Lacey's voice wound into a higher octave.

"Okay. When we get closer to home, both of you watch for a restaurant. Lacey, it will be your job to ring the bell this time."

Jacob's shoulders rose up around his ears as he trotted in front of them. Nell's eyes flooded with tears, and for a second, she felt as if she was drowning. Pulling the wire to get the bus to stop was a game they played, each taking turns. The game had come to signify regaining a morsel of control after visiting Tony. It was Jacob's turn to pull the wire this time, and God knows he'd earned the privilege, but Nell knew from the tone of Lacey's voice, she was about to have a sobbing child on her hands. And the ride home was long and hard enough without hysterics.

When the bus lumbered around the corner, Nell stepped up her pace, tugging Lacey along behind her. She knew the driver could see them and hoped he'd wait for them. But if he didn't, if they missed the bus—

"Nell." Jacob swirled round to her, his face glowing with excitement. "Look." He pointed toward the bus stop a few yards ahead. "It's Jordan."

Nell stumbled to a stop. The dark blue sedan looked like Jordan's car but what were the chances? Lacey pulled her hand out of Nell's grip and started running toward the car. "Mr. Jordan," she called. "We're here. Don't leave without us."

Jacob ran after his sister, his arms pinwheeling by his sides, as if he didn't have a care in the world.

Nell stayed glued to the spot as she watched Jordan climb out of the car, looking so tall and strong and pleased to see them. She closed her eyes and for a second, allowed herself to feel relief at being rescued from the long bus ride home. Then she forced herself to face the reality in front of her. Jacob and Lacey had grown far too fond of Mr. Jordan. He was going to break their hearts.

Nell strode up to the car. "You just happened to be in the neighborhood?"

Jordan narrowed his eyes as he leaned against the hood.

"Jordan, can I ride in the front seat?" Jacob bounced on his toes as he waited for an answer.

"No, I want to ride in the front. He likes me better." Lacey pouted.

"Both in the back," Jordan said without taking his eyes off Nell. "Nell rides shotgun."

"I still want a hamburger," Lacey muttered as she crawled into the backseat after her brother.

"You have nothing better to do on a Friday night than drive all the way out here to pick us up?" Nell asked. There was that wonderful, teasing, cocky grin of his again. He had no business looking so good in faded jeans and the snug white T-shirt he always favored. She had an overwhelming urge to stamp her foot in frustration.

"Anyone ever tell you a person can catch more with honey than vinegar?"

Nell snorted. "I'm not trying to catch anything but the bus."

He jerked his thumb over his shoulder. "Go for it. I'll take the kids home."

"You want to tell me what you're doing here, Tanner?" She rocked back on her heels. He wasn't smiling now. Which was good because life was too damned complicated to add in tangling with Tanner, as well.

"I'm looking for my supper. Let's go, I'm starving." He rounded the car to the driver's door.

She followed close behind him. "You've got to be kidding. You did not drive all the way out here to get me to cook your supper."

He yanked the car door open, leaned on it as he eyed her over the top. "We have an agreement. You said you'd cook for me. You're not going back on your word, are you?"

Nell was sure she felt steam pour out of her ears. "It's my night off," she managed to get out through clenched teeth.

"Fine." He smiled slyly as though he had her exactly where he wanted her. "But I'm still hungry and so are the kids. Are you coming or not?"

"Of course I'm coming, as you knew all along." She marched around the car and jumped into the front seat. Bewildered, she slammed the door shut, not able to shake the feeling that Tanner had gotten exactly what he'd come for, and yet made her feel as though he'd conceded a point. She wanted to stay mad at him for manipulating her, but really, she settled into the soft leather seat, what did she have to complain about? He'd driven miles out of his way to offer them a lift home. What she should be concentrating on is why.

JORDAN WRAPPED HIS FINGERS around the steering wheel and kept them firmly in place as he waited for Nell to settle in beside him. When he'd first seen the threesome stagger out of the prison grounds, they'd looked so beaten down, it had taken all his control to remain in the car and wait for them. Tony had no idea how fortunate he was to be on the inside. If he were free, Jordan would hunt him down and pound some sense into him. Or just pound him.

He flexed his fingers and glanced over at Nell as she fussed over the kids in the backseat. She had a summer dress on, a beige thing with flowers. His fingers itched to trace the thin straps that stretched over her golden shoulders. She looked tan and fit, but so fragile a gust of wind could pick her up and carry her away. How had he gotten the impression that she was tough? It was a wonder she could even swing a hammer.

He bit back a smile as he started the car. Good thing Melody, not Nell, was the psychic. Nell would drill a hole in the ground and stuff him in it if she knew what he was thinking.

"Everyone buckled up?" he asked as he glanced in the rearview mirror at the kids.

"I wanna listen to Raffi," Lacey said around the thumb in her mouth.

"Interpret." He tossed the word to Nell.

She cracked a small smile despite the shadows in her eyes. "Didn't you ever listen to Raffi when you were a kid? I'll lend you a tape of his music sometime. You'll love it."

When Jordan pulled out of the parking spot, Nell suddenly sat up straighter and stared across the street. He glanced over to see what had sparked her interest. A gray compact car sat in the shadow of a tall tree. He thought he saw an outline of a man in the driver's seat, but it was too dark to see anything clearly.

"A friend of yours?" he asked.

She shrugged and sank down in her seat. "I don't think so."

Jordan felt hot, moist breath on his neck. "Is that a GPS?" Jacob asked reverently.

"Seat belt, Jacob," Nell scolded.

"But, Nell, it's a *GPS,*" Jacob said in a voice more often used to describe one of the wonders of the world.

"You're into that kind of stuff, bud?"

"Yes." Jacob breathed on his neck.

"Jacob," Nell warned.

"Okay."

Jordan waited until he heard the click of Jacob's seat belt. "Tell you what, Jacob. You write down five different locations close to us, and some day soon, I'll show you how to program them into the GPS. We'll drive around and find the places you picked. Okay?"

"Just you and me?" The longing in the boy's voice embarrassed Jordan. Driving around with the kid was such a small thing to do.

Jordan opened his mouth to answer when Nell gave a sharp cough, more like a bark. He glanced over at her and was caught in a high-voltage glare. Apparently he'd stepped into dog doo.

"Um, well, I think—"

"I think Mr. Tanner is a very busy man, and he probably doesn't have time." Nell twisted in her seat to look at Jacob. "Perry would probably be interested in doing something like that if you asked him."

"Perry's too stupid. He can't figure out that kind of stuff," Jacob said.

Jordan bit the inside of his cheek when he glanced in the rearview mirror and saw Jacob stick his finger down his throat and pretend to gag. That was pretty much how he felt about Perry, too.

He was afraid to say anything after that. He slid Nell a sideways glance to see if she was still mad, and felt his gut tighten. Her dress had ridden up on her thighs. Her legs were a work of art, tanned and muscular; he could easily imagine what it would feel like to trace his hands up and down her sleek curves.

"*Ding, ding, ding.* There's the restaurant, Nell," Lacey shrieked.

Nell frowned. "Do you mind pulling in here? I promised her she could have a hamburger. We could go to the drive-through if you don't want to go in."

"Oh, please, Mr. Jordan, can we go in?"

"Can I stay in the car and look at the GPS?" Jacob chimed in. "You can bring my food out to me."

Jordan pulled into the lot of a generic greasy spoon and parked. He'd practically lived in places like this one when he was a kid. The food was warm, cheap and filling; a place to sit and forget what was waiting for him back home. But the smell of grease made him nauseous now. He was about to suggest he and Jacob stay in the car when Nell stiffened beside him. Jordan checked the direction she was looking. A gray compact, similar to the car outside the prison, had pulled into the back of the lot.

"We're going in together," he said, opening the car door. "You can order anything you want. I'm buying."

"Anything? Even an ice cream sundae with chocolate syrup and nuts on top?" Lacey squealed.

"What about the cherry?" he asked over his shoulder.

Lacey's eyes grew round with wonder. She leaned forward and patted his arm. "Do you like cherries, too, Mr. Jordan?"

"You bet. Let's go, gang." Had there ever been a time in his life when something as simple as a cherry on top of a sundae constituted the sum of his desires? He'd lived with a hunger in his belly so long, he couldn't remember not having a constant craving. He'd always needed more. Probably always would.

He kept his eye on the gray car as they made their

way into the brightly lit restaurant, but no one got out. The smell of grease hit him the second he stepped inside. He swallowed and tried not to look pained as he scanned the menu board. Nell negotiated the kids' orders—*if you have curly fries you can't have onion rings, but maybe your brother will trade one of his onion rings for one of your curly fries, and no you absolutely can't order more than you can eat, fries never taste as good reheated.*

"You're amazing," he said, reaching for his wallet. The kids had raced over to the condiments table to stock up on everything they'd need, and probably on a good deal they wouldn't.

"Excuse me?" Nell tore her worried gaze away from the windows. It was dark out now, and their reflections obscured the view outside.

"The way you brokered the kids' meal. You're a first-class negotiator. Did that come naturally, or is it something you had to learn?" He waved away the twenty-dollar bill she pulled out. "Your turn next time." He paid the cashier and leaned a hip against the counter as they waited for their order to be filled.

Nell chuckled. "If you try to take something away from a child, they let you know their displeasure pretty fast. But if you give them something first to distract them from what you're taking away, then..." She smiled. Jordan felt a sharp pang, but it had nothing to do with the smell of food. "Explaining negotiating to you is like explaining Buddhism to the Dalai Lama, isn't it?"

He tried to keep the heat out of his gaze, but he could tell by the way she shifted away from him and turned her attention to the kids that she'd seen it.

"Jacob," she called. "Sit over here, not by the door, please."

Jordan scanned the restaurant. There were only a dozen people in it, and all the plastic tables looked the same to him. "What's the story with the gray car?"

"I don't know."

"Have you seen the car before?"

"Maybe."

"At the house? At work? Where?" He looked around the restaurant again, checked to make sure Jacob and Lacey had chosen a table closer to them.

Nell accepted the first of the hamburgers they'd ordered. "Both." She glanced up at him, then down at the food the young pimple-faced man was piling up on the tray in front of her.

He grabbed her elbow and turned her to face him. "What's going on?"

"I don't know. I think it's one of Tony's friends, spying on me."

"How long has this been going on?"

She rounded a shoulder. "A week, I guess."

"Why didn't you tell me? Did you at least tell Perry?"

"No, I…um." Jordan felt winded, like he'd taken a sharp jab to the ribs. The delicate curve of her neck as she bowed her head made her look so defenseless.

"I was hoping I was wrong," she confessed. "There are a lot of small gray cars around."

"There's one way to find out." He headed for the door.

Nell stopped him with a touch. "Please don't. Some of Tony's friends can be nasty. I'll phone Perry when I get home, I promise."

Not if he could prevent it. Unless, of course, he thought the situation warranted police protection. "My camera's in the car. No crime in taking someone's picture and writing down their license plate number is there? You stay here with the kids."

"Jordan, wait. Take this." She dug into the huge cotton bag she'd been dragging around. She pulled out a small leather purse and held the bag out to him.

He put his hands up in front of him and backed away. "Really, let me handle this my way."

She thrust the bag into his hands. "It has beans in it, see?"

The bag felt a lot heavier than it looked. He weighed it in his hands, looking at her with a mix of admiration and exasperation. "You've been carrying around cans of beans in case someone attacked you?" He wanted to chuck the beans through the plate-glass window. Why hadn't she told him about her suspicions?

"Perry says use of a lethal weapon can carry a serious charge. I looked it up on the internet just to be sure. So, beans." She shrugged. "I could just say I was out shopping, and they happened to be in my bag."

"Wait here. I'll take care of this." He stalked out of

the restaurant, swinging the brightly colored cotton bag as menacingly as he could. He couldn't remember ever feeling so ramped up. He felt exposed and vulnerable and so damned mad, he'd gladly tear the guy's limbs from his body if he so much as touched a hair on Nell's or the kids' head.

His hands shaking, Jordan fumbled with the remote to unlock his car. What was happening to him? He didn't even know for sure that the man in the gray car was tailing Nell. And even if he was, maybe he had a legitimate reason, like… He couldn't think of one. He couldn't think at all. He was scared. Scared that someone could hurt Nell and the kids, or that he wouldn't get it right, that he would be the one who hurt them. What a mess.

The whole time Nell had been trying to protect the children from becoming too involved with him, no one, especially not him, had thought about how fond he might grow of them. Apparently, he'd become more involved than he'd realized. That wasn't part of his plan. He had to reassess the situation, devise a new strategy. But first he had to take care of the scumbag in the gray car.

CHAPTER SIX

"MA'AM? WAS THERE SOMETHING else you needed?"

Nell dragged her gaze away from the window and grabbed the tray of food. "No, this is great. Thanks."

She dashed over to Jacob and Lacey and deposited the tray on the table. "Stay right here. I'll be back in a sec." She hurried to the door, her heart thumping against her ribs. Jordan didn't understand how nasty Tony's friends could be. Even if the guy in the car was someone just getting supper, he wasn't going to like having his picture taken by a stranger.

A bubble of hysteria rose in her throat as she leaned her shoulder against the heavy glass door to open it. As crazy as it was, she had to admit she liked Jordan's take-no-prisoners approach. She hardly dared let herself acknowledge the liberating feeling that came with sharing her concerns with someone else for a change. Not that she planned to make a habit of depending on Jordan. Yes, he was dependable, but it was just part of his nature and had nothing to do with protecting her and the kids. Absolutely nothing. She couldn't let herself get confused about what his priorities were.

She stepped outside, but stayed close to the door. Jordan glanced in her direction, grimaced and jerked his thumb toward the restaurant. Apparently he wasn't used to having his orders disobeyed. Tough. She wasn't used to having someone fight her battles for her. As she stepped out into the lot, Jacob's tired voice stopped her.

"Nell?"

"It's okay. I'm coming inside in a minute." She waved her hand behind her, not daring to take her eyes off the scene across the parking lot. A huge man, a huge *angry* man, climbed out of the gray car and took a menacing step toward Jordan. She couldn't hear what he was saying, but by the angry expression on his face, it wasn't howdy-do.

"What's Jordan doing?" Jacob asked.

Nell took her time forming an answer as she watched the two men size each other up. In the beginning she'd tried to cover for Tony's nastiness, but she soon learned his children were well acquainted with their father's ways. Jacob, in particular, wanted the truth straight up. In an effort to protect him, she always presented a watered-down version, but it broke her heart to see how stoic the little fellow was each time his father delivered another blow.

"I thought maybe that guy was following me," she explained.

Jacob tucked his chin close to his chest. "That's Stan, Dad's friend. I think they met in jail the last time Dad was there for fighting."

"Stan," she repeated his name.

"He makes really stinky farts."

"He looks like he would." She glanced inside the

restaurant to check on Lacey. By the look of the girl's face, she was eating more ketchup than anything else. "You should go inside and eat before the food gets cold. Lacey shouldn't be left alone."

Jacob nodded and pulled the door open. "Nell? Don't yell at Jordan, okay? He doesn't know you're…you know."

"I'm what?"

A faint blush touched her nephew's innocent face. "That you'd never let anyone hurt Lacey and me." He watched her, as if testing the truth of his words.

She cupped her hand over her aching heart. "You've got that right, kiddo. I swing a mean hammer."

Jacob shot her a sweet smile and slipped into the restaurant. Nell took a second to swallow her tears before turning back to watch Jordan. It took all her self-control not to march over to the two men and throw in a few verbal punches of her own. But as much as she hated to admit it, this might be one time when Tanner was right. At the very least, he had size on his side.

"WHADDA YA THINK YOU'RE doing?"

The heavyweight stepped toward him, but Jordan held his ground, thankful it was fat, not muscle, that padded the guy's body. Although he knew from experience fat guys could be misleading. Some of them knew how to use that extra weight to their advantage in a fight.

"I'm taking a picture of your license plate. I could write the number down, but this is easier. And now—"

he raised the camera to eye level "—I'm taking a picture of you."

"You can't do that." The fat guy lunged for the camera, but Jordan easily sidestepped him.

"I just did." Jordan made sure he kept his shit-eating grin in place. "Want to tell me why you're following Nell Hart?"

"Who?"

Jordan turned as if to leave. "Okay, I guess I have everything I need. I'll email this to my friend at the police station, get an ID and turn everything over to one of the many lawyers I know. Some of them are very creative. I'm sure they'll come up with a list of things to charge you with."

Fat guy rubbed his hand under his nose. "I haven't done nothing."

"Yet," Jordan added. "Now that I'm alerting the police that you've been following her, if anything happens to Nell or the kids, they'll look at you first."

Aw, geez, what had he done? As if someone had flipped a switch, the guy's eyes narrowed into mean slits that disappeared into folds of fat. He looked like the nasty SOB he probably was. He looked like one of the creeps his mom used to drag home.

"But the damage will already be done, won't it?" The guy leered.

Jordan held on to his grin as if it were a lifeline. If he thought it would help, he'd take the clown on right now. But that was exactly what the guy wanted, a physical confrontation. He thought he could take Jordan. Maybe he could, but Jordan had his doubts. He hadn't been in a fight for years, but that didn't mean he'd forgotten how. Fighting only delayed dealing with the real problem, which wasn't the creep standing in front of him. The real problem was the kids' father, Tony Bleecher.

"You're a friend of Tony's?"

He looked disappointed that Jordan hadn't reacted to his taunt. "I don't gotta tell you nothing."

"No, you don't. But I want to thank you. If you hadn't been so obvious in your attempt to follow Nell, we wouldn't have been alerted to the potential danger. Thanks to you, we'll take measures to mitigate this new challenge." It had taken years, but Jordan had eventually learned to use his brain, not his fists.

Although, man, he'd love to knock out a few of the guy's teeth.

"Mitigate this." The man gave him the finger, slid into his car and roared out of the parking lot.

Jordan took a minute to pull himself together before heading over to where Nell waited. He felt as if someone had given him a hard shake; everything was stirred up inside. The creep hadn't denied he knew Bleecher. What did they have planned? Were Nell and the kids in jeopardy or was Bleecher just messing with them? How had he become so involved?

All he'd wanted was to give Nell and the kids a drive home. And now this. He couldn't possibly walk away from the threat Bleecher posed. Who else did Nell have to help her? He closed his eyes and sighed. Mrs. T? Rodney, who could barely walk? Up-in-the-air Melody?

Bozo Perry? At least Perry had a gun, which was kind of scary now that he thought of it.

Whether he liked it or not, he felt obliged to help in any way he could until the adoption went through. There hadn't been many helping hands held out to him during his childhood, but there'd been a few. It was time to repay the debt.

"YOU SHOULD HAVE STAYED inside with the kids." Jordan scowled at her as he approached.

Nell snorted. "You mean I should let the big, tough guys duke it out by themselves?"

"Damn it, Nell." He shoved her bag into her hands. "You've got trouble. That guy's a creep."

Nell clutched the bag to her chest. "Jacob recognized him. His name is Stan, and he's a friend of Tony's, just as I suspected. Apparently, they met three or four years ago when Tony was in jail on an assault charge."

Jordan's face tightened. "We're calling Perry as soon as we get home."

She should have told Perry her suspicions earlier. She sighed, thinking of how complicated this would make things. Maybe she should call the police station and talk to someone else, but then Perry's feelings would be hurt. She knew he struggled with his job, that some of the other officers made fun of him. How cruel was it that Perry was a gorgeous, buff man, but dumb as a rock?

Beulah had had a heart attack a few months after Nell moved in, and Perry arrived seconds after the am-

bulance as was customary. He'd been stopping by ever
since and asking her out on dates. She'd tried to explain
to him she wasn't interested in anything beyond friendship, and frankly there were days when she wasn't even
interested in that. But he kept showing up, had even
talked her into attending a few police functions with
him. Sometimes she wondered if he was eventually
going to talk her into marrying him out of pity.

It made her tired when she realized he'd be stopping
by the house every day to check on them once he heard
what was going on now. Which was the point, wasn't it?

The smell of warm food rushed to greet her as she
and Jordan walked into the diner. Despite the dark
cloud Stan had cast, she'd seen a ray of light. For the
first time Jordan had called Dunstan Lane *home*. It was
a silly thing to fixate on, and, really, what did it matter?
But sometimes stupid and silly where exactly what a
person needed to get through the day.

While she and the children devoured most of their
food within minutes, Jordan picked around the edges of
the meal. Nell wondered if the altercation in the parking
lot had upset him more than he let on. But she changed
her mind when they started in on the sundaes. Jordan
gulped his down in half the time it took Lacey and
Jacob to eat theirs. Nell smiled to herself as she stole a
spoonful of ice cream from Lacey's sundae. She liked
it that the six-foot tough guy had a sweet tooth.

By the time they arrived home, both children had
fallen asleep. Jacob, predictably, woke and insisted he
was too big to be carried upstairs. With gratitude, Nell

allowed Jordan to take Lacey's limp, sleeping body from her. She'd carried Lacey up the three flights of stairs many times, but her niece had grown over the summer and was almost too heavy now.

"Thanks," Nell said as Jordan gently deposited Lacey on her bed. "She's growing so much." She swept her niece's hair out of her eyes, then kneeled to pull her tiny, red sneakers off. They'd found the sneakers in the secondhand store last week, and Lacey had worn them to show her father. But Tony had been so consumed with berating Jacob, there hadn't been a chance to mention the sneakers. Why couldn't he see how precious his children were? Did he even care? Nell arranged the sneakers neatly by the bed where Lacey would see them first thing in the morning.

She glanced up to see Jordan watching her from the doorway. "Would you mind checking on Jacob?" she asked as she dug under the pillow for Lacey's baby doll pajamas. "Tony was hard on him this time."

Jordan wiped a hand over his face. "I don't get how a guy can act like that toward his own kids. Or any kid, for that matter."

"Could we talk about this later?" She pointed at her ears, then at Lacey.

"Of course." Jordan disappeared from the doorway. A couple minutes later, warmth filled her when she heard the low, comforting murmur of Jordan's deep voice as he spoke to Jacob. Nell was used to handling damage control on her own after a visit to prison. It was comforting to know that, if only for tonight, she had help.

When she went to check on Jacob after tucking Lacey in, she was disappointed to discover Jordan was gone. The man had driven miles out of his way to pick them up on a Friday night and bought them supper. Not to mention scaring off the bogeyman. What more could she really ask?

Afraid to answer that question, she circled Jacob's room, straightened his bedside lamp and pulled the bamboo shade down on his window. "You okay?" she asked.

He had pulled his blankets up so she could see only his nose and eyes. "'Course."

She sat on the edge of his bed. "Your dad—" The comforting words she wanted to say wouldn't come.

Jacob burrowed deeper into his bed. "My dad's an a-hole."

"Sometimes," she admitted. What was the use of pretending otherwise? "But he's still your dad. People mess up, Jacob. You think it's your fault, but most of the time, the truth is, it has very little to do with you."

"You mean Dad wasn't really mad at me?"

"I don't know for sure, but chances are someone else made him mad before we showed up, and he took it out on you. I'm sorry. I wish things were different."

"Jordan says when he was little and bad stuff happened, he'd make himself think about good things. He says I'm lucky 'cause you love me."

Nell cleared the huskiness out of her throat and

kissed his forehead. "Did he mention how lucky I am to be your aunt?"

Jacob's eyes fluttered closed. "Maybe. Can we work on the tree house tomorrow?"

Relieved to have things back to normal, she smiled. "If I don't have to work, sure. Good night, champ."

"'Night."

Nell switched off the lamp and slipped out of the room. She wandered through the living room, picked up some of the day's debris. After depositing the items into her laundry basket of things-to-be-sorted, she went into the kitchen and stared inside the half-empty refrigerator much longer than it merited before closing the door.

She felt restless and out of sorts, a mood she hadn't experienced in a long time. Her must-do list was always too long and too demanding to allow for boredom. She had at least two loads of laundry she wanted to get done tonight, and there was a stack of bills in the top kitchen drawer, waiting to be paid. Instead, she flopped down on the couch.

She didn't want to think about Tony and farty Stan, but ignoring her brother-in-law's threat to interfere with the adoption wasn't going to make the situation go away. She hated to involve Perry and give him a reason to hang around more. He was a nice guy, but so needy. She didn't have the energy to take on another lost soul. But if she didn't tell him, Jordan would, and then she'd have to deal with the fallout from Perry's misguided possessiveness.

Despite her repeated attempts to communicate that no, they were not a couple, they were *not* dating, Perry either refused to believe her or couldn't grasp the concept that they were just friends. It was definitely better to call Perry herself. She'd make sure he understood she was asking for his professional help only.

But not tonight. She slipped her sandals off and wiggled her bare toes. Teressa, the social worker from Child Welfare assigned to their case, would have to be contacted in the morning, as well. Maybe Teressa would come up with more suggestions on how to combat Tony's latest maneuver. Not that Nell really needed to be told what not to do. They'd been over it several times, and it basically came down to providing a dependable and predictable home life. Starting a romantic relationship right now was one of the worst things she could do. She needed to keep her focus on the kids and their needs. Her own would have to wait. Not that there was anyone noticeably available and willing to start a relationship with anyway. Well, besides Perry. And that wasn't happening.

Feeling downright grouchy, she curled up on her side and closed her eyes. She was tired, that was all. Jordan's disappearing had nothing to do with the peculiar emptiness she felt inside. All she needed was rest.

"Whoa. Sorry."

Nell jackknifed upright at the sound of Jordan's voice.

"Sorry," he repeated. "It's only nine. I didn't think you'd go to sleep so early."

"No, I, ah…was just resting for a minute. I thought you'd gone out."

"I went to get some wine from my apartment." He waved the bottle in front of him. "I know you prefer beer, but it's all I had on hand. I thought you could use a drink. Don't get up," he continued when she moved to stand. "Just tell me where to find the corkscrew. I know where the glasses are."

"Second drawer down, on the left," she said. She scrambled to her feet and made a beeline for the bathroom as soon as he disappeared into the kitchen. Her hair was a mess, and the dress she'd put on earlier to bolster her spirits was wrinkled and had a streak of chocolate near her knee. God, she looked like a…like a tired, single mom. Which is exactly what she was. And Jordan was just being kind by offering her a much-needed glass of wine like any good neighbor would. No more, no less.

Nell chucked the hairbrush into the basket on the back of the toilet and ran a hand over her crumpled dress. No illusions, kiddo. She smiled wryly at her reflection and scooted out to the living room.

Jordan was sprawled on the couch, a glass of wine in one hand. Nell watched with fascination as he skimmed his hair back off his forehead. Her fingers ached to do that for him. She grabbed the glass of wine from the coffee table and wedged herself into the small children's chair across the room.

He raised an eyebrow. "There's plenty of space over here, Nell."

She sipped her wine and savored the rich, full taste on her tongue as much as the sound of his deep voice saying her name. She was way out of practice with this kind of stuff—adult conversation. "I'm okay," she chirped.

"So—" Jordan looked around "—you never did tell me where you sleep."

She rocked forward. Jordan was right, she didn't fit into the little chair comfortably. But other than bringing a chair in from the kitchen, she was stuck where she was. Sitting beside Jordan on the couch seemed too... she shied away from the word *intimate*. She was being ridiculous, and she couldn't believe she'd already drunk most of her wine.

"You're sitting on my bed. I used to have Lacey's room," she explained as she set her glass on the coffee table between them. "Lacey and Jacob shared the other room. When Jacob turned nine last winter, he suddenly needed more privacy, and so did Lacey."

Jordan grinned, a mischievous glint dancing in his eyes. "It must play hell on your sex life."

Nell snorted before she could stop herself. She blushed. How graceless could she get? Jordan filled her wineglass, deposited the bottle on the floor beside him and held his hand out to her.

"If you don't sit with me, I'll have to leave. I can't handle watching you squirm in that chair."

"You're right. I'm being stupid." She took his hand and allowed him to pull her out of the chair. She inserted herself on the opposite end of the couch and put her bare feet up on the coffee table. "This is good wine. Cheers." She toasted him.

"It's one of my favorites." He held up his glass to look at the wine before taking a sip. "I have an extensive collection at home."

Home, in this instance, wasn't the pitiful room downstairs. "You have a condo in Seabend?"

"Yeah. It's nice there. You should see it sometime."

"Sure." She'd have to remember not to wear her overalls and leave her tool belt at home. Har, har.

"Alex is staying there for the next few months." He laughed. "I think Alex and Melody had a date tonight."

She sat up straighter. "No."

"I'm not certain, but I think I saw Alex's car as I was leaving."

"Wow."

"That surprises you?"

"I don't know Alex, but I doubt they have a lot in common."

"What is that, inverted snobbery?"

"Hardly. Melody's into touchy-feely stuff. Matter of fact, I could have sworn she didn't like him at all when she met him last week." Nell paused and savored another mouthful of wine, letting the heat of the alcohol spin through her. She couldn't remember the last time she'd had wine. Which was a very good reason to take it slow.

"Alex, on the other hand…" she continued, leaning her head against the back of the couch.

Jordan sat forward and rested his arms on his knees, looking suddenly alert. "What about Alex?"

She squinted at him. "He's your friend, right?"

"We met at university."

"He's okay, I guess."

Jordan grinned. "Just okay?"

"I'm betting he's used to getting what he wants."

"You say that like it's a bad thing."

Her foot jerked when he reached for it. He grabbed again and caught it this time. "You keep wiggling your toes like your feet are sore. Let me give you a foot massage. I'm good at massages."

Not just *foot* massages, but massages. As in full body? Not going to go there. Thinking about Jordan's hands all over her body would open floodgates that had to remain closed. No need to review all the reasons why. That was fast becoming old ground, well trampled.

A groan escaped her as he pressed both thumbs against her instep and slowly worked his way up the length of her foot. "Ohh, that feels so good."

Everything, she realized, felt good at the moment. The wine, their conversation, the massage. The tension from her horrific day vaporized. Her eyes drifted closed as she concentrated on the warmth of Jordan's hands. She'd give herself five minutes to savor the delicious feeling, then pull herself together. Five minutes wasn't too much to ask, was it?

JORDAN TRACED THE DELICATE line of Nell's instep as he studied her face. She had such an expressive face, it wasn't difficult to guess what she was feeling. Which suited him just fine; he liked knowing exactly where he stood. At the moment her eyes were closed, which was probably lucky, because if she could read his thoughts as easily, she'd be gone before he could blink. He turned his attention to each individual toe, rolling them between his fingers. The corners of her mouth lifted in appreciation.

What he wanted was to hear her groan again. Her soft, throaty purr had shot straight through him. He'd be happy to sit here all night massaging her feet if it meant he could hear the intoxicating sound again, except for one problem. He dropped her foot into his lap, picked up her other foot and went to work. Her legs looked smooth and muscular, and he figured he could spend at least another hour running his hands over them before he needed more. And therein lay the problem. He wanted more from this woman. Much more. He wasn't used to not going after what he wanted.

He squeezed her foot and laid it down beside the other one. Then held his breath as she wiggled her toes and came into contact with the physical evidence of his wayward thoughts. Her eyes shot open, and she jerked upright, her face a lovely, dark rose. She even blushed prettily.

"Sorry. I must have drifted off." She shoved her wineglass onto the coffee table so abruptly, wine splashed over the rim.

"It was just a foot massage, okay?" Who was he

trying to reassure, her or himself? "Sorry I upset you. These things happen."

"I'm not upset. I'm—" She leaped to her feet. "Actually, I am upset. I like you, and I think we can be friends, but that's as far as it can go. So, this—" she waved her hand at the space between them "—this isn't going to happen."

He relaxed back into the couch and tried not to smile. He loved the way her green eyes sparked when she got riled up. Damn if he didn't want to tumble her down onto his lap and kiss her senseless. He folded his arms against the temptation. "I know, Nell. I got that part."

She looked around the room as if searching for a quick exit. "You should go," she said.

"That's probably a good idea, but I've got a problem." He hadn't planned to tell her about the newlyweds tonight, but it was just what he needed to distract her. She had enough to worry about. He didn't want her worrying about him hitting on her, too.

"And that would be?"

"It's the new tenants, Lisa and Tom. They, uh, they kind of…" How to put it politely?

"They what?" Curiosity lit Nell's face. At least he'd succeeded in distracting her.

"They make a lot of noise. All night, if you get what I mean." He should have taken care of the problem himself.

"All night?" A small giggle bubbled out of her. His lips twitched upward in response to the sound.

"All night, every night. And in the afternoon when they get back from work."

She covered her mouth with her hands. "You're making that up."

"I wish. They're driving me crazy. If I don't get a decent night's sleep soon, I think I'm going to lose it."

"Have you ever—" She started laughing so hard she couldn't speak. She dropped down on the couch beside him.

He grinned. He loved her no-holds-barred laugh. It was a sound he didn't hear often in his carefully constructed world. "Have I ever what?" he prompted.

"Earplugs." She gasped.

He felt a rumble of laughter inside, her giddiness infecting him. "I don't think I've painted the picture clearly enough. They're very…verbal. And I think they have their bed pushed against the wall between our rooms."

Giggling, she bent over at the waist and tilted toward him. "That's why you…supper here," she managed to get out.

He stopped laughing to inhale her scent. She smelled like lemons. Clean and fresh with a zing, perfect for Nell. "At first, yeah."

"Why didn't you tell me?"

"I just did. Any great ideas of what we're going to do about the situation?"

"I'll have to think about it." She wiped tears from her eyes. Another giggle rippled out of her.

"What?"

"You could do the same thing when they're home."

Oh, he liked that idea. "You mean have wild sex all night long?"

Her eyes turned dark green and she grew still, as if holding her breath. "No, I, uh…" She tore her gaze away from his, glanced around the room, and then as if against her will, slowly turned back to him.

When she opened her mouth to speak, he leaned toward her. "I think we could manage that, don't you?"

Not giving her a chance to respond, he skimmed his lips over hers, then returned to catch her sigh as he sank into the feel and taste of her. Oh, yeah, they could manage that and so much more. Her mouth felt hot and yielding and demanding all at the same time. Their teeth clashed, and she started to pull back but he swooped in for another taste. And another.

Wanting her closer, he tugged her into his lap, where he'd wanted her all along. Where she belonged. He could kiss her all night until she begged—

Nell put her hands on his shoulders and pushed. "No."

He closed his eyes and leaned his forehead against hers. The last woman who had said no to him had probably been Aunt Beulah. Even understanding why Nell was putting on the brakes, he didn't much like it. Especially with that passionate look in her eyes she hadn't yet managed to douse. Or her swollen mouth that begged to be kissed again.

"Right." He picked her up off his lap and placed her on her feet in front of him. "Sorry."

She crossed her arms, looking cold and forlorn. "I think we've already covered all the reasons."

"At least a couple of times. Doesn't seem to be sinking in, though. You and me, hon. We've got something going on here."

He watched the last of the heat die away from her eyes, leaving behind a hint of sadness. She tried to smile. "If I'm ever looking for a quick fling, I'll know who to call."

Was that supposed to be a joke? 'Cause he never felt less like laughing. "I won't hold my breath."

They took each other's measure before she turned away to pick up one of Lacey's dolls that had fallen off the couch. He had to leave before he said something he might regret. It wasn't so much that he was angry; true, he didn't like being rejected, even if he understood why, but he knew how to handle rejection. In his line of work, he aggressively cultivated clients. Sometimes it panned out, sometimes not. Sure, he was bummed when the results weren't in his favor, but he'd never had this hollowed-out feeling in his gut before. The intensity disturbed him.

He stood. "I'd better go."

She nodded and kept on picking up the kids' stuff with a weariness that made him want to drive his fist through the wall.

"Look, I'm sorry."

She stopped and looked at him. "It's okay. I knew better than to let us…you know."

He shook his head. That wasn't what he meant at

all. If he was sorry about anything it was they couldn't explore the connection they seemed to be forging between them. He'd never met a woman who captured his attention so completely.

He went to the door. "Good night, Nell." But she'd already slipped away from him, disappearing into the kitchen. With grim determination, he descended the stairs to his musty room.

He'd run into his share of roadblocks on his way to success. That's all the attraction between them was, a minor detour. Somehow Nell and the kids had distracted him from his vision of success. He had to narrow his focus, get back on track. He'd cut out having supper with them, work longer hours and phone Sandra. She was always up for pulling together a dinner party. A dinner that included scintillating conversation and gourmet food. Anything but mashed potatoes and frozen vegetables.

CHAPTER SEVEN

IT WAS HAPPENING AGAIN. She was hurting the people she loved. If Tony did gain custody of his children, would he insist they get in the car with him when he'd been drinking? Would he disappear on a bender for days like he used to and forget all about them? Nell wiped tears from her eyes as she huddled inside the dingy garage.

The day had started out beautiful. She poked her head out to check on Lacey and Jacob playing in the tree house. It still was a clear, sparkling Saturday morning. But the promise of the day had disappeared with the phone call she'd just received from the social worker. She clutched the cordless phone to her chest and squeezed her eyes shut.

Tony had called in a complaint to Child Welfare. He claimed she was prejudicing his children against him, and that she had also influenced Teressa. Maybe she had, because Teressa felt obliged to call her on a Saturday with the warning that Nell would be getting a new worker on Monday. She'd cautioned Nell that the new worker, Mrs. Cripps, was not the kind of person to consider extenuating circumstances. Either you scored enough points to adopt or you didn't.

The situation hadn't changed, except the adoption

had become even more delicate. Tony was in jail for killing his wife, for God's sake, and she was doing her best for the kids. They loved her. She just had to *keep* doing her best. No distractions. It wasn't as if she had woken this morning and thought Jordan's kiss had changed everything. Okay, it was the last thing on her mind last night before she fell asleep—the kiss, how good his hard, masculine body felt against hers. And before she'd opened her eyes this morning, Jordan was right there in her thoughts, as if she'd spent the night in his arms. Her mouth turned dry at the idea. With a savage jerk, she yanked open a bag of rags Mrs. T. had refused to throw away, found a worn tea towel and scrubbed the evidence of tears from her face.

She hadn't needed the phone call to refocus her energy. Before she'd gotten out of bed, she'd already made up her mind she and Jordan did not and would never have anything "going on between them," as he'd put it.

She stuffed the towel in the back pocket of her shorts, and watched from the garage door as Lacey used a whisk to sweep the floor of the tree house. The pending adoption was only one factor that made her decision easy. Easy? No, it had been anything but, because she had to admit that Jordan was right. There was a connection between them. No sense in pretending otherwise. She hadn't been looking to get involved with anyone, especially now. And she was certain career-minded, sky's-the-limit Tanner hadn't been looking for any kind of commitment, either. Certainly not with her. Single mom, two kids, potential farmer. Her mouth quirked. Could you find two more different people?

"Hello there, anyone home?" When Melody laid a gentle hand on her arm, Nell jerked herself back to the present.

"You're smiling, but your aura's very dark. Why are you hiding inside the garage? What's going on?" Melody asked.

"Not much. We're going to work on the tree house this morning." She followed Melody out into the sunshine. "My, my. Don't you look gorgeous. What's up?"

"This and that." Melody twitched the full skirt of her buttercup-yellow summer dress.

Nell grinned, relieved to think of something else besides her problems. "This and that wouldn't go by the name of Alex by any chance?"

A surprising un-Melody-like blush crept up her throat. "Who told you?"

"Jordan. He saw Alex's SUV last night. So, you and Alex." She raised her eyebrows. "That seems… unusual."

"I know. I'm a little confused."

"In what way?"

Melody frowned down at her sandals. "The first day I met him I got this feeling. Here." She pressed her hands against her stomach. "I thought *this man belongs to me.* I've never felt anything so strongly. It scares me. I mean, *Alex.* He's a lawyer, for heaven's sake. I know it's not right, we're not right. We can't be. He's black and white, and I'm all colors of the rainbow." She smiled sadly. "But I can't seem to help myself. I only met him a week ago, but I think I'm falling in love with him. What am I going to do Nell?"

Fresh tears popped into Nell's eyes as she hugged Melody. She didn't know if she was crying because she was happy for her friend or sorry that she'd probably never get to experience that head-over-heels feeling. Perhaps she was just feeling particularly emotional today. "Follow your heart, Mel. Like you always have. If it's meant to be, things will work out. Isn't that what you always tell me?"

"You're right. Thank you. We've only had one date. I'm probably getting ahead of myself. Okay, your turn. Jordan."

"Nothing to tell." Nell grabbed the old wicker basket she used for picking vegetables and scooted over to the tomato patch. She and the kids would have tomato sandwiches for lunch.

"I like your dress, Melody," Lacey sang out from her perch on the tree house porch.

"Thank you, honey. Those are seriously cool red sneakers."

Lacey grinned down at them. "They're my faves."

Melody turned back to Nell. "I don't believe it."

"They really are her favorite shoes."

"I'm talking about you and Jordan. The air sizzles when you two are in the same room."

Nell nodded, plucked a plump ripe tomato. No sense in trying to bullshit Melody; she had a direct pipeline into Nell's psyche. "That may be, but I've flipped the off switch. No more sizzle."

Melody lowered her voice. "Because of the adoption?"

"Partly." She stood, wiped a trickle of sweat from her forehead. Not wanting the children to overhear the conversation, she wandered over to the shade beside the garage. She put the basket of tomatoes on the grass beside her.

Melody followed her. "I've watched him with Jacob and Lacey. He's good with them. I don't see the problem."

"Come on, Melody. Jordan's never made any bones about what he wants. He's after money in a big way. There's no place for someone like me and the kids in his life."

Melody's eyes widened. "You're scared."

"Don't be ridiculous." Nell looked away from her friend's intense scrutiny.

"Does this have anything to do with your parents' and your sister's deaths?"

"Of course not." She hated the gruff sound in her voice.

"We've been over this, Nell. You deserve to be happy. No matter how much you love someone, you can't control their lives. You're no more responsible for that man shooting your parents than you are for Tony making your sister get in the car with him when he was drunk. Mary could have refused to go with him. Your parents could have—hell, they should have—closed the store early and gone home to look after their sick daughter."

Except Nell hadn't been sick. She'd lied. When she was twelve, her parents had owned a mom-and-pop corner store and had worked fourteen- or sixteen-hour days. When she wasn't in school or at home looking after her younger sister, she was expected to work at the store, helping stock shelves. Knowing she'd never have a normal life like the girls at school, Nell read books to escape. That Wednesday night, Halloween night, she was supposed to help her father at the store so her mother could have a break. But the school librarian, who always made the time to ask how Nell and her sister were, had saved the newest *Sweet Valley High* book for her, and she wanted to read it right away. So she called her parents and told them she wasn't feeling well so she could stay home.

The small deception hadn't seemed a crime at the time. It wasn't as if she was stealing out to go trick-or-treating with other kids or leaving her sister at home by herself. She just hadn't factored in the guy dressed as a skeleton who pointed a gun at her father's head and demanded the money in the till. Her father had refused, so the skeleton man shot both her father and mother on the spot.

Logically, she knew Melody was right. She wasn't responsible for anyone's death, and yes, she deserved to be happy. But she didn't know how to lay down the burden of what-if. The only thing she could do was try to make Lacey's and Jacob's lives as happy as possible.

She smiled at her friend. "You're right, and I'm trying." What was Melody's favorite refrain? Cut the cord, let the guilt float free.

"Visualize." Melody moved her hands through the air as if she were conducting an orchestra. "Happy Nell. Laughing Nell. Loving Nell."

Nell laughed. "Thanks, Melody. You're a good friend."

"But you're still not going to give Jordan a chance."

Nell yanked the old lawn mower out of the garage. "The social worker phoned this morning." She squatted down and pried the top off the motor. It had been sputtering last week and needed a tune-up.

"They work weekends now?"

"No." She got up, went into the garage for her toolbox and came back out. "Tony filed a complaint. He claims I'm turning his children against him and that my social worker is prejudiced, as well. I get a new worker next week. Mrs. Cripps, a regular dragon lady according to Teressa."

"I'm so sorry, Nell."

"Yeah, me, too." She selected a ratchet, backed the spark plug out of its slot and wiped it on her rag. Other than the basics, checking the oil and spark plug, she had no idea how to tune up a motor. She dug in the toolbox again and came up with a new spark plug. If that didn't fix the sputter, maybe Jordan would spring for a new mower. Or, at the very least, a better secondhand one.

She glanced up at Melody's concerned face and tried

to smile. "Looks like the fun and games are over." Not that they'd ever started.

"Tony's such a pisser. I wish someone in prison would take him out."

"Melody!"

"Well, it would be the perfect solution to your problems. You'd automatically get the kids, and you and Jordan would be free to explore your potential as a couple."

Nell swiped at the drops of sweat on her forehead. "Nice fantasy, but I don't see that happening anytime soon. Take a look behind you."

Pushing away a sudden bleak feeling that took the shine off the morning, Nell cranked the new spark plug into place. Alex and Jordan were walking up the driveway with the most beautiful woman in the world between them. There was no mistaking which man she was with; she had a proprietary hand clamped on Jordan's forearm. They looked like they were made for each other, the woman's long blond hair and tall, willowy body a perfect foil for Jordan's dark, masculine beauty. He had it all, money, a solid career, friends and probably any woman he gazed at with those soulful, gray eyes.

And that was the real reason she and Tanner would never happen; he didn't need her. One thing she knew for certain, if you wanted a place in someone's life, they had to make room for you, to need you. People talked about love, and Nell understood it on a theoretical level, but in her experience, if a person didn't need you, sooner or later they'd find a reason to leave. No, better to avoid the whole thing entirely. Especially now.

Jordan had kissed her. That was all. No big deal.

Nell glanced up from the lawn mower to watch Alex stop beside Melody and run his hands up and down her bare arms. "You're looking particularly beautiful this morning." He leaned closer and murmured something in her ear that brought a delicate pink blush to her friend's face. Nell almost toppled over into the dirt when Melody giggled. Melody was not the giggling kind—at least not until now. The two of them couldn't keep their hands off each other, gently bumping shoulders, holding hands. Nell shot to her feet and forced a smile. She loved Mel and refused to be jealous of her friend's happiness.

"What a lovely garden, Jordan. Is this your gardener?" The willowy blonde smiled at Nell.

Jordan looked confused, maybe a little embarrassed as he rubbed his free hand against the back of his neck. "Um...well, Nell is...."

"The gardener. And the caretaker, as well. I'd shake your hand but—" Nell held up her oil-stained hand. "Don't think you'd appreciate it."

"My mother always has such a difficult time hiring a good gardener. I don't suppose you'd let her borrow yours?" Blondie leaned into Jordan as she gazed up at him from under long, luscious lashes.

Borrow her? What did Blondie think? She was nothing more than lawn furniture? Nell pulled the rag out of her hip pocket and meticulously cleaned her hands as she counted to ten.

"That would be between your mother and Nell. Do you do landscaping for other people, Nell?" Jordan asked.

"Sometimes." She bent over and flicked at some dirt on her legs to avoid looking at him. She had never been skilled at hiding her feelings, and Jordan had proven to be particularly adept at deciphering her expressions. It was never a good idea to let your boss know exactly how stupid you thought he was.

"NELL'S VERY EXPENSIVE, she's—"

"I doubt if Nell—"

Melody and Jordan spoke at the same time, stopped and exchanged a knowing look. *Defuse and run.* Nell looked as though she was about to explode. Jordan had no idea what Sandra was up to; he'd never heard her use that snooty tone before. He pried her hand away from his arm, preparing for a tackle in case Miss Nellie went after her. Not that Sandra didn't deserve to be taken down a notch or two for talking about Nell like she was a fixture, but not in front of the children. He choked back a laugh. What was it about Nell that made him feel so good?

Melody chattered on about Nell's skills being in great demand and how expensive her services were. He made a mental note to think about how he could use her in PR as he studied the steaming dynamo in front of him. The *dirty,* steaming dynamo. Nell had one black streak on her forehead and another down her left cheek. He wanted to wipe the streaks away but knew he'd get swatted for his efforts. She looked hot and sweaty, and there was hardly anything left of the ragged, cut-off jean shorts she wore. But her butt filled the disreputable shorts just fine, and her tanned, muscular legs were a work of art. As for the rest of her… His gaze locked onto her breasts, and he felt an instant stirring that could prove to be very embarrassing if he didn't get a grip. She wasn't wearing anything under her thin T-shirt.

Jordan swallowed with difficulty, tore his eyes away from her breasts and met her gaze. Heat arrowed straight at him from the green depths of her eyes. She folded her arms over her beautiful small breasts, but not before he saw her nipples pucker against the cotton.

"Jor-dan." Sandra broke his name into two syllables, underlining her impatience.

"Sorry, I, ah… Anyone else find it incredibly hot today?"

Melody snorted and linked her arm through Alex's. "We're off. Are you going to be okay?" she asked Nell.

Nell hitched her shorts up. "Of course. The kids and I are probably going to hang out here."

Jordan cleared his throat. "Um, about the mower." He wasn't sure this was the best time to raise the issue, but it looked as if Nell had the thing half-ripped apart. Rodney had approached him a couple days ago to tell him the mower wasn't running properly. The old man had, with the greatest respect, explained Nell hadn't a clue how to fix it. Not that the small inconvenience would stop her from trying. Apparently small-engine repair was one of Rodney's hidden talents. It was up to Jordan to find a way to convince Nell it was in everyone's best interest to let Rodney have a look at the mower.

"It's got a sputter, but I replaced the old spark plug. That should fix the problem." She squatted down, snapped the lid back over the engine.

"Fine, but if the problem persists, Rodney's going to take a look at it. He's good at small-engine repair."

"You want Rodney to fix the mower." She rose slowly, as if it pained her to stand. Man, did she have to look as if he'd just taken away her puppy? He'd expected a few fireworks, maybe, but she looked so dejected he wanted to tell her to go nuts. Tear the damned thing to pieces.

"Only if it doesn't work," he assured her.

Sandra looked from one to the other, a puzzled look on her face. "You are talking about this old thing, aren't you? It's ancient. Why not just replace it? Or did I miss something?"

Unfortunately, she hadn't. Somewhere along the way, he'd started looking at things differently when Nell was around. And he was enjoying the change. After his rocky childhood, he'd craved material things to show the world he'd made it. Even if it was just a new lawn mower. But he also loved a challenge, and Nell kept him on his toes. She'd probably be crushed if they threw out the old mower. How was it possible someone so sensitive could be so strong? She was an amazing woman. A caretaker, yes, but she was a damned fine one.

When Sandra slipped her arm through his, Jordan couldn't think of a way to put some distance between them without looking surly and offending her. After all, he'd called her this morning, asking if she'd like to have a look at the house as a prelude to inquiring if she'd be interested in arranging a dinner party. Most of the time, Sandra was a kind person. He had no idea what possessed her to treat Nell as if she were a commodity to be traded.

If he didn't know better, he'd almost think she was setting the scene, a technique she used to get clients to agree to her proposal. One would think that meant presenting the idea or person in the best possible light. But humans were complex, and sometimes to get a yes, you had to aim for no. So, was that what she was doing? Treating Nell badly to make him realize her true value? Why would Sandra do that? He already appreciated Nell. Besides, it wasn't anyone's business what he thought about his caretaker.

"I've been telling Jordan he shouldn't stay in that stinky old room. I think he should live in the remodeled apartment on the first floor, but he says there are tenants renting it already." She bumped him with her hip. "What's the point of owning the building if you can't live in whatever apartment you want?"

Okay, now he knew for sure Sandra was up to something. Yes, she'd scolded him for living in the bedsit, and he'd actually thanked her for the reminder that he deserved better. But he'd be the one to decide where he lived. He pulled his arm out of her grasp and put a good couple of feet between them. "Sandra, I don't think—"

"You may be right," Nell interrupted him.

"What?" Was this some kind of woman-bonding thing? Gang up on Jordan?

"I meant to talk to you about that," Nell continued. "I saw the better half of our newlyweds this morning." The corners of her mouth twitched. "Before I had a chance to talk to Lisa about that little…problem, she dissolved into tears. She's pregnant. Go figure, eh? Just married and boom—pregnant, just like that. They want out. She wants to move back to the city where she'll be closer to her family and her doctor."

"They signed a year's lease." Yes, he wanted them to be quiet, but a contract was sacrosanct in his world.

Nell shrugged. "So? This would make the problem go away, and you could move into the apartment and have loads of room."

"This way you'd have a home office," Sandra added. "You're always complaining about how there are too many distractions at work. We could get in some late-night strategizing sessions."

Jordan opened his mouth to ask her what she thought she was doing when she sent him a sly wink. Oh. He relaxed. Sandra, the queen of marketing, was making him look desirable and in demand. Wait a minute, more desirable to whom? No way could she have picked up on his attraction to Nell. Even if she had, since when did he need help with women?

"When do they want to move out?" he asked. With Alex covering the mortgage payments on his condo, Jordan could easily afford to pay the rent for the apartment, which meant the building would still look okay on the books. He smiled, warming to the idea. No more stinky room. No more being kept up all night.

Nell smiled back. "Why don't you talk to them? Their car's across the street, so they're still home."

Nell's cordless phone rang. She plucked it out of a basket of tomatoes sitting by the garage and answered it. Her mouth flattened into a thin line and her shoulders drooped while she listened to the caller. Jordan shifted closer to her, wondering if it was Tony making more demands. He had no idea what he could do if it was, but he knew in intricate detail what he'd *like* to do to the scumbag.

"Hello, Mr. Jordan." Lacey's sweet, high voice sang out from the tree house.

Jordan smiled up at her and waved as Nell disappeared into the dilapidated garage. If he were staying, he'd tear the garage down before it collapsed and build a shed with lots of room for Nell's gardening equipment. Maybe even a greenhouse off to one side.

He channeled his thoughts in a saner direction. "I see kitty cats can climb trees as well as dance."

Lacey giggled. "We have a staircase, silly. Back here."

"What a darling child. Is she Nell's?" Sandra asked.

"Yes." She wasn't their birth mother, but in all other aspects she was their mother.

"Hey, Jacob. What's up?"

Jacob was laying on the floor of the tree house, alternately reading his book and checking out the action below. "Not much. Just waiting for Nell to stop yammering so we can work on the tree house."

Yammering sounded like a word Tony's fat friend Stan would use. Of course he'd thought about how hard it must be for Nell, losing her sister and having to deal with her brother-in-law, not to mention giving Jacob and Lacey the love and security they so desperately needed. But the day-to-day reality of the difficulties she juggled was slowly sinking in.

How many wrong turns would he have avoided in his life if someone had done the same for him? Sometimes, especially recently, the idea that he'd missed something in his drive to attain financial stability haunted him. Which was ridiculous because he'd always known exactly what he wanted, and he was well on his way to getting it.

The sound of something solid striking wood came from inside the garage. Nell, working out her frustration. "Excuse me," Jordan said to Sandra. "I think I'd better check this out." He hustled into the garage before Nell brought the old building down singlehandedly.

"Nell." She held an axe, almost as big as her, above her head. Without looking in his direction, she sunk it into the block of wood perched on a huge stump. "Tanner, just—don't." Her voice broke on the last word.

He stuck his hands in his pockets, hating the helpless feeling in his gut as Nell dropped the axe and crumpled down onto the stump. She swiped at the tears on her cheeks.

He took a cautious step forward. "What can I do to help?"

"You?" She glanced at him. "Nothing."

He wasn't used to being dismissed so readily. "Perhaps if you tell me the problem."

"Which one?" She shot to her feet, assumed her fighting stance, hands on hips, eyes shooting sparks. Much better. She'd been momentarily down, but not out.

"How about the most current one? The phone call obviously upset you."

"You don't want to get sucked into my problems, Tanner. Why don't you go on your way with your pretty lady and enjoy the day?"

With a jolt, he realized no matter what he did today he wouldn't be able to enjoy himself, knowing Nell was miserable. "I thought we agreed you'd call me Jordan."

"Okay, Jordan, here's your get-out-of-jail-free card. Take it and run along with your girlfriend. I'm sure she's had enough of slumming for one day."

"Sandra and I are colleagues, that's all. She just dropped by to see the house." Why was he explaining himself to her? He couldn't remember the last time he'd felt obliged to explain his actions to anyone.

"Not that it's any of my business." She smiled.

"Not that it's any of your business. So." He leaned a hip against an old three-legged end table. "The phone call."

"They want me to come into work, and I can't find anyone to babysit. You'd have been proud of me, Tan... Jordan. I wanted to tell them to stuff the job, but I didn't." She kicked at a piece of kindling by her feet. "Then they gave me an ultimatum—show up today or don't show up at all."

"Can they do that?"

She shrugged. "Apparently. Even though I'm a manager, I'm a seasonal, part-time employee. They can do what they want. I only need another six weeks, and I'll be able to get employment insurance for the winter. In the spring I can look for another job, but at this time of year, there aren't any. At least not ones that I'm qualified for."

"Does Mrs. T. ever look after the kids?"

She shot him an incredulous look. "Not hardly. Besides, she went to the walk-in clinic. Her gout's acting up in this heat. No telling when she'll be back."

"How about Rodney? Jacob and Lacey like him."

"He went to his farm today. It's the first time he's gone back since he's been here." She frowned. "I hope he's okay."

Unbelievable. Even with her own problems, she was worried about the old man.

"What about their grandparents?"

"My parents are dead, and Tony's are...unacceptable."

How much had Nell and the children had to endure? On top of everything else, now the grandparents were unacceptable. There was a word that covered a multiple of sins. He took a deep breath. "I'll babysit," he said before he could change his mind.

"You?"

Okay, now he was insulted. "How hard can it be?"

"You're kidding me, right?"

"I do have some people skills, Nell. I can handle two children. It's only for a few hours, right?" Two kids for part of the day, what was the big deal?

"What about your girlfriend? No offense, but she doesn't look like the wash-and-wear type."

"She's not my—" He stopped, angry that he was explaining himself again. "She just dropped by for a few minutes."

"I don't know, Tanner." She shot him an impish smile. "I mean, Jordan. I guess if things got out of hand you could bring them to the garden center. Are you sure?"

"Not as sure as I was five minutes ago. You keep talking like that and I'm withdrawing my offer."

"Nothing to worry about. They're generally good kids. I should be able to get back by seven. Thanks, Jordan. I'll pay you back somehow."

As she scooted past him into the sunshine and called for Lacey and Jacob, a feeling of disquiet crept over him. He hated words like *generally*. It reminded him of clients who were *hardly ever* in the red or had *mostly* dependable customers. He called them quicksand words; when people started talking like that, the chances that their business was sinking out of sight rose dramatically.

Plus, he'd never been left alone with a child before, never mind two. But Lacey and Jacob were good kids; he could probably even get some work done. And having Nell indebted to him—well, he could think of a few transactions he wouldn't mind discussing with Miss Nellie. It never hurt to have the upper hand.

CHAPTER EIGHT

JORDAN, JACOB AND LACEY stood in the doorway of the apartment and watched Nell disappear down the stairs. She'd given him a frigging book of lists of what the kids could or couldn't do, what they liked to eat, what they should eat, who they were allowed to play with, along with a whole page of phone numbers—the garden center, doctor, neighbors. Jordan stuffed the notepad in his hip pocket and looked down at his two small charges. By the suspicious looks on their faces, they obviously weren't convinced he was the best man for the job. Time to put his people skills to work.

"Okay." He rubbed his hands together. "What's on the agenda for today?"

"What's a 'genda?" Lacey asked, her finger stuck up her nose. Was that on the can't-do list? It should be.

"It's a list of what we're going to do. Don't do that, Lacey."

"Lacey's a booger baby." Jacob snickered.

Lacey's bottom lip trembled. "Am not."

"Are, too."

Yikes. They were at it already, and Nell had barely disappeared from sight.

"Don't tease your sister, Jacob."

"Don't tell me what to do," Jacob snarled.

Jordan hadn't the slightest idea how to respond to the nine-year-old. His mother, or one of her boyfriends, would have slapped him up the side of his head for talking that way. Likely Nell had her own manner of dealing with insubordination, but damned if he knew what it was. The kids had always been so well behaved when she was around. "What did you and Nell have planned for today?"

"We were going to work on the tree house," Lacey said. She took her finger out of her nose and stuck her thumb in her mouth. That was a security thing, wasn't it? So, that meant what? They didn't feel secure around him? That was reasonable. This was the first time they'd been left alone together.

He squatted down and smiled. "What were you planning to do?"

Lacey eased close enough to lean against him. "You like me better than Jacob, don't you?" She batted her short, spiky lashes at him.

Jordan laughed. "I like you very much, but I also like Jacob a lot. I'm glad we're all friends."

"We were going to add another room." Jacob watched him with bright eyes.

"Another room." Just his luck. A paintbrush he could handle, but he didn't know the first thing about carpentry. He stood, rubbed the back of his neck. Might as well fess up, although it wasn't going to earn him any brownie points.

"I don't know how to build."

"Anything?" Jacob looked at him as if he were a bug on the end of a pin.

"Nothing. Sorry, bud."

"Do you know how to fix a car or a lawn mower?" the boy persisted.

"No."

"How about cook?"

"I can make grilled-cheese sandwiches. Open a can of soup."

Jacob's jaw dropped. "That's it?"

"Well, I can make coffee, but I don't think that counts."

"I can cook lots of stuff." Despite being more than a foot taller, Jordan felt as if the kid was looking down his nose at him.

"I can, too," Lacey piped up. "Don't worry, we'll take care of you, Mr. Jordan."

Jacob snorted. "What *can* you do?"

He had a feeling analyzing complex businesses to identify their strengths and weaknesses, and creating and implementing dynamic business plans wasn't going to impress his young critics. Who knew kids could be so tough?

"I can take you to the beach or the movies," he said.

"No, you can't. Look at the list. I'm allergic to salt water, and movies give Lacey nightmares." His disgusted expression more eloquent than words, Jacob disappeared into his room, slamming the door behind him.

Jordan sank down onto the couch, wondering if it was too early for a beer. He yanked the notepad out of his pocket and started to read. He'd thought Nell was being overprotective when she'd produced "the book," but maybe there was more to this kid thing than he'd realized. There it was: #3. *Don't go to the beach.* Jacob was allergic to water and Lacey burned much too easily, even with sunscreen.

Lacey walked over, leaned against his knee and stared at him until he looked up from the list. She was such a sweet little girl. "What is it, honey?"

"I have to change my clothes."

"You look great. You don't have to change." Jordan went back to the list. *No sugar.* Nell had to be kidding. Sugar fueled the world, especially a kid's world.

"Mr. Jordan?"

"Yes, Lacey."

"I have to change my clothes." Her voice held a slight quaver that made him think of a tremor before an earthquake.

He tossed the notepad on the couch beside him. "Okay, go change your clothes. Then we'll decide what we're going to do."

He relaxed when her thumb came out of her mouth. "I need your help," she said.

"With what?"

"Getting dressed, silly."

"With buttons and stuff. Sure. You go get ready and yell when you need help."

When Lacey skipped off to her room, he eased back into the couch and studied the room. Man, it was hot in the apartment. He spotted the window air conditioner unit, got up and flicked the power button several times. Nothing. Why hadn't Nell told him it was broken?

He tried opening the window, but it took all his strength to raise it three or four inches. Apparently his little caretaker hadn't given him the full scoop of what upgrades needed to be done. With a sinking feeling, he wondered how extensive the list was.

"I'm ready, Mr. Jordan," Lacey called from her room.

No way was he spending the rest of the day cooped up in the hot, stuffy apartment. "Oh." He stopped dead at the door to Lacey's room and started backpedaling fast. "I thought you said you were ready."

"I am."

He turned his back to her and shielded his eyes with his hand for good measure. "You don't have anything on." Except for a pair of panties that had bees or ducks, something on them. He hadn't looked long enough to know.

"You have to help me pick out what I'm going to wear."

The warble in her voice was back. "Yeah, but…you know. Um…" Think, man. There had to be a simple way out of this. "How about you put something on, and I'll tell you if I like it or not." Was he good or what?

"That's not how Nell does it. She helps me p-p-pick…out… I want Nell," she wailed.

Jacob shot out of his room. "What are you doing to my sister?"

"Nothing." Jordan raised his hands as if to show

he was innocent of...well, everything. "She wants to change her clothes," he explained over Lacey's full throttle wails. Wow, for a little kid, she sure could kick up a ruckus.

"So?" Jacob brushed past him and glanced into his sister's room. "Cut it out, Lacey."

"She's naked." Her caterwauling increased another ten decibels. Jordan's throat tightened and he couldn't breathe. He wasn't going to start hyperventilating, was he?

"She's just a kid. She doesn't know better." Jacob headed back to his room.

"If you desert me on this one, bud, I swear I'll hang you out to dry."

As soon as the words were out of his mouth, Jordan wished them back. He liked Jacob and he didn't want to upset him. Besides, he had a reputation to uphold. Where were his famous people skills now?

Curiosity lit the boy's face as he pushed his glasses up on his nose. "What does that mean, 'hang me out to dry'?"

Jordan heaved a sigh of relief. A second person crying would've sent him over the edge. "It means I'll—"

The door banged open and Melody rushed in, her face tear-streaked. "You," she snarled when she saw him. She bolted across the room and shoved hard against his chest with both hands. "I loathe you and your despicable friend."

Jordan staggered backward. The furies of hell had

been unleashed. He rubbed his chest; Melody could really pack a punch. Her wails seemed to feed Lacey's, the phone started ringing, and Jacob slunk toward his room.

Enough. "You," Jordan shouted, pointing his finger at Melody. "In the kitchen now. And splash some cold water on your face. You're a mess. And you." He picked up the phone and slammed it down as he whirled round to Jacob. "Help your sister get dressed. We're leaving in five minutes."

Melody disappeared into the kitchen, her crying reduced to sniffles. With a baleful glare, Jacob scooted into his sister's room, and Lacey immediately quieted. She was probably sobbed out anyway, all over changing some frigging clothes. Jordan sucked in his first real breath since the kid had started crying. He grabbed Nell's list and tossed it into the garbage can on his way into the kitchen. Until Nell got home, they were playing by his rules.

SEVERAL HOURS LATER, Jordan sank into his lawn chair, took a long pull on his cold beer and congratulated himself. Once again, the king ruled. He'd come up with a brilliant solution to most of their problems, if he did say so himself. Nell was going to be wowed when she got home. Which should be—he looked at his watch—any minute now. Probably a good thing because just maybe he'd been a little too liberal with the s'mores rations.

Nell had specified no sugar on her list, but they'd burned the notepad and danced around the outdoor metal firepit he'd bought as if they were escapees from the looney farm. He'd gone a little nuts at the store and bought the whole package—tent, sleeping bags, mattresses, even a lantern. When they'd returned home, the kids had helped him pitch the tent in the spare lot beside the house.

He was embarrassed to admit it, but he'd bought the camping gear as much for himself as for Jacob and Lacey. He'd forgotten how he'd longed to go camping when he was a kid until he was in the store today and looking at different tents. Almost everyone he knew got to do something cool during summer vacation. Not him. It had been pretty much the same old, except he didn't have to squeeze school into his schedule. It wasn't his mother's fault. Wasn't anyone's fault. Life sucked, everyone had a childhood, so get over it.

Somehow, the tough philosophy didn't sound as good as it used to. Especially when he applied it to Jacob and Lacey. He wanted only good things to happen for them, because life hadn't been kind to them up to this point. But they had Nell. He was guessing that made up for a lot.

He eyed the tent, thinking of how he wouldn't mind crawling inside right about now for a little shut-eye. He'd been pleasantly surprised by how peaceful it felt when he'd helped make up the beds. He'd even bought a sleeping bag and air mattress for Nell. The tent was one of the bigger models, with plenty of room for everyone. Although the thought of him and Nell in the tent, alone, somewhere off by themselves— Yeah, he could really get into this camping thing.

He drank more beer and checked on his charges. Performing her kitty cat dance for maybe the fifteenth time, it was possible Lacey was a little hopped up on sugar. Definitely too many s'mores and root beer. Jacob wasn't far behind her. For the past half hour, he'd been running around and around behind Melody, hoping for a chance to drive the new ride-on lawn mower Jordan had also bought.

As for Melody, she was beautiful even when she was half in the bag. He'd promised her the most expensive bottle of wine she could find if she'd stop crying long enough to tell him what was wrong. Alex, the idiot, had told her they were running out of time to get the house on the market and had decided to ask Nell to leave.

The taste of beer turned sour in Jordan's mouth. He'd already told Alex that wasn't a viable option. He and his partner had some serious talking to do because he couldn't envision asking Nell to leave. Where would she go? Her financial situation wasn't going to change anytime in the near future, which meant she wouldn't be able to pay more rent.

He kept telling himself he'd deal with the problem after the adoption, but what exactly would be different then? Nell still wouldn't have more money, and she and the kids would still need a place to live. He rubbed a hand over his eyes. He'd think about all that later. He was exhausted from just keeping up with the kids, never mind trying to stay one step ahead of them. How did Nell make it look so effortless?

Jordan tipped the bill of his baseball hat over his eyes and slouched down in the lawn chair. For now he was going to bask in the glow of a job well done. For his first try at babysitting, Nell couldn't help but be impressed.

NELL ROARED OUT OF THE GARDEN center parking lot. Wouldn't you know Mr. Fitzgerald, the little worm, had decided to work in the office all afternoon. He could have minded the store. If they wanted to pay her to sit on her hands and wait for nonexistent customers to show, that wasn't her problem. Heaven knows she had a boatload of her own, with Jordan reigning at the top of the list. She was going to tear a strip off him when she finally tracked him down.

She'd called as soon as she'd arrived at work to say maybe it wasn't a good idea for Jordan to babysit. Maybe she should go home. She'd called, really, for a bit of reassurance. Someone on the other end of the line had picked up the phone and slammed it down, but not before she heard what sounded like a whole lot of crying. She called again, praying she'd dialed a wrong number. Same pick up and slam down, but no crying. After that, the line had been busy, as if someone had left the phone off the hook. Trying not to panic, she'd called Jordan's cell phone. No answer.

Desperate with worry, she'd been about to call Melody to ask if she would check on them when a landscaper rolled into the lot, needing around a hundred plants for a job. As she was the only one working that section, she had to help with the order. And then Worm had arrived and there was no making personal calls without losing her job. Jordan would have phoned if something was wrong, wouldn't he? He was a smart man, responsible.

She stomped on the gas pedal. What had she been thinking? She should never have left the children alone with him. She'd sped home on her lunch break only to find the apartment and yard deserted. They hadn't talked about Jordan taking them anywhere, but he had the list. All he had to do was read it to know what Lacey and Jacob were allowed to do. Remembering Jordan's sweet tooth, she rationalized that they'd probably gone out for ice cream. Yes, no sugar was on the list, but she didn't expect anyone to follow every single rule exactly. Putting down no sugar usually guaranteed the babysitter would limit the amount the kids ate. At the apartment, she'd hung up the phone, then raced back to work.

Her stomach heaved, and she slowed for a minute to take her hand off the shaky steering wheel and cover her mouth. What had gotten into her? She'd made a pact with God, the Earth Mother, whomever was out there listening, if she could adopt her niece and nephew, she'd always, always, always, do the right thing. Hadn't she known, even before she left Jordan with the kids, that it was a bad idea?

Exactly the same way she'd felt the weekend Mary

had died. Nell had been so exasperated. *She* hadn't chosen Tony. And hadn't she already given up enough? When Mary had gotten pregnant with Jacob before they were married, Tony had broken up with her and said he didn't want the baby. Mary was only eighteen—just a child herself—so Nell put her dream of going to college on hold and used the money she'd been saving for school to pay Mary's medical bills. But when Tony's parents, the Bleechers, discovered they were about to be grandparents, they threatened to terminate his trust fund unless he married Mary. Then everyone got to go on the hellish roller coaster ride of their marriage.

As much as she loved her sister, Nell had longed to be free, to not always be on call to break up fights between Tony and Mary, or to bundle Lacey and Jacob up in the middle of the night and hustle them off to her place. So when Mary had said *go,* Nell left for a skiing weekend with her boyfriend, ignoring every instinct that told her to stay.

After Mary's death and their son's arrest, the Bleechers, stunned they couldn't buy Tony's way out of jail, went on to traumatize Jacob and Lacey. Although Nell had taken them to court to make damned sure they wouldn't get near her niece and nephew again, even now when she thought of them, she still got a panicky feeling in her chest.

This morning had echoes of the same trapped feeling, that there wasn't enough room in her life for, well, her, and just maybe it was driving her crazy. Tony and the new social worker. The kids' disappointment that she had to go into work. And yes, Jordan turning up with his girlfriend when she was covered with grease and dirt and sweat. Which was worse? Losing her job or trusting Lacey and Jacob with a man she barely knew. She pushed the old truck until it shuddered with resistance. She'd never, ever make a stupid, selfish decision again. Just let her get home without the truck breaking down. Let her darlings be okay.

The sound of a police siren cut into her prayers. Nell eased off the gas and glanced in the rearview mirror. *Perry.* Of course. She'd called him early this morning and told him about farty Stan. He'd wanted to come over right away for a statement, but she'd been called into work and had to put him off. At least this way she could get the interview out of the way. She pulled over to the side, folded her arms on the steering wheel and rested her forehead against them. What was she thinking? Perry would be dogging her every move from now on. There would be no getting rid of him.

"Can I have your license and registration, please?" he said through her open window as if she were a stranger. He already had his ticket book in his hand.

"Hey, Perry." Nell summoned a tired smile as she dug into her purse and pulled out the required paperwork. He'd ticketed her before, so she expected it. In Perry's world, rules were rules and couldn't be broken. He wasn't trying to be mean; he just didn't grasp the concept that sometimes he was allowed to give people a break. Especially when it came to a speeding ticket.

"Do you know how fast you were going?"

"No."

He started writing out the ticket. "Seventy in a fifty zone."

"I was preoccupied. I'll pay attention to my speed. I promise."

"This is a residential area, Nell." He handed her the ticket along with her license and registration. "It's important to drive slow through neighborhoods."

"I'm in a hurry to get home. I'm worried about Lacey and Jacob. Sorry."

"Is something wrong with the kids?"

"I couldn't find a babysitter and had to leave them with Jordan."

Perry straightened away from the truck. "The new landlord?"

"It was either that or lose my job. No one's answered the phone all day."

"That may have not been a good idea, Nell."

No kidding. "I've got to go, Perry. We'll talk later."

"What about this man who's been following you? What should I do about that?"

Shouldn't he be the one telling *her* what to do? She sighed. "I think now that we've confronted him, he'll leave us alone. He's one of Tony's jerky friends."

"I'm going to fill out a report and get you to sign it. It's important to have this kind of thing on file in case something else happens. I'll follow you home. We'll do it there."

Not bothering to argue, Nell tossed the ticket onto the seat beside her and pulled out. Perry was right about the report. Besides, regardless of what she thought, he'd continue on as if she'd cooperated, anyway.

Ten minutes later, she pulled into her driveway. Jordan's car was parked in his spot. Thank God they were home. Her truck had barely stopped moving before she was out and running for the steps. She took them two at a time, but was greeted by dead silence in the apartment. Her stomach bottomed out. She raced from one room to the other which took all of a minute. The place was a mess. Lacey's clothes were strewn all over her room, and it looked like Jacob had built another fort in his. What had he needed to seek refuge from this time? This was her fault. She shouldn't have left them with Tanner.

She circled back through the apartment, looking for clues of where they'd gone. From the kitchen window, she noticed someone moving around the side lot. Someone driving a ride-on lawn mower. Nell shoved the window open and crawled out on the fire escape. Melody?

"Nell, you here?" Perry called from the living room.

"On the fire escape."

What did Melody have on her head? It looked like a hat with great gobs of plastic fruit stuck to it, an apple or orange bobbling by her ear like an oversize earring. Although she was sitting down in the mower seat, she listed to one side and was holding... Nell bit back a shout. Melody was brown-bagging it. Melody, who rarely had more than one glass of wine because alcohol turned her into a sloppy, albeit happy, drunk.

"What are you looking at?" Perry asked from inside the kitchen.

Nell moved to block his view. Was there a law about driving a lawn mower while under the influence? Because if there was, Perry would be all over Melody. Not only would it be a hassle for everyone here, but it was this kind of stuff—arresting someone for drinking and driving a ride-on lawn mower—that reinforced Perry's reputation on the force as a saphead.

"Melody's mowing the lawn."

She peeked over her shoulder. For some reason, Jacob was chasing her. He looked goofy, wearing an oversize cowboy hat and slapping his thigh as if he were riding a horse. His feet tangled, and he went flying headfirst onto the ground. Nell waited for his wail, but he just curled up on his side and giggled hysterically. Dear God, what was going on? And where the heck were Jordan and Lacey?

She slipped back through the window. "This is a really bad time for me to talk about Stan Whats-his-name, Perry. I promise I'll write up everything that happened and email it to you." Or not. The downside of reporting Stan was that if anyone went after him with, say, a hammer, the police would know exactly where to look.

Perry shuffled his feet. "I guess it's not a good time to ask you about going out to dinner, either."

Oh, great, he was doing his gosh-golly act. She really hated it when he laid that on her. Why her? If he needed a woman, all he had to do was walk into a bar—any bar. Women would be all over him in two seconds flat.

"Perry, everything in my life, and I mean everything, is on hold until the adoption goes through. After that happens, we'll talk. Okay?"

He adjusted his heavy police belt and nodded, switching immediately to officious and professional. "I understand, Nell. We have to wait until the children are taken care of first. Make sure you send that information, though. The report has to be filed."

"Of course. I'll get right on that. See you later, Perry." She waited until she heard his car start, then flew out the door and down the stairs.

She should never have left Lacey and Jacob with Tanner. He didn't know a thing about children. And where was he? She hadn't seen him in the yard. Had he left them with Melody? Obviously, he'd been around for a while—where else had that lawn mower come from? And, man, she didn't want to get into *that* right now. If he preferred to waste a boatload of money on a new machine rather than let her do her job, it was no skin off her…nose. It wasn't like she didn't have a ton of other work to do around here.

Halfway across the yard, she spied the tent under the trees at the back of the property line. She pulled a one-eighty and bore down on Jordan who was slumped in a lawn chair outside the tent. He had a cap pulled over his eyes and a beer bottle dangling from one hand. The muscles in her neck corded as pressure built inside her head.

"Tanner," she barked when she was within a couple feet of him.

He stirred, pushed his hat to the back of his head and smiled at her. "Nell."

His smile was dreamy and full of sweet promises. He looked young and happy, the way he'd look if life hadn't left scars. He was so…beautiful.

She licked her dry lips and reminded herself to breathe. *Oh. No.* She wouldn't let him distract her that easily. She *would* stay focused.

"Nell." Lacey crawled out of the tent and tumbled over to her. Still reeling from the impact of Jordan's smile, Nell scooped her sweaty little niece into her arms and inhaled deeply.

"Miss me?" She smiled at Lacey.

"A little bit at first, but Mr. Jordan bought us the tent 'cause everyone was crying. The tent's ours, he said we could keep it. And the sleeping bags and everything. And he bought everyone a hat. Except you." She patted Nell's cheek. "Don't worry, Mr. Jordan will buy you a hat, too."

Nell lowered Lacey to the ground. It sounded like Mr. Jordan had been busy today. "That's okay. I have lots of hats already. It's a beautiful tent. Did you thank Jordan?"

"About a million times." She ran over to Tanner and jumped up and down as though she had a bungee attached to the top of her head. "Can I have another s'more, Mr. Jordan?"

He shot a sheepish look toward Nell. "You've probably had enough for now."

No kidding. Lacey was doing a good imitation of Tigger. *Bounceity-bounceity-bounce.* Nell took note of the six empty root beer bottles and the mostly empty bag of marshmallows and raised her eyebrows. "You didn't read the list?"

"We burned the list." Lacey cackled and raced over to chase Melody with Jacob. Her nephew hadn't even acknowledged her arrival, although Nell knew he'd seen her. So much for being missed. She glared at Jordan.

He unfolded his lean body out of the chair and loomed above her. At least he had the grace to look embarrassed. "I can explain."

"What are you going to explain, Tanner? How you got Melody drunk or fed the kids too much sugar? Or that you deal with problems by buying your way out? What kind of message do you think you're sending to Jacob and Lacey?"

When Jordan's face hardened, Nell felt a moment's regret. Part of her wanted the happier, softer man back. He'd seemed so open and lovable, but now the old chill was coming off him again. Good. She was much safer with this Jordan. The businessman.

"I'm sorry you don't approve of the way I handled the situation, but I did the best I could. What's the problem? The kids are happy. Yeah, they had too much sugar, but it's not going to kill them. We were having a good time until—" He clamped his mouth shut and tucked his chin tight against his chest, as if he didn't trust himself to say more.

Okay, she was a party pooper. But someone had to make sure that the children were safe. She crossed her arms and stared across the lawn at Melody. The kids looked silly—happy—chasing after Melody and each other. They looked like kids were supposed to.

She swallowed hard and blinked a couple of times. Had she tried so hard to make everything okay that she'd stifled Jacob and Lacey? Hung on too tight? Been too strict? Jordan had a point—a little sugar once in a while wouldn't hurt them. But being too rigid could.

The thought knocked her breathless. In her rush to do everything right, to protect Jacob and Lacey, she'd suffocated them. They hadn't complained or rebelled. They wouldn't, would they? Not after all they'd been through.

She needed space, and she needed time to think. She spun on her heel, but Jordan stepped in front of her, cutting off her escape.

"Come on, Nell. I didn't mean that. I was mad because I hoped you'd be pleased the kids were having a good time." He stood close enough that she could feel the heat from his body. She wanted to lean into him, the same way Lacey had, and soak him up.

She kept her gaze trained on her work boots. "I've had a rough day at work, and I have a headache. Everyone seems to be having a good time, so I'm going to take a bath."

"But I thought we'd…" Without looking up, she heard him sigh. "Never mind. We're good. Go for it."

Nell nodded her thanks and hurried toward the house. She felt as if she was running away from both the past and the future. She needed a time-out from her life. Hell, she needed another life because this one was too crowded, and there wasn't room for her anymore.

CHAPTER NINE

NELL CLICKED THE SEND BUTTON and turned off the computer. She hoped an email account of the encounter with Stan would suffice for now. That taken care of, she slid into her tepid bathwater that she'd run half an hour ago. It was too hot outside for anything more than lukewarm anyway. Too bad her body wasn't getting the message. She sank farther down until her head slipped below the surface. She'd managed to keep thoughts of Jordan at bay for a while, but now, free to let her mind roam, the first one it landed on was how gorgeous he'd looked in the yard. For one unguarded moment, she'd wanted him in every way a woman could want a man.

Fine, so she was sexually attracted to him. She sat up and let the water sluice down her shoulders. She was okay with that. Sexual chemistry was something that, if she worked hard enough at, she could, well, not ignore, but maybe control somewhat. It was the subtext of the chemistry between them that bothered her more. In that one moment, they'd connected on another level. Like soul mates. With just a look.

She dove under the water again and came up sputtering and cursing. If she was going to drown herself, it wasn't going to be because of a man. She had so many problems at the moment, she didn't even know why she was wasting time thinking about Jordan. Except he seemed to be the source of several of those problems. Not all, but enough that she couldn't ignore him.

Having an affair with Jordan was not an option. And that's all it would ever amount to. He'd made his position clear from day one—no farmer wife, no kids, nobody getting in his way to success. Fair enough because she wasn't going to let anything get in the way of the adoption. And being distracted by an affair with a man right now would definitely do that.

She squirted shampoo on her hair, scrubbed for a couple minutes and rinsed. What she should be concerned about was that he didn't need a caretaker for the house. It had been different with Beulah. She rarely left her apartment, and in the last few months of her life she hadn't gone out at all. Beulah had needed Nell to be the contact for the residents, make sure the rent was collected and keep up with small repairs.

Jordan was more than capable of doing most of those things. He may not be handy with a hammer, but he could sign checks with flair and hire people far more skilled than her. He'd already made a huge concession by delaying the sale until the adoption went through. And now she expected him to reduce her rent in exchange for work he didn't need done? God, how had it come to this?

She'd been fighting so long, fighting for Jacob and Lacey and against Tony, Child Welfare, the Fitzgeralds. When Jordan showed up, she hadn't tried to see the situation from his point of view; she'd just kept right on fighting. It had to stop. She couldn't keep bulldozing her way through life. It wasn't healthy for the kids or for her. Everything had to change.

She'd explain it all to her social worker, or try to. Getting a full-time job that hopefully paid better was a good thing, right? She wrung out the facecloth and laid it over her eyes. Her life was crap, pure and simple. Regardless, she had to smarten up and stop feeling sorry for herself. She'd start looking for work on Monday. Might as well check out apartments, too.

But, oh, how she hated the thought of making the kids move. They loved living here. She'd work twice as hard to make their new place even better than this one, because no way was she freeloading off Jordan. And no child of hers was ever going to have to endure the crappy feeling of being a charity case.

How many times had her aunt bought her new jeans or a blouse, only to remind Nell over and over again how lucky she was to have relatives who cared about her? No matter how many dishes or floors or clothes Nell washed, it was never enough to pay her aunt back for taking them in. Nell had done what was necessary to make sure she and her sister had a home, but as soon as she was eighteen, she left, taking Mary with her.

She sat up, scrubbed her face hard. Jacob and Lacey were never, ever going to feel they deserved less than the best.

So, new job, new apartment, but most of all, she had

to make life more fun for them. Hell, she might as well whistle down the moon while she was at it.

JORDAN WATCHED WITH trepidation as his caretaker approached through the gathering dusk. It had been a rough half hour. Nell could have warned him that one drink too many turned Melody from happy-happy to a howling drama queen. He'd managed to convince her to go sleep it off in her apartment just as Jacob and Lacey started crashing from their sugar high. That hadn't been pretty. Once he'd gotten them in their pajamas and tucked into their sleeping bags, it hadn't been so bad, especially when Lacey had snuggled up to him until she drifted off. It had made him think of his mom, how she loved to cuddle when they were alone. Which had never been often enough, but still they'd had some good times together.

Next time, he'd know to go easy on the sugar and the booze. And he wouldn't piss Nell off so she'd stick around. Half the fun of the day had been anticipating Nell coming home. Which both worried and excited him. He was starting to care too much about these people, and he couldn't let that continue. Sure, the kids were fun, and Melody was amusing for a time. And Miss Nellie—his pulse sped up as he watched her draw near—Nell was the most fascinating woman he'd ever met. And he didn't know what he was going to do about it. Or even if there was anything he *could* do about it. He knew where he was going in life, and he knew he had to go there alone. Or did he?

"I'm sorry I left you with putting the kids to bed. Thank you for taking care of them today." Nell spoke in a rush, as if afraid to leave space for what she really wanted to say. It didn't take too much imagination what that something else might be.

"You're entirely welcome. Sit." He indicated the other lawn chair. "Would you like a cold beer?"

"That would be nice. Thank you." She sat, crossed her ankles and clasped her hands in her lap.

This proper little lady was not the Nell he'd been waiting for. Fatigue pulled at him as he flipped the cooler open and handed her a cold one. "How was work?"

"Boring. There was only one customer the entire day."

"Why didn't you close up shop and leave?"

Her mouth turned down at the corners. "Fitzgerald didn't think that was a good idea."

"If you hate the job, Nell, you should quit."

"That's not an option until I find another one." She picked at the label on her beer bottle.

"I know people. I'd be happy to give you a letter of introduction and reference."

"Thanks, Tanner, but I'll have a look around on my own first."

"Jordan," he snapped before he could stop himself. That got her to look up from the damned label she had half peeled off.

"Jordan," she repeated. "Your mom picked a nice

name. I've always hated mine. Nell. Sounds like a workhorse."

"It suits you."

She raised her eyebrows. "Don't hit me with the compliments all at once. They might go to my head."

He poked at the embers in the fire pit and added another stick of wood as he carefully considered his answer. "Nell sounds like someone you can depend on, someone you can trust. What's it short for?"

By the wilting look on her face, he could tell he wasn't scoring any points. What was wrong with being dependable and trustworthy? They were honorable traits in a world that seriously lacked accountability.

"Eleanor. Which isn't any better."

"You said you were twelve when your parents died?"

"Yes. Are you sure the kids are asleep?"

About to take a sip of his beer, Jordan halted. He knew how hard it was to talk about losing a parent, but up to this point Nell had been so straightforward, her evasiveness now gave him pause. "You never told me how they died," he probed.

"A man wanted the two hundred and seventy-nine dollars and thirty cents in the till at the convenience store, and my father refused to give it to him. The guy shot both my parents."

"Did the police catch him?"

"No. It was Halloween. He was dressed in a costume. A skeleton. Ironic, isn't it?"

"It's sad, is what it is. Where were you?"

"Home reading the latest *Sweet Valley High* book."

She grabbed her beer and took a long swig. "I was supposed to work that night, but I told my mom I was sick. I wasn't."

Jordan leaned forward, barely restraining himself from pulling her into his arms. "You think it was your fault."

"Melody says there's no such thing as fate." She was working hard on the beer label again. "There's only the decisions people make, and the consequences of those decisions." Finally, she looked at him. "I know the drill, Jordan. I was only twelve, just a child. It wasn't my fault. But I still have to live with what-if. I'll never know if my being at the store might have changed the outcome."

"Well, here's something I know for sure." His voice had turned raw with emotion. "You're a good person, Nell Hart. I'm glad you stayed home that night. And I'm betting there are a lot of people who feel the same way I do."

"Thanks, Jordan." He had to lean forward to catch her whisper.

There were a number of other things he wanted to say to her. Mostly he wanted to hold her in his arms and tell her...well, how important she was to him. How glad he was to be her friend. But she'd drawn into herself with her head down and her arms tucked tight against her sides. Her body language screamed *back off.* Besides, feeling the way he did right now, holding her wasn't going to be enough. And he wasn't convinced taking their relationship a step further was a good idea for him or for her. Funny how that had changed. At first Nell had been one more obstacle to overcome. Quirky and interesting, yes, but still an obstacle.

Now—he studied her in the firelight. The night was warm, and she'd put on shorts and one of those cropped T-shirts that drove him crazy. Heat gathered in his belly as he thought of how much he'd love to peel that shirt away from her body. He wanted her. Not exactly a news flash. But the way he wanted her was different from the women he'd known before.

Jordan shifted in his chair. He wasn't used to analyzing his relationships with women. They either worked or they didn't. But with Nell, something kept nudging him to pay attention, telling him that what was happening between them was important. And that just maybe things were a little out of his control. Like he was on a ride he hadn't asked to take, and either he didn't know how to jump off or he didn't want to. One thing he did know—he'd been in the driver's seat most of his adult life and he didn't like being a passenger.

Nell unwound herself. "It was a good idea to buy a tent and camp out here. This is nice."

Jordan relaxed. He knew an olive branch when he was offered one. "Not bad, eh? Next time, though, I'll know to lay off the sugar and keep Melody away from the booze."

"Is she okay? She doesn't usually drink more than one glass of wine."

Way to stir up trouble. He had to mention Melody. "She and Alex had a fight. She'll get over it."

Nell toed the end of a burned branch into the fire. "What did they fight about?"

"Just a misunderstanding. I think you're right, they aren't very well suited." Truth was he was pretty sure Alex was caught, hook, line and sinker. He couldn't keep his eyes off Melody. Jordan snickered to himself. They had a standing bet which one would stay single the longest. It was beginning to look like Alex was going to owe him one very fine bottle of Scotch.

"You said you met Alex at university?" Nell asked.

"Yes."

"You know a lot about my family, but I don't know anything about yours." Nell held out her empty beer bottle for him to take. He added it to the two empties in the box beside him, then offered her a fresh one.

"No, thanks. Mornings are hard enough."

"I had no idea that kids could be so all-consuming." How had his mother, a child herself, coped? For the first time, he allowed himself to consider the possibility that she wasn't dead, that maybe she'd run away because life became too much.

"Do your parents live nearby?" she prompted.

"I never knew my father, and my mom…. She disappeared when I was fifteen." Now it was his turn to pick at a beer label. "She worked in a bar and one night she just didn't come home. The police couldn't find any trace of her after she left work. Eventually, they figured she was probably dead." He glanced at Nell who had leaned closer to him. "She was nice, you know? Sweet. But she had really lousy taste in men. She always had these bastards hanging around her." He stared out at the black night around them. "She was a good mom, though. She wouldn't have willingly left me on my own."

Nell reached over, slipped her hand into his and stared into the fire. After a few minutes, Jordan felt his tension slowly evaporate. Alex was the only other person who knew about his mother. He wasn't sure why he'd told Nell, but it seemed important to do so. She'd understood it wasn't sympathy he needed, but understanding. It felt good to be understood. Especially by someone like Nell.

THE NIGHT HAD BEEN MADE for people like Jordan, Nell thought. His eyelashes looked indecently long as they shadowed his mysterious gray eyes, and his wide shoulders blocked the night surrounding them. She felt protected. At ease. As if, for once, she was exactly where she should be. And if she kept staring at the way the fire highlighted his dark hair or the way the muscles in his arms bunched every time he raised his beer to his mouth, that ease was going to combust into a wildfire. He was going out of his way to be friendly and kind, and all she could think about was pressing her lips against his throat and tasting his salty skin. For starters. She had to stop thinking like that right now. Not only was it embarrassing to be caught drooling over her boss, but somehow she knew if they ever did spend the night together, one night—hell, a hundred nights—wouldn't be enough.

"Is something wrong? Want to change chairs or something?" Jordan's voice brought her heated thoughts to a screeching halt.

"What?"

"You're twitchy, like your chair isn't comfortable. Want to try mine?"

Twitchy. Great, he was bone-melting hot; she was *twitchy.* She pressed her back into the lawn chair and willed herself to sit still. "I'm fine. Thanks."

Jordan rested his forearms on his thighs, his hands dangling between his knees. She'd never seen him wear shorts before, and she hoped he never did again. They made it too easy to imagine his long muscular legs entwined with hers. She clutched the armrest to keep herself still.

"Are you worried about work?"

"Work?" She tore her gaze away from his legs and stared at the fire. "Yeah. I mean, no. I am, but I don't want to talk about it tonight." Apparently, she wanted to babble instead, because that's the kind of thing that really turned guys on.

"Fine, but I was serious. If you decide to look for another job, I'll help all I can."

"Maybe you could have a look at my business plan sometime soon." Another brilliant idea. Bring up a subject he thought was downright stupid.

"If you want, of course I will. You know, most businesses don't turn a profit for the first year or two. Some as long as five." His voice held a cautionary note.

He thought she was stupid and twitchy. Fantastic. "I

know that, Ta…Jordan. I can work and start my own business at the same time. It doesn't have to happen overnight as long as I make a start. You have a job, but that hasn't stopped you from working toward other goals as well, has it?"

She *wasn't* stupid. She'd done her research. Her plan was as viable as his, only more modest. She didn't want to own half the world.

"But I don't have two children to take care of, and my job is more…secure."

Nell stood and moved to the far side of the fire. "I plan on looking for a new job next week." She hadn't meant to mention that, but what did it matter?

"Good idea. I'll keep my ears open for any available part-time jobs."

"I need a full-time job."

His head jerked up. "Full-time? You can't. You work here."

"Doing what? Riding that thing?" She pointed at the ride-on mower that was parked beside the tent. "If Melody can drive that dead drunk, you don't need me to operate it. And as you pointed out, Rodney's much better at repairing stuff around here. He can have the bedsit back once you're done with it. It's time for me to move on."

No. JORDAN BIT BACK THE WORD. Nell would hardly be open to taking a directive from him. But damn it, no. "You can't just leave." Something akin to panic fought its way to the surface as he stashed his empty bottle in the box and folded his arms over his chest. "We need you. The house needs you."

"No, you don't. And now that I'm thinking about it, Rodney's lost, and this place will anchor him. The caretaking work will be perfect for him. And you've got money." She plowed on. "You can afford to hire people to do whatever he can't."

This was not good. His gut felt all screwed up and his head started to pound. *Play to her strengths. Tell her why she's so important to 879 Dunstan Lane.* "You take care of all of us. I'll never find someone else who'll feed Mrs. T. a couple times a week just to make sure she's eating properly or listen to Rodney reminisce about his wife. And what about Melody? If I have to deal with her the next time she has one of her crying fits, one of us is out of here."

He needed her, too. He liked having dinner with Nell and the kids, liked the feeling of fitting in, as if he were part of something more than…well, more than one person. And he liked that she didn't let him get away with anything. Not that he couldn't get along without her. Of course he could. A few more weeks, and he'd probably be living in his condo again. He frowned, the thought not as soothing as it used to be.

"I sure know how to collect lost souls, don't I?" she said.

"That's not a bad thing. It means you're compassionate."

"Sure." She blinked a couple of times, as if she was trying not to cry.

He grabbed at the first thing that came into his head. "Moving won't help with the adoption."

"As long as I find a place in a good neighborhood, maybe it wouldn't make too much difference. I'll have to discuss that with the social worker." She spoke slowly, as if feeling her way. "And if I get somewhere not too far away, Lacey and Jacob could go to the same school."

The kids. He cricked his neck from side to side and rolled his shoulders, certain he'd won the argument. "They're not going to like the move at all. They need stability, not change."

"What are you doing, Tanner?" She sat on the edge of her chair, her glare slicing through his complacency. "If you get rid of me, it'll be simpler for you to sell the house."

Jordan sat, stunned. She was right. She was giving him an easy out, and he was trying to convince her not to. Unless…why couldn't he have it both ways?

"Finding another job doesn't mean you have to move. Making too many changes at once isn't always a good idea, especially when it involves the children." He stopped talking, wondering if he'd gone too far. But the place wouldn't be the same without Nell.

"If I'm not the caretaker anymore, I can't afford the apartment." She spoke as if talking to a five-year-old. Or an idiot.

"I couldn't get that much more for it. The windows only open a couple inches, the air conditioner is broken, the appliances are old. God knows what else. Apparently, the caretaker doesn't think it necessary to keep the landlord fully informed."

When she narrowed her eyes, he felt a chill waft toward him from across the fire. "It's a two-bedroom. Invest a bit of money, and you can ask at least seven hundred. I can't afford it."

She was driving him crazy. A couple of weeks ago, she'd worked hard to convince him that he needed her. How in God's name had the situation reversed itself? He shot to his feet. "You're getting ahead of yourself, aren't you? You still work for me. I'm moving into 1A tomorrow, and I need your help. I'd like to rent your truck for the day to move a few of my belongings from the condo."

He hadn't completely thought it through, but now that he'd told her, it sounded like a great idea. Nell thought they didn't need her? He was going to prove otherwise.

"Why don't you rent a moving van?"

"Because I need someone to help me pack some stuff and load and unload. That's the kind of thing caretakers do, isn't it? You helped Lisa and Tom move into their apartment, and now you can help me." He turned to go.

"I'll have to bring Jacob and Lacey," she said to his back.

"Even better. I'll have someone sane to talk to. Good night."

His heart ping-ponged inside his chest. What the hell had he just done? He hadn't been spontaneous since he was fifteen years old and realized it was up to him to change his life. This is exactly why he'd carefully constructed a plan over the years and stuck to it. He hadn't been thinking with his head tonight; he'd been thinking with his...he hadn't been thinking. Period.

Yet there'd been an element of truth to what he'd said. Sure, Rodney was the better candidate for doing repairs. And Jordan had already contacted a roofing firm to give him an estimate on a new roof. So he didn't really need Nell as a caretaker.

But for once in his life, he'd encountered something he couldn't put a price on. Nell gave the house heart. She scrubbed and polished the old oak staircase in the front hall every week. Inside the front door, the subtle scent of lemon oil and a cheerful bouquet of flowers from her garden made the house feel like a home, not an apartment building. Whenever Nell was around, he heard laughter, the children's, hers, Melody's. Sometimes even old Mrs. T. She kept the lawn mowed, the flower beds weeded and the windows clean. Despite the faded purple exterior and the obvious need for more extensive repairs, the house looked loved.

And then there were the kids. When Lacey hurtled herself with complete trust into Nell's arms or Jacob followed her with his eyes, as if needing reassurance she wasn't going to disappear, Jordan understood he was being given a rare view into how life could be if... well, if he were someone else. Someone who believed he deserved to be part of a family. Someone whose mother hadn't disappeared from his life.

Of course he'd known about families before he

moved here, but only in theory. Now that he had a working knowledge of the intimacies of family life, he recognized a need that demanded attention. Which made sense, now that he thought about it. He was in his thirties and all of his material ambitions were within his grasp. It was time to think about the nonmaterial ones—a family and a real home.

He'd take care of that problem after the house sold and his new business was up and running. He'd waited this long for a family. What would a few more months matter?

CHAPTER TEN

NELL RUBBED THE SLEEP from her eyes and stumbled out of bed. It had taken ages for her to fall asleep last night, her brain zipping every which way, trying to figure out what Tanner was up to. She'd handed him the solution to his problem of selling the house, and he'd rejected her idea without even thinking about it. There had to be an angle, but for the life of her, she couldn't figure out what it was. And now he expected her to spend her one day off helping him move. He still had no idea how cranky and unreasonable a hot, tired child could get, but if this job needed more than one trip to Seabend, he was going to find out in a jiffy.

Tanner had looked after the kids yesterday, and she owed him one. But after today, every spare moment she had would be used to look for a full-time job. Nell stood and arched her back to work out the kinks, wishing, as she did every morning, for a proper bed to sleep in.

Lacey was already up when Nell emerged from the bathroom. Sitting at the kitchen table, she was munching on the granola and milk she'd poured for herself.

"Hey, sunshine." Nell grabbed the coffeepot and filled it.

"My head hurts," Lacey complained.

"You've got a sugar hangover." Nell dropped a kiss on the top of her blond curls on her way to the refrigerator. Lacey likely wasn't the only one suffering this morning. After her first infusion of coffee, she'd take some down to Melody, along with a couple of painkillers.

"What's a hangover?"

"It's when you have too much of one thing and your body's mad at you."

Lacey nibbled on a raisin. "Mr. Jordan's fun. Can we move into Mrs. Winer's apartment with him?"

"No." She grabbed the half-filled carafe and poured a cup of coffee before it finished dripping. It was going to be one of those days.

"Jacob and I could both have our own room."

Nell smiled across the table at her niece. "What about me? You guys going to leave me here all by myself?"

"No, silly. You and Mr. Jordan can share the biggest bedroom, just like the other moms and dads."

A pang of longing startled Nell. She placed her mug on the table, aligning it precisely, handle to the right, the bouquet of painted violets centered in front of her.

"Lacey." She cleared her throat. Damned if she knew how they'd gotten here, weaving dangerous fantasies about a man who was a temporary fixture in their lives. She should have worked harder at stemming their growing involvement with Tanner. Now she was going to have to break her sweetie's heart and tell her the truth—that Mr. Jordan didn't really care about them. He was just passing through. Better she do the telling, and better sooner than later. The situation was out of hand.

"I know Jordan's fun, but…" She searched for the right words. "He's not going to be around forever."

"I know." Lacey plowed her spoon through her cereal.

Relief swamped her. Lacey had just been playing a child's game of "let's pretend." "You do?"

"Of course. Mrs. T. told me we're all going to die some day. Like Mommy."

Nell sighed. She needed to have a talk with Mrs. T. again. Last time it had been how you couldn't trust men. At the moment, Nell was inclined to agree on that one.

"Most people live a long, long time."

Lacey continued stirring her cereal. "Will you?"

"I can't wait to play with your children."

A giggle rippled across the table. Lacey looked up from her cereal. "You have to be married to have children, silly."

"In that case we better start looking for a husband for you right away. I need grandchildren."

"Maybe Mr. Jordan will wait for me to grow up."

Right. Mr. Jordan. Nell knew she'd gotten off track. She reached across the table and patted Lacey's hand. "Jordan's our friend, but he's not going to be around for long." She rushed to explain when Lacey's sparkle dimmed. "He has another apartment and a whole bunch of friends. You know this, Lacey. We've talked about it before." They had, hadn't they? If she hadn't talked to

Lacey and Jacob about it, she'd meant to. How, in the course of two weeks, had he become such a fixture in their lives?

"Then why are we helping him move here today?"

"Jordan told you about that yesterday?" Before he'd asked her? Things were really getting out of control around here.

"He called this morning. You were still asleep."

"What did he say?"

Lacey spooned up the last of her cereal. "That he was ready to go when you were, and to tell you Jacob was already downstairs with him. But I told him he'd better wait 'cause you're kind of cranky if we wake you up before you're ready."

Nell sunk her head in her hands. It was a miracle Lacey and Jacob even talked to her. She was a terrible person, a horrible aunt. She hadn't even realized Jacob wasn't in the apartment. From now on, she was going to make an extra effort to be sensitive to their needs. And look for a job. And an apartment. She closed her eyes as a wave of weariness swept over her. She'd take Melody some coffee and something for her headache, and hopefully, get a good dose of rah-rah-of-course-you-can-do-it for herself.

"I just have to take this coffee to Melody, and then we'll help Jordan move. Go brush your teeth."

"Jacob said he was going in Mr. Jordan's car," Lacey said in a teeny voice.

Nell stopped at the door. "And you want to go with him, too."

"Will you be lonely all by yourself?"

She didn't deserve such kindness. "I'll be fine. But you have to ask Jordan if it's all right with him, okay?"

"He won't mind." Lacey put her bowl and spoon in the sink. "He likes me."

Today, yes, and probably tomorrow. But a year from now? He wouldn't even remember their names. How do you explain that to a four-year-old? Thank goodness school was starting soon. It would be much easier to curtail the amount of time the kids spent with Jordan.

"Brush your teeth. I'll wait for you, and we'll walk down together."

A few minutes later, she watched Lacey climb into Tanner's car from the window outside Melody's door, then used her key to let herself into her friend's apartment. With the curtains drawn against the bright sunny day outside, she could barely make out a lump on the couch. Melody hadn't even made it to the bedroom last night.

"Melody?" she whispered.

A groan rose from the couch a few feet in front of her. "Don't talk," Melody moaned.

"Okay, but I'm leaving in a minute to help Jordan move some of his stuff. Take these pills first, they'll help with the headache. Here's some coffee," Nell said in a hushed voice.

Melody sat up and clutched her stomach. "You're going to Jordan's condo?"

"Yes, and I'm taking the kids with me. Ouch! You look terrible. Here." She thrust the pills at her friend, doubting they'd do much good. Melody's face was a sickly shade of green. She'd probably spend part of the morning hanging on to the toilet.

Melody heaved herself off the couch and galloped toward the bathroom. Nell ran a glass of cold water while she waited. Melody was always so cautious about the amount she drank, which meant the fight with Alex must have been a doozy.

Everything had been so much simpler before Jordan came onto the scene. A little boring, yeah, but she'd accepted the fact that her life wasn't her own anymore. It was all about Lacey and Jacob, at least until the adoption went through and they were a bit older. Okay, a lot older, like young adults. Nell sank onto the couch, trying to ignore the sounds coming from Melody's bathroom.

When Jordan had moved in, it was like a door to a room that she'd kept locked had swung open. A room where her wishes and dreams resided. Her first reaction had been to slam it shut, but now she was beginning to wonder if maybe she'd taken the wrong approach the past couple of years.

She couldn't remember her parents ever laughing. They'd always been so serious and worried. She and Mary would be fine at home until her parents arrived from the store. There'd be a tension in the air, and she and her sister would grow quieter and quieter until Nell wondered if she was even visible. Was she doing that to Jacob and Lacey? Letting her worry infect their lives?

She needed to make some changes. Yes, Lacey and

Jacob were important, and yes, it was her duty to take care of them the best she could. But maybe she had to take care of herself as well. She needed to reclaim a portion of her life, keep her personal dreams alive.

Melody opened the bathroom door. "Did you say something about painkillers?"

"Come and get them." Nell held up her hand.

Melody slid onto the couch beside her. "Bless you."

Nell handed her the coffee after she'd swallowed the pills and water. "I can only stay a minute. The kids and Jordan are waiting for me downstairs. Are you going to be all right?"

"Yes. No. Oh, God, Nell. My heart feels like it's broken. Really. I have a pain right here." She placed a hand over her chest.

"Melody, honey…" Nell stopped. She didn't want to be insensitive to her friend's pain, but Mel had only dated Alex twice.

"I know what you're going to say 'cause I keep telling myself the same thing. I barely know the guy. But, Nell, he's *The One*. I just know it."

"Okay, say he is. What's the problem?"

Melody picked at the hem of her wrinkled T-shirt. "He's a louse."

As she'd thought earlier, one of those days. "So, you don't love him?"

"No, I do, but he's…misguided. I can feel all this goodness inside him, but he's so focused on making money, that he's not paying attention to that part of himself."

"Small wonder Alex and Jordan are friends."

"Jordan's light-years ahead of Alex. He may be zoned into making money but he, at least, questions what he's doing. I think Jordan realizes he's looking for more than just money. He's looking to be loved."

Who wasn't? Nell stood. "He's quite a package, good-looking and successful. I'm sure he won't have a hard time finding someone to love him."

"I think he already has." Melody sent her a sly smile.

"Mel, hon, don't start. Please. I admit I wouldn't mind having him to myself for a few days. I'm sure we'd be capable of entertaining ourselves. But that's as far as it goes. I mean, look at me." She spread her arms and grimaced at the overalls she'd put on. Tanner had asked for a caretaker to help him today, and that's what he was getting. "I'm not corporate-wife material or whatever you call it. I'm just me. And I have kids. Tanner and I are not going to happen. Ever." Repeating it wasn't making the reality any easier to accept. "I gotta go. I'll check on you when I get back."

"Nell?" Melody's soft inquiry stopped her at the door.

"Yeah?"

"I had a fight with Alex because he said he was trying to convince Jordan to raise your rent. He claims he told me because he thought you should be warned, but that doesn't change what they're doing. They want you gone. According to Alex, your job is obsolete." She stopped, as if to let Nell absorb the information.

Nell's stomach lurched. She had to find another

job and apartment much sooner than she'd thought. "Thanks for telling me."

"That's not all. When I confronted Jordan, he was really angry. He said he'd told Alex to back off for a while. I think he's in love with you, Nell. He might not have admitted that to himself yet, but those are not the actions of someone who doesn't care."

When a horn blasted down in the driveway, Nell moved toward the door. "I think you're reading too much into the situation," she said. "Jordan feels guilty. That's all. He'll get over it when someone offers him money for the house. You'll see."

She escaped down the stairs. Melody was wrong, wrong, wrong. She and Tanner didn't have a chance, and it was cruel to think otherwise.

Tanner looked a little unstrung by the time she reached the driveway. Standing up in the backseat, Lacey had wound her thin arms around his neck. Jacob was wearing Tanner's expensive sunglasses and bouncing on the front passenger seat to loud music that pulsed with a heavy bass. It would have been hard to find a man who looked less enamored about inheriting someone else's children.

She rapped her knuckles against Jacob's window. "Turn that music down or you'll give Ta…Jordan a headache. Lacey, sit down and do up your seat belt. You should have given me your address and gone ahead," she said to Tanner.

He raised his eyebrows when he noticed the overalls, but didn't say anything. He didn't have to—the way his mouth tightened indicated he thought she was over-doing the caretaker bit. He was right. She was wearing the overalls like armor. She was the caretaker, he was the rich dude with the pricey condo.

"I don't trust that truck of yours to make the trip without breaking down," he said over Jacob's head. "Try to keep close to me, okay? How's Melody?"

"Suffering for her sins. Everyone strapped in? Good." She smiled for the children's sake. "Let's get to work."

ONCE AGAIN JORDAN HAD TO ADMIT he had no idea how Nell pulled it all off. Kids, lousy job, grouchy neighbors, the pending adoption. And him. No sense pretending he hadn't added to her workload and her anxiety. She should be nominated for sainthood.

Jacob and Lacey had peppered him with questions the entire forty-five minutes it had taken them to drive to his condo. Kids' brains were weird. A little kooky and sometimes entertaining, yeah, but weird. How was he supposed to know how the moon stayed up in the sky? He wasn't an astronomer.

When he found Alex's car in his private parking space, he pulled into the visitors' lot. If he had to listen to one more Raffi song, he planned to personally hunt down the singer/songwriter and strangle him. Although Raffi had been a definite improvement over that stuff Jacob called music. The kid's education had been pa-thetically neglected; he didn't even know who Led Zeppelin was, for Pete's sake. Jordan planned to remedy that. He had their entire collection up in his condo.

It wasn't until he started to open his car door that he realized the kids had gone completely silent. Jordan glanced at Jacob, then over his shoulder at Lacey.

"What?" he said into the void. They'd closed down, their usual bright faces dark with worry.

"Where's Nell?" Lacey asked around the thumb in her mouth.

"There." He pointed as her rusty old truck groaned its way into a parking spot. "This is where I usually live," he explained. "We're going to go up and pack some stuff that I need and take it back to Dunstan Lane."

Maybe they hadn't understood what they were doing today. Maybe a string from the sun really did keep the moon in the sky. He had absolutely no idea what was going on, but he didn't like it. Both kids crouched back into their seats as if they were afraid. This had something to do with their SOB of a father, he was sure of it. How, in God's name, did you fix a child's fears?

"Come on, gang. We've got work to do." Nell's sunny face appeared at Jacob's window.

One look at the children, and her expression turned murderous. When she ripped open the back door, Lacey sprang into her arms. Jacob clamored out and shuffled around until he stood just behind her, close enough to be her shadow.

"What happened?" Nell sent a killer look over the

top of the car at him where he stood waiting for her to make everything right.

"I honestly don't know. Things were fine until we parked." He draped his arm on the roof of the car and hung his head. He'd never felt so helpless in his life. There was nothing he hated more than not knowing how to fix a problem.

"It's not Jordan," Jacob said.

She squatted down, set Lacey on her feet and gathered both children into her arms. "Okay, we're in the safe circle now. You can say anything you want."

"Is this where Grammy and Grampy live?" Lacey asked in a small voice.

Nell's face relaxed into a small, sad smile. "No. Remember what the judge said? If they want to see you, it has to be at our place. And only if you want to see them."

Lacey leaned closer to her aunt. "Are you sure they don't live here?"

"I'm sure, sweetpea. They live in France. You know France is far away. But this building looks just like theirs, doesn't it? And so does that one." Nell pointed at another new building across the street.

"And that one, except it's a different color." She pointed to an apartment building farther down the street that was beige instead of gray.

"I'd forget where I lived if I lived here," Lacey said.

Nell laughed. "Me, too. The buildings all look the same."

Jordan hung on to the car door and barely restrained

himself from lashing out. He honest-to-God saw red for a minute. Whatever the grandparents had done, it must have been bad for the judge to lay down such stringent conditions for visitation. How could anyone hurt Jacob and Lacey? They were so sweet, so special. He wanted to grab them and hold them; he wanted to hide them away so no one could ever hurt them again. He clenched his fist and rapped it against the side of his leg until he had himself under control.

What was happening to him? He knew he liked the three of them, but this…this was different. It felt as if someone had crossed into his territory, and he wasn't going to stand for it. But what exactly did he think he was going to do about the situation? Nell seemed to have it well in hand. Was there anything the woman couldn't do?

"Okay, enough standing around talking. We've got work to do." Nell waved them toward the truck. "Everyone has to help bring the boxes upstairs."

Jacob and Lacey dragged their feet as they followed her. Jordan locked the car and brought up the rear. This wasn't how he'd expected the day to go. He hadn't realized until now how much he'd been looking forward to showing Nell and the children his condo. For some reason, it had seemed important they see this side of his life. He felt like the kid with the coolest bike but no one around to admire it. Geez, Tanner. He rolled his shoulders. Get over yourself.

They all squeezed into the elevator and had pressed the button for his floor when two young girls, close to

Jacob's age, jumped on board. The girls checked out the company as the doors shut, looked at each other and giggled.

Jordan couldn't tell for sure, but he imagined they were wearing kids' designer clothes. At any rate, the stuff they had on made Jacob's and Lacey's clothes look faded and worn. Lacey's thumb had popped back into her mouth and she squeezed in behind Nell as far as she could. Jacob stared down at his sneakers, his shoulders hunched, as if waiting to be attacked.

The gesture instantly took Jordan back to his childhood, a place he'd sworn to never return. Kids could be so cruel. Never mind the labels, he'd counted himself lucky if his clothes were clean. Laundromats had been a safe haven during his childhood. They were warm, never crowded, and without one of his mother's boyfriends calling him a snot-nosed delinquent or yelling for another beer, a great place to get his homework done.

"Where in France do your grandparents live?" He directed his question to Jacob.

Jacob's head jerked up. "What? Oh, I dunno."

When Nell glared at him, he inclined his head toward the giggling twosome. He suspected they were working their way up to an insult. Lacey, and especially Jacob, were an easy target.

A corner of Nell's mouth lifted. "You know, I don't remember the name of the town. It's just outside Paris."

The giggling stopped.

Jordan plowed on. Spinning facts was his speciality. "Have you been to Paris, Jacob?"

Jacob looked at him as if he'd grown two heads. "Yeah."

"Did you like it?"

Jacob tucked his hands under his armpits. "Some parts are nice, but everyone smells like garlic there."

That earned him a genuine laugh from one girl, and a smile over her shoulder from the other.

The elevator stopped at Jordan's floor, and he shepherded his crew safely out. He felt a small kick of pride when Jacob saluted the two girls still on the elevator before the doors closed. Atta boy. He wanted to tell Jacob and Lacey they were every bit as good as those girls, but some things were better left unsaid.

When Jordan let everyone into the apartment, Alex was slumped in a chair by the wall of windows overlooking the bay. His usually crisp Brooks Brothers shirt was wrinkled as if he'd slept in it. By the blank look on his face, Jordan realized Alex had either forgotten they were coming today or he hadn't heard the message Jordan had left on the answering machine this morning.

Nell and the kids lined up silently behind him. If he'd thought about it at all, and apparently he had, Jordan would have imagined Jacob running over to his top-of-the-line sound system and asking a dozen questions. He realized now he'd been looking forward to that, as well as watching Nell's reaction to the stuff in the kitchen an old girlfriend had talked him into buying, hand-painted dishes from Italy and all kinds of pots and pans. Lacey should be doing blackflips on his king-size bed.

But with Alex glowering at them, all he wanted to do was throw a bunch of things in boxes and get out.

"Rough night?" he asked his friend.

Alex ran a hand over his morning beard and cast a wary glance at his entourage. "Look at this, the inmates of Dunstan Lane have been set free for the day."

Nell shoved her boxes on the solid oak dining table and marched over to confront Alex. Aw, geez, he should have seen this one coming.

"Nell," he cautioned.

She held up her hand to stop him as she drilled Alex with a glare. "You're not welcome at Dunstan Lane. Do you understand?"

Jordan cursed under his breath. No one went toe-to-toe with Alex without coming away bruised. He dropped his boxes and started toward the duo.

"Well, gee, little caretaker lady, it's not really your place to say, is it."

Nell leaned closer. "I talked to Melody this morning. You're no longer welcome at Dunstan Lane. Do you understand?"

Alex's face paled. When he pulled himself out of his chair and loomed above her, Jordan stepped up behind Nell. Sometimes he forgot how small she was.

"Put like that, it's hard not to. Here's something for you to chew on. I was around long before you came on the scene, and I assure you I'll be here long after you're gone. If you knew Tanner at all, you'd know he's not into kids. He's got more important things to think about, like selling that crappy house." Alex turned and left for the bathroom.

Jordan stole a glance at Nell to see if he had to do damage control. If Alex's comments upset her, she hid it well. He wasn't sure he was as successful. Everything Alex had said was true—and yet not. He didn't know what to think anymore. It had been stupid to bring Nell and the kids here. He wasn't so usually inept at handling people, but with her, he continually felt off-kilter.

Take the ridiculous overalls she insisted on wearing. They hung on her slender frame, giving her absolutely no shape at all. Yet every time he looked at her, the only thing he could think about was how much he wanted to explore what was underneath.

"Sorry about that," he said to Nell. "I didn't realize he'd be here."

"I'm sure he doesn't know what he was talking about." She tilted her head in Jacob's direction.

Jordan took in the small boy's pinched expression. "He hasn't got a clue. Forget him. He's in a bad mood. Jacob." He dragged a black leather chair over to the stereo. "Sit."

Jacob slid into the chair, his eyes darting between the panoramic view in front of him and the CD player Jordan was turning on. "We'll start with Led Zeppelin. Listen to one full song, and if you don't like them, see if you can find something you do like. Headphones."

Jacob accepted the headphones with the respect they deserved. "Sit back and enjoy, my man." Jordan squeezed the boy's thin shoulder, wishing he could erase Alex's words. But all he could think to do was continue with what he'd planned.

"Lacey," he said. The little girl peeked out from behind Nell's leg.

"Want to check out my big-screen TV?" Nell's TV was pathetically small, and she didn't have cable. He couldn't wait to watch Lacey's reaction to his. He adjusted another chair in front of the television.

"No," Lacey whispered around her thumb.

Jordan halted. For a minute he'd felt like a magician, showing the kids his tricks. He'd forgotten who he was dealing with. "Are you sure?" He switched on the TV and starting flicking through the channels. "There's probably a channel with just kids' shows."

"I wanna stay with Nell." Lacey's bottom lip trembled. She wound her arms around Nell's leg.

Nell frowned down at her. "There's Dora the Explorer. I thought you liked her."

"I don't want to go over there."

Jordan looked around. "Over there" was five feet from where she was now. Kids, he'd never get the hang of them. "That's okay. I'll leave the TV on in case you change your mind. Do you want to help pack some stuff?"

With tears clinging to her eyelashes, she nodded. Jordan looked at Nell, but she shrugged. If Nell didn't know what was going on, he wouldn't beat himself up.

"We might as well start in the kitchen," he said to Nell. "You can tell me what I need to bring in order to start making more than sandwiches and coffee. It's about time I learned to cook."

"Lacey, I can't move until you let go of my leg. We're just going to the kitchen."

Jordan smiled to himself when he heard the frustration in Nell's voice. Good to know even Ms. Perfect had her limits.

"I wanna watch Dora." Lacey hiccupped, and the same panicky feeling he got when she'd cried yesterday hit him again. He knew that full-on sobs were only a blink away. He shouldn't have turned the stupid TV on.

Nell freed herself from Lacey's death grip, but before she could pick the little girl up, Jordan scooped Lacey into his arms. He'd created the problem, he was going to find a solution if it killed him.

"If you don't tell us what's wrong, we can't fix it," he said in as gentle a voice as he could muster.

Lacey picked at the top button of his shirt, one fat tear rolling down her cheek. And he'd thought the kids would get a kick out of seeing his condo. *Idiot.*

"I'm afraid of the air," Lacey said.

"The air?" He glanced over her head, but Nell was gazing off into the distance. She had a weird look on her face, like she'd forgotten to turn the stove off.

Lacey laid her head on his shoulder. "My stomach feels sick when I look at all that air. You smell nice, Mr. Jordan."

Everything softened inside him. He made a big deal

of sniffing under her ear. "You do, too, princess. I think I have a solution for you."

Her arms tightened around his neck as he crossed the room to the coffee table. He grabbed the remote for the floor-length curtains, then returned to the other side of the room. "Watch this." The curtains swished closed. "Pretty cool, eh?"

Lacey took the remote from him and opened the curtains. Then closed them. Opened them. Closed them. He'd have to remember to buy new batteries for the remote after this. She squirmed out of his arms and sat in the chair by the TV. *Dora the Explorer* couldn't compete with this new marvel of technology. Open. Close. Open.

"I think it's safe to go to the kitchen now," Nell said. "Good job, Tan…Jordan."

Jordan was flooded with relief when the front door slammed as they escaped into the kitchen. He'd half expected Alex to charge back out and verbally attack Nell. Alex was the closest he had to family, but he wouldn't have stood by and let him tear into her. Not that he didn't think Nell could take care of herself. But— Jordan stumbled. He *wanted* to take care of her. And Lacey and Jacob. The enormity of the realization frightened him.

What did he know about taking care of anyone? He couldn't remember feeling that way about anyone except his mom, and she'd been gone for years.

He wasn't qualified to be responsible for anyone.

But that didn't seem to make a difference. The drive he felt to protect Nell and the kids was compelling, and he didn't think it was going away anytime soon.

CHAPTER ELEVEN

FOUR HOURS LATER, NELL swiped at the sweat that trickled down her neck as she swerved to avoid hitting a pothole. It was fried-egg-on-the-sidewalk hot, and Tanner had insisted they take her truck back to his condo for another load. Thank goodness Melody had recovered enough to take care of Jacob and Lacey. It was too hot to do much of anything, certainly too hot to haul the kids back to Seabend.

Nell hadn't felt completely comfortable leaving them behind. She couldn't quite put her finger on why, but something was off with them. Surprisingly, Lacey had asked to ride home with Nell in the old truck. Jacob had gone with Jordan, but he'd hardly said a word the entire time. The contrast between the nonstop chatter on the way to the condo compared to the near silence returning had disturbed Jordan enough that he mentioned it to her.

Nell didn't know what to think. A big salad for lunch had restored some of Lacey's usual sunny mood. When Nell had left for the second run to Jordan's condo, Lacey looked drowsy, and Melody was reading to her, hoping she'd have an afternoon nap.

In an attempt to find out what was bothering

Jacob, she asked what he thought of Jordan's condo. He shrugged and muttered an unenthusiastic "okay." Which was a huge step up from the absolute terror both children had felt when they first saw the high-rise building, but still not what she'd expected. She'd assumed Jacob would find the whole scene pretty cool. The stereo, the big-screen TV—he'd even had a turn at operating the remote for the curtains.

Jordan had seriously impressed her with how good he'd been with the children at the condo. Plugging Jacob into his stereo had been nothing short of brilliant. She reviewed what had been said, searching her mind for what could have upset Jacob. It had to be the similarity of the building to his grandparents'. What a nightmare that had been. Just thinking about the kidnapping nauseated her; no wonder Jacob was feeling strange.

She glanced over at Jordan who seemed to be nodding off for his own afternoon nap. He'd surprised her when he decided not to bring his expensive stereo back from the condo. After the big deal he made about showing it to Jacob, she'd assumed he was as proud of his music collection as he was of his wine. Apparently he wasn't ready to move everything from the condo, though, since he'd left both stereo and wine behind. Which was reassuring in a way. Lines were blurring, territories trespassed upon, and she was beginning to feel there wasn't a thing she could do about holding back the inevitable.

It wasn't just Jacob and Lacey who were falling for

Tanner. The image of Lacey in his strong arms kept replaying in her head. It had been such a turn-on watching him play the protector with her fragile niece. But that's all he'd been doing—playing. It was getting harder and harder to keep that fact front and center. She'd already lost the battle of convincing Jacob and Lacey that Tanner wasn't for keeps. They were sunk if she didn't keep her own head above water.

"Exactly how much stuff do you plan on moving?" She shifted in her seat, wishing she hadn't insisted on wearing her stupid overalls. Tanner had his arm along the back of the bench seat, and although he was wearing his seat belt, it felt like he was sitting way too close. Despite the intense heat and no air conditioner, he smelled delicious. Spicy. She smelled like the turpentine she'd spilled on her overalls last week.

"I'll leave most of the furniture, except for my bed. But don't worry." His finger brushed her bare shoulder. Then stayed there. She knew she should shrug it off, but the pressure of his hand felt nothing short of heavenly. "A moving company will get it tomorrow. Today, I need to pack a few more sheets and towels. Stuff like that."

All of his belongings were the very best. Her hands had trembled when she'd wrapped his beautiful dishes in paper. The fused glass platter and serving dishes were exquisite. Tanner had superb taste, and he was way out of her league. Her shoulders drooped right along with her spirit. She was setting herself up for a big fall. A humongous fall.

"Tell me about the grandparents."

Her grip tightened on the wheel. "The Bleechers. Tony was their only child, and you can see what a number they did on him. They're rich and self-absorbed, and truly think if they want something all they have to do is take it."

She yanked on the wheel too hard and the tires screeched as they took the corner. "Sorry. They're not my favorite subject."

"What did they do to Jacob and Lacey?"

She heard the rough emotion in his voice and glanced at him sideways, but nothing showed in his face. "Right after Mary died, Tony was in jail and I had temporary custody of the children. We were just getting by one day at a time. The Bleechers had come back from France for Tony's trial, and a few weeks later, out of the blue, they asked to have the children for a weekend. They'd never spent time alone with the kids before. I should have known something was up." She shoved back the terror that rose every time she remembered.

"I knew they were self-serving idiots, but they're the kids' family. I didn't know if I could do it all on my own. We were such a mess. I needed help. Hell, we all needed help." She swallowed a couple of times so she could get the words out. She wanted Jordan to understand what they'd been through.

"They took them to Paris." His voice went flat.

"They tried to. Airport Security stopped them, thank God. Tony had told them where to find the kids' passports, but hadn't given them a letter of permission.

Jacob and Lacey were terrified. So was I. It was all my fault. I failed them." The story of her life.

"How was it your fault?"

She pulled into his parking lot and turned off the engine before answering. "Because Jacob and Lacey were my responsibility. They trusted me to take care of them, and I let them down."

"We could argue that for hours, but I see your point." He squeezed her shoulder.

"You do?" After the hours she'd spent listening to people tell her she couldn't hold herself responsible for the action of others, it was a relief to have someone understand how she felt.

"I'd feel the same way. Lacey and Jacob have been through a lot. They deserve the best in every way."

"Exactly." Nell unclipped her seat belt and started to open the door.

Jordan touched her arm to stop her from slipping out. "That's not to say you're not the best, Nell. Those kids are lucky to have you."

A blush stung her cheeks. She kept her gaze on his long fingers wrapped around her wrist. "Thanks."

"What about money? Surely they help you with expenses."

Obviously, she hadn't painted a clear enough picture of the Bleechers. "They set up an educational fund for both kids so they can go to university later if they want."

"That's it?"

She pulled her arm away. "Jacob and Lacey have everything they need."

"I was thinking of you. It must be an incredible strain on you to support them."

"Sometimes," she admitted. What was the use of denying the truth to Jordan? He hadn't become successful by being stupid. "Most of the time I don't think about it because I love them and can't imagine not taking care of them."

She glanced over at him. No dreamy poet eyes today. His brows had lowered, his gaze intense, as if he was working out a puzzle. When he caught her looking at him, he smiled. "What do you say we buy some ice cream on the way home? For the kids," he added.

"For the kids, eh?" she teased. "That sweet tooth of yours wouldn't be acting up, would it?"

When he laughed, she scrambled out of the truck. Dear God, she was ready to jump the man in public. Because he laughed. She looked at the apartment building, then at Jordan who was still smiling as he came around the back of the truck. She hadn't thought about being alone with him in his condo. Just the two of them.

She hitched up her overalls, straightening them at the waist. Okay, she was the caretaker. *The caretaker.* Nothing was going to happen. She was being silly and, yeah, nothing was going to happen.

She followed him into the elevator. "Mrs. T.'s gout is doing better." Like Jordan needed to know that.

"Good."

"It is good, because she gets really cranky when her

gout acts up in this heat. Poor Rodney, he's been bearing the brunt of it. That was nice, you know, to let him move back into the bedsit. I know he won't be paying the full rent."

She glanced up. Jordan's head was cocked to one side, and he was squinting, as if she was speaking a foreign language and he was trying to interpret it.

"What?" She blasted him with her don't-mess-with-me glare.

A smile slowly stretched over his face. "You're nervous."

"Don't be ridiculous. What's to be nervous about?"

His smile widened as he hooked a finger through the hammer hoop on her overalls and tugged her toward him. "I like this little doodad. It's handy."

"It's for my hammer," she croaked.

"Of course it is. And these. Intriguing." He traced a finger up and down the pencil pockets that covered one breast.

"Tanner." His name came out sounding more like a sigh than the intended scolding.

"It's Jordan, remember." He tucked an errant curl behind her ear, massaged her earlobe between his thumb and finger. "I've been wondering what it would feel like to do this." He lowered his head and caught her earlobe gently between his teeth.

A groan purred out of her. "What are you...what are you doing?"

"What I've wanted to do from day one." He brushed

his lips against hers, then pulled back and smiled as if he'd lapped up a bowl of cream.

Oh, yikes. When he smiled he was irresistible. It wasn't fair. He'd caught her off guard. She wasn't ready for this. Any of it.

Like hell she wasn't. She clutched a fistful of his shirt and pulled him to her, his throaty chuckle vibrating against her mouth just before he kissed her. Her heart pounded in her chest, matched his beat for beat.

Oh. My.

Her knees turned rubbery, and she held on tighter to keep from falling. His lips were soft but firm, and about a second into the kiss, she grabbed the back of his head and pulled herself up his big, hard body. Felt his heat, his urgency. He eased her back against the wall of the elevator, pushed his leg between her thighs. With intent. There was no mistaking what he wanted.

Trembling, she drank him in. She could taste the fresh tomato he'd eaten at lunch. And under that, something dark and spicy and rich. She'd never get enough of his taste.

"Nell." Her name sounded beautiful for the first time in her life. He nibbled on her bottom lip, darted his tongue into her mouth. She met each parry, feeling a giddiness build inside her. She could become addicted to this man. The way he smelled, the sound of his voice, everything, everything, everything about him.

The elevator pinged, signaling its arrival on Jordan's floor.

"Come." Jordan draped his arm over her shoulders, keeping as much body contact as possible.

Nell stifled the giggle that threatened to escape; she was stomach-quivering nervous. It had been so long since she'd made love, what if she'd forgotten how? What if she blew it? *Stop thinking.* She wanted this. Needed it. Needed Jordan. Even if it was just for one afternoon. They could do that, couldn't they, and not hurt anyone? She could walk away from him after that.

"Do you have a condom?" she asked as he unlocked the door. He raised an eyebrow. Stupid question. He probably brought beautiful, sophisticated women home all the time. She felt like weeping—she was wearing her overalls.

"I'm not using any birth control because, you know, I haven't done it for so long," she babbled with the finesse of a sixteen-year-old girl. "Why waste the money? I mean, I do keep a box of condoms hidden in my dresser, but they're probably past the due date. Do condoms have a due date?" *Someone shut her up.* She felt shaky inside and out. She wanted him too much.

He ushered her inside and shut the door behind them. "Nell?"

She gulped for air, her heart galloping inside her chest. "Yes?"

"Shut up." He said it with the most beautiful smile on his face, so all she could do was grin at him like an idiot.

"Come here." He held out his hand.

She let him tug her toward him, surprised when he

spun her around and pulled her back against him. "I have been dying to do this from the first day we met." With a deep sigh of satisfaction, he slipped his hands inside her overalls and covered her stomach with his large, capable hands.

"You're kind of kinky, Tanner."

He laughed in her ear. "You think so? Wait a minute. Oh, God," he groaned. "This is good." He skimmed his hands over her bare midriff, then traced the bottom edge of her T-shirt that came just below her breasts. "This is very, very good."

That was the best he could come up with? Good? It was breath-stealing fantastic. Her stomach trembled as he slipped a hand up under her shirt and brushed against the bottom edge of her breast, the light calluses on his hand scraping deliciously against her skin.

When he cradled her gently in his arms, Nell sank into the embrace, reveling in his hardness. It had been so long since someone had held her. She shivered, feeling cherished as his fingertips brushed tantalizingly close to her breasts, his breath warm on her ear. But this wasn't just any man holding her; it was Jordan who cradled her as though she were fragile. Precious. No one, not once in her life, had ever made her feel that way. But Jordan did.

Despite all their differences, there'd been a connection between them almost from the first day they'd met. As if they recognized each other. As if they'd been waiting all their lives for the other to come along. The timing couldn't be worse. They were on such diverse roads, and no matter how much she wished for things to change, the reality was nothing could. And yet, here she was in his arms, and it was the only place in the world she wanted to be.

Despite his low murmur of protest, she turned and held his long, lean body against hers. She wanted Jordan. All of him, heart and soul. Whatever the price, she was willing to pay. She raised herself on tiptoe and kissed him with all her heart. She was falling in love with Jordan Tanner. She had been since the first day they met, and that wasn't going to stop anytime soon. Just this once, she'd take what she wanted, and in return, she'd reserve a small corner of her heart for him.

JORDAN FELT A FLICKER of heat as he took in Nell's bright eyes and the heightened color in her face. He undid the clasps on her overalls and tried to breathe as they slid to the floor. She stood before him wearing nothing but a pair of lacy green panties and a minuscule T-shirt that molded itself to her breasts. No bra.

His body pulsed with desire. He knew lust, and he knew what it felt like to care for someone. But he'd never before felt the raw hunger and gut-wrenching need that consumed him. Nell looked wild and beautiful, and everything he'd ever wanted in a woman. He just hadn't realized it until now.

He raised her hand to his mouth and kissed her palm, kissed his way up her arm to her elbow. Her skin was unbearably soft against his lips. But underneath the softness, the muscle was firm and toned.

He slowly worked up to her shoulder, savoring the taste of her skin, exploring the delicious hollows at the base of her throat. There was so much to discover about her, and also so much he instinctively knew.

She was the bravest, strongest woman he'd ever met. He smiled, and took her mouth with his again. No matter how many times he held this woman in his arms, it would never be enough. He was on fire for her.

"Let's do this right." He scooped her into his arms and headed for the bedroom.

She nipped his jaw, then ran the tip of her tongue along his mouth. "You're not going to go all conventional on me now, are you?"

He stumbled. "Conventional?" He wanted her so badly, his brain had stopped working. She was so sexy; her soft moans alone had almost made him lose it. But her body. Who could have guessed that those overalls hid an exotic, sylphlike woman? He wanted to see all of her. Now.

He strode to the bed, set Nell on her feet and tried to slow his breathing. He felt as though he'd been running in a marathon. "Right now I—" He dragged in an extra breath. "I could probably come up with a few innovative things, but right now, I just need to get you naked."

Her face lit up. "Ditto." She reached for his shirt and stripped it off him. He swelled with pride when he heard her gasp of pleasure.

"Hey, what's this. You have a tattoo?"

He kept meaning to have it removed, but had never gotten around to doing it.

"*Mom?* That's so sweet." She smiled as she traced the word on his arm.

"I was young."

"How young?"

"I don't remember. Seventeen, eighteen. Too young to know better."

"No one's too young to love someone, Jordan." She reached for his belt, but he put his hands over hers to stop her.

"This first." He took her into his arms and dove into the sweet, dark mystery of her mouth. He needed to do this right, because no matter what happened between them, he wanted her to always remember this time together. He didn't want to think about why.

He tore his mouth from hers and pulled her T-shirt over her head. Her breasts were perfect, small and perky. He gently lifted one in his hand and blew softly, watched with satisfaction as her nipples hardened. "You're so beautiful. Perfect."

"It's been a long time, Jordan. I'm not sure I can handle much foreplay."

He needed hours to explore her body, but her desperate plea spurred him on. They had all afternoon, with time for doing it right later.

She crawled onto the bed and curled up on her side as he rummaged in the bedside table drawer for a condom. From the corner of his eye, he saw a frown flicker over her face, but it disappeared when he turned toward her and she caught sight of his erection pressing against his jeans.

A laugh burst out of him, and he shucked the rest of his clothes and stretched out beside her. Trust Nell to make him laugh at a time like this. "Anyone ever tell you that every thought shows on your face?"

She buried her face in his shoulder and pressed her body against his. "I know. I am so totally not cool."

"No, but you're very, very hot. I like knowing what you're thinking."

She looked pleased with herself as she trailed a hand up his thigh, traced the muscles in his back with her fingertips. "Really."

He groaned and closed his eyes. He wanted to take his time, savor her. But he didn't think he was going to be able to control himself.

He rolled on top of her, parting her legs with his knee. "You fascinate me. Every part of you. Let me in, Nell. Don't hold anything back." The words unfurled from a dark, lonely place inside him. He needed this woman. He understood now it would always be this way for him. Because he was in love with Nell Hart. Had loved her from the first day they met. She completed him. He would always need her.

NELL WRAPPED HER LEGS AROUND Jordan's muscular thighs and pulled him toward her. There was no way to put her need into words. She had to show him. She buried her face in his neck, and reveled in the feeling of his hard, warm body surrounding her—the hair on his chest and legs grazing her skin, the weight of him between her legs, his taste on her tongue. She lifted her hips, and he slid into her. And then there was just the two of them, soaring. Clinging to each other as they fell.

Again. Forever. Impossible words pressed down on her as she rested her head on Jordan's shoulder, their heartbeats slowly returning to normal. She wanted to stay nestled in his arms forever. At the same time that she wanted to roll out of bed and run as far and as fast as she could. She'd lied to herself, something she'd promised never to do. Jordan Tanner was the man of her dreams, and she couldn't have him.

She shivered when he rolled off her and headed to the en suite bathroom without a word. Talk about coming back down to earth with a crash. She hadn't expected a declaration of undying love, but a gee-whiz-that-was-fantastic would have been nice. She jerked upright, drew her knees up under her chin and wrapped her arms around them. No sense leaving herself on display.

She tensed when he returned and sat on the side of the bed. Perched at an angle and staring at the floor, he took her hand in his. "That was…something. Thank you."

"Something," she croaked.

Still not looking at her, he patted her hand before placing it on the mattress between them. "Yeah, really, really…something."

Nell scrunched into a tight ball. "Geez, Tanner. Don't knock yourself out."

He sent her a sharp look. "The name is Jordan."

"Not today." *Not ever.* With as much dignity as she could muster, she swept up her clothes and dashed for the bathroom.

She closed her eyes and sagged against the wall once the door was closed. If he'd driven his fist into her gut, he couldn't have hurt her more. She'd thought the sex was oh-my-God-I-can't-get-enough good. But for Jordan—*Tanner*—it had been so mediocre he couldn't even find a word to describe it. She knew she was rusty, but come on.

She sank to the toilet and tried to think rationally. There'd been nothing wrong with the sex. Tanner was scared, afraid she'd read too much into the act. And, oh, how tempted she was to do just that. Because she knew what had happened between them was more than just sex. They'd connected—again. If this were a fairy tale, she'd say she'd met her prince. But life wasn't a fairy tale. At least, not hers.

Nothing had changed. She still had to find a new job and apartment, Tony was still a bastard and the adoption was yet to be finalized.

And yet *everything* had changed. Before Jordan had come into her life, she'd plodded along like a horse wearing blinders, accepting the guardianship of the children and all the joys and sorrows that came with that responsibility. She hadn't allowed herself to dream that life could be different, that she could have her own desires—and go after them.

She leaned over and turned on the water, anxious to wash the episode away. Time to get on with the rest of her life.

JORDAN SAT ON THE EDGE of the bed and dropped his head in his hands. *Something.* What a stupid word to use. How about life-altering? Earth-shattering? Soul-connecting. Anything but *something.*

He strained to hear if Nell was crying in the bathroom. She had to be hurting. He'd seen it in her beautiful, expressive face right before she'd escaped from the bedroom. But for the life of him, he didn't know what to do.

He was scared. He imagined Nell had already figured that out. When he heard the sound of the shower running, he pulled fresh clothes from his dresser and headed for the second bathroom down the hall. Falling in love with a little spitfire who knew more about fixing a rusty old furnace than which fork to use at the table did not fit into his plans.

How was he supposed to fit Nell and Jacob and Lacey into his life?

Right off the bat he could forget buying his own company. He couldn't risk every penny he had if he had a family to support. Which in turn meant he'd have to keep on working in his present job to provide for them. Not that he didn't like his job, but he'd gone as far as he could within the company. He'd have to give up his condo because it was only a two-bedroom. The kids needed a yard to play in. And—

He stepped into the shower, welcomed the hot spray of water over his tense muscles. *Face it, Tanner. You made a mistake.* He should never have let his attraction for Nell get out of hand. He didn't know how he was going to fix it, but he'd come up with something. He winced. That bloody word again.

Nell was waiting for him when he came out of the bathroom. For once he couldn't read what she was thinking, her face tight and closed. He didn't like that look on her, especially when he was the jerk who'd put it there. She seemed smaller somehow, and he could see her brace herself as she met his eyes.

"You were stupid. I was stupid. It won't happen again. Now, can we grab some of your stuff and get out of here?"

In spite of the hollowness in his gut, Jordan bit back a smile. He should have known Nell would attack the problem head-on.

"I owe you an apology," he offered.

"Yes, you do. Apology accepted. Now, what do you want to take with you?"

Ridiculous to feel miffed that she wasn't weepier. He wouldn't have minded a chance to explain why he'd acted the way he had. He needed to explain.

"I think we should talk about what happened here," he said in the authoritative voice he reserved for boardroom discussions.

Nell sent him a withering look. "Why? Will it change anything?"

She was right, of course. Talking wouldn't change a thing except maybe make him feel better. Way to go, Tanner. He'd officially sunk to a new low.

"No," he admitted.

She closed her eyes as if absorbing a blow, then turned her back on him. "Sheets, you said, didn't you? And towels?"

"Yes." His voice sounded hollow to his ears as he went to get some bags to put the sheets and towels in. He gave the bags to Nell and pointed out the linen closet, then muttered something about packing more clothes and fled to his bedroom.

He'd followed the same path for so long, he didn't think he could change. Or maybe the truth was he didn't want to change. The part of him that craved stability was still there, would always be there. He'd worked his entire life to reach financial security, and he almost had it. Like Nell said, they'd made a mistake. Some day he'd look back on this and marvel at what he'd almost given up.

CHAPTER TWELVE

THE RIDE HOME WAS excruciating. Not only did Nell's truck seem grittier and crankier than usual, the piercing silence between her and Tanner was agonizing. If he sat any farther away, he'd be perched on the running board. She glanced over at him. Arms crossed, staring straight ahead, his mouth grim. Well, hell. Either she was as lousy in bed as his reaction would have her believe, or the sex was as mind-blowing as she thought, and he was...what? Disturbed by it? Plotting to get her alone as soon as possible?

As if. She flicked on the radio. More likely none of the above. They'd stepped over a line they had no business crossing. Yes, they liked each other. Okay, there was a good chance she was in love with him. But it was time to grow up and accept the inevitable. Heaven knows, she'd had lots of practice facing reality.

And another thing. She sat up straighter, rolled down her window and rested her arm along the bottom edge. Since the day she'd met Tanner, she'd been spinning in circles, always arriving at the same point. He's hot, he's smart and funny. He's good with the kids. And he's off-limits. She'd had enough. It was time to forget about him and move on with her life. She had a job and a new apartment to find. She had a family to adopt. The sooner she got to it, the better off they'd all be.

Nell started humming along with Robbie Robertson as he took her down the lazy river. Having made a decision, she felt better, more in control. Everything was going to be fine, and in about two minutes when they got home, the knot in her chest would disappear. Because she didn't have time to sit around feeling sorry for herself.

Jordan shifted toward her as they turned onto Dunstan Lane. "I feel I should say something."

"Some things can't be fixed, Tanner. I'll survive." Her heart blipped when she noticed the police car parked in front of the house, but it settled when she realized it was just Perry. Another idiot.

He unfolded his arms. "I apologize. I took advantage of you."

"Oh, please. Living in this old house is getting to you. You sound like someone out of the Victorian age."

She frowned as they pulled into the driveway. She couldn't remember ever seeing Mrs. T. sitting on the front steps before. Lacey was huddled against the elderly woman's knees. Even from the truck, Nell could see the misery on her sweetpea's dirty face. Strange that Jacob wasn't close by. He liked to pretend his little sister was a pain, but he'd taken on the role as her protector with a vengeance.

Nell shoved the truck into Park and clambered out. Lacey streaked across the lawn, tears brimming in her eyes. Something was definitely wrong. "What's going on? Where's Jacob?"

Lacey barreled into her, and Nell squatted to gather her niece into her arms. "It's okay, baby. I'm here. It's okay," she murmured as she stood up, her eyes darting from Perry to Mrs. T.

When Jordan came and stood beside her, she let herself lean back against him for a second.

"We can't find Jacob." Lacey sobbed into her neck. "Perry says he's run away, and the b-b-b-bad guys will get him." She howled.

Son of a— Jordan rested his hand on Nell's arm. She jerked away from him, but the gentle reminder had been enough to help her focus. She turned to Mrs. T. "Tell me."

The elderly woman worried her bottom lip. "Melody lay down with Lacey after lunch for a nap. She says Jacob promised he was just going outside to work on the tree house."

Nell felt a twinge of guilt. How many times had she canceled plans for the tree house over the past couple of weeks? "But he wasn't there?"

"We don't know where he is." Perry joined the cluster of people.

She whirled on him. "Then why aren't you looking for him? Is *anyone* looking?"

Perry hoisted up his gun belt. "'Cause we don't know if he's run away."

Would she go to jail if she took a swing at him? "If he's not here, Perry, and we can't find him, I think it's a reasonable assumption he's run away." The alternative was simply unbearable.

Perry blinked twice. "No need to get snarky with me."

"Melody and Rodney are going door-to-door, asking if anyone's seen him," Mrs. T. interrupted. "Alex is driving around the neighborhood. He showed up, looking for Mr. Tanner. No one answered the phone at your old apartment, and you didn't answer your cell," she said to Jordan.

He patted his pockets, but came up empty. "I must have dropped it at the condo."

When Nell had ripped his clothes off. Oh, God. Her knees started to give out. Jordan plucked Lacey out of her arms and took her arm. "Maybe you should sit, Nell."

She jerked herself free a second time and dragged both hands through her hair. Recriminations would have to wait until later. At lunch, she'd sensed something was wrong with the kids, but she'd ignored the warning signs. It was her fault Jacob had run away.

Before today, he'd never shown any inclination to explore beyond the immediate neighborhood. He was a responsible child, and under normal circumstances, if he'd decided to go somewhere new, he would have told someone. What had happened today to change that?

"Nell, do you really think Jacob's run away? Should I call it in now?" Perry sounded as if he was starting to panic. How did he ever pass the exam to become a police officer?

"Call it in," Jordan said. "Give them Jacob's description, his home address, that kind of thing."

Perry sent Jordan a dirty look. "I know what to tell them."

Nell bit her lip to stop herself from yelling at him to get to it. Perry didn't react to pressure well. Honestly, the man should not be walking around with a gun.

"How long has he been missing?" Jordan asked Mrs. T.

Good question. One Nell should have thought of herself, but she had too many accusations running around in her head. *You should, could have. Why didn't you? How could you?*

"We don't know because Melody thought he was in the tree house. She didn't check on him until an hour or so after she woke from her nap." Mrs. Trembley put her hand on her chest. "The poor thing, she says this is all her fault."

"You looked everywhere? The apartment? The toolshed? Basement?" Nell heard the rising anxiety in her voice.

"Three times at least."

"I'll check the apartment. See if anything is missing."

"Nell," Lacey called.

Nell pivoted back. Knowing Tanner probably felt as guilty as she did, she'd deliberately avoided facing him. She couldn't deal with him or them or anything but finding Jacob. But surprisingly, his stricken expression as he put Lacey into her arms calmed her slightly.

She didn't have to go through this alone. Her friends, even Tanner, would help her find Jacob.

"Can you check your apartment?" she asked him. "And the basement. Maybe the tent. He likes you," she admitted. "If he's close by, he may come out when you call his name."

Tanner looked as though he was having trouble swallowing. "I'm on it."

She nodded her thanks and headed for the garage, Lacey clinging to her like a monkey. "Did Jacob say anything to you, Lacey?" She set her niece down and yanked open the door. "Jacob?" she called.

Lacey followed her inside. "N-n-no." Her bottom lip trembled.

Nell checked under an old sofa, behind an ancient chest Mrs. Trembley insisted was an antique. An antique pile of junk is what it was. Jacob wasn't here. Nell couldn't explain it, but she felt his absence.

She took Lacey's hand and headed for the house. "Did you check all of Jacob's hiding places?"

"Uh-huh."

When they entered the apartment, Nell immediately knew Jacob wasn't there, either. She took a quick tour through the rooms, but there was nowhere to hide in the small unit. When Lacey trailed after her into the kitchen, Nell poured her a glass of orange juice and leaned against the counter. Despite their age difference, Jacob and Lacey were unusually close. Nell had prayed for the day when both children felt confident enough to become normal, self-absorbed kids with friends their own age. But right now she hoped their unique closeness would pay off.

"I need you to think, sweetpea. What's the first word that pops into your head when you think of Jacob?"

Lacey pulled her thumb out of her mouth. "Sad."

There was a bucket load of that going around. "Do you think he was sad all summer?"

"He likes sleeping in the tent," she offered.

"Yes, he does. You think he got sad after that?"

"Mr. Jordan likes me best, doesn't he?"

Nell was about to tell her to forget about Jordan, but stopped herself. "He likes both of you. Is Jacob afraid of Jordan?"

Lacey licked the rim of her glass. "No," she said after taking a drink. "He likes Mr. Jordan. He says Mr. Jordan doesn't want kids. But maybe he'll want me because I'm a girl."

Nell sank into a chair and rested her head on the table. Her beautiful, intense nephew thought she was going to leave him. Just as his mother had, his father, his grandparents.

Lacey patted her back. "Are you going to marry Mr. Jordan?" she asked.

Nell was an insensitive, selfish person, and she didn't deserve Lacey's and Jacob's love. She pulled herself upright and opened her arms to her niece. "I'm not going to marry Jordan. You know what I think?"

Lacey snuggled into her arms. "What?"

"When the adoption goes through, I'm going to marry you and Jacob."

Lacey giggled. "Big people don't marry little people."

"We'll be the first then. If we're married, you can't get rid of me ever."

"Okay. Nell?"

She smoothed down Lacey's curls. "What?"

"I want Jacob to come home."

"Me, too." She set her niece on her feet and stood. "He didn't tell you where he was going?"

"No, but his new school knapsack is missing."

"That's a start. Let's go find him." Please, she prayed, before anything happens to him.

AFTER CHECKING ALL THE PLACES he could think of and coming up empty, Jordan hustled back to the front of the house. Perry was getting into his car.

"There goes one dumb cop," Mrs. T. announced from the steps.

Jordan stuck his hands in his pockets as he watched a car pull into the spot Perry had vacated. He wanted to hit the streets to look for Jacob, but he needed to talk to Nell first. "Did he get a description of Jacob out to the other police on patrol?"

"He did manage that, at least. What do you suppose this woman wants?"

He tensed as he watched a middle-aged woman climb out of her car, grab a notepad and study the house. Aw, hell. He recognized that blue polyester suit, the brown hair flecked with gray and those sturdy never-wear-out shoes. Every Child Welfare worker who'd hounded his mother had worn the same damned thing. Had someone called them?

"I'm looking for Nell Hart," the woman said as she approached them.

It was all Jordan could do to nod. He felt as if he'd stepped back in time twenty years, facing the same grim woman who'd made up her mind about his mother before she'd even talked to her. His mother may have been young, and yeah, a little flaky sometimes, but she'd loved him. The social workers hadn't cared about that part.

"Nell's upstairs." Mrs. T. used the railing to pull herself upright. "Jordan will get her for you."

"That's okay." A dim smile creased the newcomer's face. "Just point me in the right direction and I'll find her myself."

Mrs. T. shot Jordan a worried look before straightening her spine. To his surprise she transformed into an imposing figure. He'd dismissed her as an old lady with swollen ankles, but now he wondered where or why she'd learned to look regally down her nose at people. "Nell's busy at the moment," she addressed the for-sure social worker. "We're like family here. If you'd like to give me a message, I'll make certain she gets it."

The woman consulted a list on her notepad. "Are you Guinevere Trembley or Melody Northrop?"

Guinevere? Really? Maybe that's how she learned the regal thing.

"I'm *Mrs.* Trembley."

Apparently finished with old Guinevere for now, the

social worker zeroed in on Jordan. "Do you live here as well? I don't have a man on my list."

"I don't believe I caught your name," Jordan said.

She gave a small nod, acknowledging the stalemate. "I'm Mrs. Cripps. I work for Child Welfare, and I need to ask Ms. Hart some questions."

"Do you always work on Sundays?" Show No Weakness had always been his motto when it came to dealing with anyone in the system.

"On occasion. Do you live here?"

"I've just moved in. Jordan Tanner." He offered her his hand, knowing that he wouldn't help Nell by ruffling Mrs. Cripps's feathers. "I own the house."

Mrs. Cripps scribbled his name down and frowned at her notes. "I have a Beulah Winer as owner."

"My great-aunt. She left the house to me when she died." And his life hadn't been the same since. A month ago he wouldn't have considered living in a run-down, old house. He would have been concerned about a runaway boy—he'd pulled the same stunt several times himself when he was a kid—but he wouldn't have this chewed-up feeling in his gut.

He wanted to shove Cripps into her car and send her on her way so they could get back to concentrating on finding Jacob. But he knew things would go a lot more smoothly if they gave her a bit of time and information. *Then* he could shove her into her car.

"How do you like living here?"

Jordan bit back the urge to tell her to mind her own business. It wasn't unusual for social workers to check out the neighborhood, and what better way than to ask a new resident? Theoretically, he'd be less prejudiced in his views.

"I like it." That rolled off his tongue as though he actually meant it. "Most of the places have nice big yards, so there's lot of space for kids to play in. The people are friendly. Like Mrs. Trembley said, people are like family here." He shot a tentative smile at Mrs. T. Maybe she hadn't meant to include him, but whatever it took to impress Cripps.

"Are any of the residents transient?" She looked at his bags in the back of Nell's truck.

"No." But if Nell left or he sold the building, all that would change. Damn it, he'd been looking to make a fast buck, not inherit an entire family, complete with problems and eccentricities.

"And Ms. Hart works for you?" Cripps went back to writing.

"Part-time, yes. She's the caretaker. It's an old house, and Nell knows how to keep everything running smoothly. I don't know what we would do without her."

"Do you see Nell's living and working situation changing in the immediate future?"

Jordan stuck his hands in his pockets and crossed his fingers, an old habit from his childhood. Lying had been a survival skill for him when he was a kid. "No," he said, relieved to see Lacey racing down the stairs in front of Nell. If he hadn't thought Nell might need his support right now, he'd have been out of here as soon as the Child Welfare worker had gotten out of her car.

Lacey flew over to him, jumped into his arms and wrapped her arms around his neck. "Nell's not going to marry you, Mr. Jordan, 'cause she's going to marry me and Jacob."

He took in Nell's guarded expression over the top of Lacey's head as he processed what she'd just said. He'd had a feeling Jacob's disappearance had something to do with him and Nell. Hadn't he also been jealous of the boyfriends his mom had dragged home? Even that was an understatement. He'd hated every one of them. His gut tied into even tighter knots. Nell had warned him something like this could happen, not that he'd needed to be warned. But even knowing the havoc he could potentially create, he hadn't been able to stay away from them. Not just Nell, but Lacey and Jacob, as well. He'd fallen in love with all three of them.

"This is Mrs. Cripps from Child Welfare," he said, louder than necessary. Lacey tightened her hold around his neck.

Everything Nell was feeling raced across her face. Fear, disbelief, panic. Wanting to hold her in his arms, he edged closer to her.

"You're here on a Sunday?" Nell's voice rose in disbelief.

"Is that a problem?"

"I told you she was busy," Mrs. T. said from her perch on the steps.

"Can't we do this in a couple of days?"

Cripps studied Nell closely. "This will only take a few minutes. There are things we need to discuss." She turned to Lacey and smiled. "You must be Lacey."

Jordan gently extracted Lacey's thumb from her mouth. "Yes," she said in her little girl voice.

Cripps smiled. "You have beautiful hair."

"Thank you." Lacey smiled back.

"Is Jacob here?" Cripps turned to Nell. "I'd like to meet him, too. Maybe we could go up to your apartment so I can talk to the three of you together."

Nell had a wild look in her eyes, like a cornered animal. Jordan was an idiot. He should have been concocting a reason for Jacob's absence instead of thinking about the changes in his own life.

"Jacob ran away," Lacey piped up. "We're going to find him and then get married. Aren't we, Nell?"

For a second, tears filled Nell's green eyes. She bit down on her bottom lip—hard, by the looks of it—and straightened her spine. As if she was facing a firing squad. It took every ounce of his self control not to go to her.

Cripps's facial expression remained impartial, and Jordan had to give her credit for not freaking out. "Is that true? Jacob's missing?"

"Yes," Nell admitted. "I was helping Mr. Tanner move—I'm the caretaker and he asked for my help. When we got back a few minutes ago, Jacob was missing."

Cripps's gaze roamed over the property. "Any idea where he may have gone?"

"No." When Jordan heard the catch in Nell's voice, he passed Lacey to her, knowing that holding her niece close would bring her a small measure of comfort. He wished he could console her himself, but he didn't think that would go over well at the moment.

"What effort is being made to find him?" Cripps asked, flipping to a new page in her notepad.

Alex pulled into the driveway as Nell began to outline what had been done so far. Before Alex even got out of the car Jordan could tell by his grim look he hadn't found Jacob.

"Look. I know you must think I'm a terrible mother, but right now all I care about is finding Jacob. I can't stand around talking. I need to look for him."

Cripps flipped her pad closed. "I'll come with you. Are you staying here?" she asked Mrs. Trembley.

"Yes. Do you have a cell phone? Nell doesn't, and I may need to call you."

"Jordan, we need to talk right away." Alex strode across the lawn to him.

Jordan put up his hand to hush him. "I'm going to look for Jacob as well. How about I take everything east of the neighborhood. Nell, you go west. If I see Melody or Rodney, I'll stop and check in with them." He turned to Alex. "I need your cell."

"Fine." He tossed the phone to Jordan. "But we have to talk." He edged closer and lowered his voice. "I've got a buyer for the house."

"Give Mrs. T. the number, okay?" Jordan asked.

"Didn't you hear me?"

Jordan held up the phone. "The number."

Alex rattled off his phone number.

"Did you get that, Mrs. T?"

She didn't look up from her scribbling. "Got it."

Alex grabbed Jordan's arm and dragged him a few feet away. "I need you to focus now. I have a buyer for the house. He's interested in investing in real estate in this area. As we thought, it's going to be the next Seabend. But he's only in town today. He wants to meet you and take a quick look at the house." He tugged on Jordan's elbow. "This guy moves fast, and he doesn't have any time to waste."

Jordan felt as though his mind had been filled with thick, sluggish mud. He understood what Alex was telling him, but he was numb inside. There was no sharp jab of excitement. No great sense of relief that he'd finally be free to go back to his own life.

He rubbed his forehead. "Does he know about Nell and the low rents?"

Alex grinned and slapped him on the back. "Not a problem. He said he'd take care of them."

"What does that mean?"

"It means, you doofus, that you can sell any old time you want. You can move back to your condo, pick up where you left off." Alex grinned again. "We're on our way, man. Once we have the money, it's just a matter of waiting for the right deal to drop into our laps. We're going to be rich."

Rich. The adrenaline rush Jordan had expected finally surged through him. He could sell the house, move back to his condo and resume his life. Not only resume, but forge ahead. The sky was the limit.

Automatically, he turned to Nell to share the good news and felt like someone had clobbered him over the head with a hammer. If Nell's face got any paler, she'd turn into a ghost. Obviously, she'd heard what Alex had said. Jordan took a step toward her, but faltered when she turned her back to him.

He needed to say something, to reassure her that everything would be all right. Even if he sold and moved back to Seabend, he'd make sure she found a good job and a nice place to live. It would all work out. He opened his mouth but there was nothing to say. He couldn't lie to her. If he sold the house today, not only would he jeopardize the adoption, but Nell and the kids would be uprooted from their home before they had another place to move to.

Aside from all that, Jacob was out there on his own, probably scared and nervous. He passed the phone back to Alex. "Call the buyer. Put him off for as long as you can. I need to find Jacob before I do anything else."

Alex groaned in frustration. "He's not going to go for it. He's scheduled to fly out in three hours."

"Then we'd both better start looking for Jacob. Nothing happens until he's found."

Jordan strode to his car and slammed the door. He had to get out of here before he blew up. As irrational as it was, he was angry at Jacob for choosing now to run away—and angry at himself for intruding into these people's lives without considering the full consequences. And did Alex really think he would leave Nell alone right now? Alex knew him better than anyone else, so what did that say about him? Was he really that heartless?

But beneath the anger, Jordan realized he was afraid. He'd fallen in love with Nell and her beautiful little family, but the hard truth was, he didn't deserve their love. As much as he wanted to, he didn't know if he could become the person they needed him to be.

CHAPTER THIRTEEN

NELL WAS AMAZED SHE STILL had the ability to feel anything as she watched Jordan back his car out of the driveway and roar away. Where was he going? To meet the man who wanted to buy the house or to look for Jacob? Yesterday she wouldn't have even considered the question. But all bets were off now.

When she'd discovered Jacob was missing, she'd turned into a block of ice. She felt clumsy and awkward and stiff. She knew she was in shock, and welcomed it. Because if she started to feel, she'd come apart at the seams. She'd lost her nephew, and now she was about to lose her home and her job—all in front of the woman with the power to take Jacob from her for good.

There wasn't enough of her to go around, so she'd shut down. She had to find Jacob. Everyone else was going to have to take care of themselves. Except Lacey, of course. She hugged her niece, needing the child's warmth and love.

"Is that your truck?" Mrs. Cripps asked.

"Yes."

"We better take it. Jacob's probably scared by now and if he sees the truck, chances are he'll be only too happy to come to you. Unless there's something you haven't told me," she added.

Like she'd been making love—no, having sex—with her employer while her nephew ran away from home because he thought she didn't love him? "Can we talk once we're on the road? I need to get out there and start looking."

"Of course."

Nell was strapping Lacey into her car seat when Melody pulled in beside her. "Nell!" she wailed before she even turned off the motor.

Nell closed her eyes. She didn't blame her friend. Not really. Jacob running away was her fault, no one else's. By the time she stepped out of the truck cab and turned, Melody was coming at her, arms spread, sobbing openly.

"I'm so, so sorry. Forgive me," she whispered as Nell patted her on the back.

"It's not your fault, Melody. You couldn't have predicted this." She pulled back. "Did you find anything?"

"The neighbors I talked to didn't see anything, but I bumped into Rodney a few minutes ago. He said Mrs. Nowlan saw Jacob." She pointed to the Nowlans' house three doors down. "She said he was wearing a knapsack and was walking toward the downtown, like he knew where he was going." She wiped away her tears with her fingertips. "Rodney's going to keep on knocking on doors. I thought I should come back to see what was happening."

Waterside's downtown consisted of two small blocks

that included a few shops, the library, the bus station and a Laundromat. Not exactly a threatening place. It was one of a string of small communities along the coast that even the locals had trouble distinguishing from each other. Jacob wasn't headed for a huge metropolis, but he was by himself, and small communities had many of the same problems as big ones.

"I'll head downtown," Nell said. "Jordan may have gone toward Seabend. Maybe you could drive to the beaches? I don't think Jacob would go there because of his seawater allergy, but I didn't think he'd run away, either." She squeezed Melody's shoulder. "We'll find him. We just have to keep looking."

Melody lowered her voice. "Who's that woman in your truck?"

Nell tried to keep her voice steady. "Mrs. Cripps, from Child Welfare. She decided to visit us today."

"Are you serious?"

"It doesn't get more serious than this."

"She's going with you?"

"Yes." Nell could only pray the woman wouldn't take both children away from her when they found Jacob. "I have to go."

"I'll check the beaches." She hugged Nell. "We'll find him."

"I assume that was Melody Northrop," Mrs. Cripps asked as they backed out of the driveway.

"Yes."

"You have good friends."

"I'm very fortunate." She glanced in the rearview

mirror to check on Lacey. She had her thumb in her mouth, her eyelids drooping. Usually after an afternoon nap, Lacey was full of energy, but it would be a blessing if she slept again.

"Lacey's asleep," Mrs. Cripps said a few minutes later as they headed for the downtown. "She's a lovely child. If I hadn't read her case file, I wouldn't have guessed the trauma she's been through. I suspect that's mostly thanks to you. It's evident you love her a lot."

Nell's heart swelled. "She's easy to love."

"And Jacob?"

"Absolutely," she answered without hesitation. "He's a bit more of a challenge because he's older, but he's so smart and funny. He has a harder time of it, though."

"Because of his father?"

Nell chose her words carefully. "Tony is a difficult man. I don't know the details of his childhood, but unfortunately, I've met his parents."

"The kidnapping incident is in the file. Why didn't you press charges?"

She flexed her hands on the steering wheel. "What would I have gained? I got the kids back safely and they don't have to see their grandparents again unless they want to. And at that point I still hoped the children could have a relationship with their father. Charging his parents would have compromised that."

"And now?"

Nell slowed for a second when she saw three boys close to Jacob's age walking along the sidewalk, then stepped on the gas when none of them looked familiar.

"Truthfully? I think seeing their father does them more harm than good."

"You mean because he does things like hiring Stan Pugsley to follow you and the children around." Mrs. Cripps had been watching out the side window for Jacob, but now she turned her attention to Nell.

The truck jerked to a stop when Nell hit the brake instead of the gas. A car horn blared behind her. "Sorry." She accelerated carefully. "I didn't realize that was in the file, too."

"You filed a report with the police. That was a smart move."

Finally, knowing Perry had paid off. Except it had been Jordan, not Perry, who'd insisted the run-in with Stan be reported.

"The children's case history makes interesting reading," Mrs. Cripps said. "But I often find it beneficial to hear the entire story firsthand."

"Now?" Nell glanced at the older woman. She looked interested, and not in a judgmental way. Mrs. Cripps had probably seen it all before, at least a dozen times or more.

"I think this is a good time to talk about what happened. Just don't forget to keep an eye out for Jacob."

Nell shot her an as-if look. Either Mrs. Cripps was a great actor or she wasn't all that bad. Either way, Nell realized it wouldn't hurt to tell the entire story from start to finish.

She tried to keep to just the facts, but Mrs. Cripps— Elizabeth, as she asked Nell to call her—kept interrupting with questions that clarified some things and made Nell look at others in a different way. By the time they pulled into a parking spot across the street from the library, Nell felt as if she'd known Elizabeth Cripps for much longer than an hour. And maybe Elizabeth knew her better than any other agency worker.

Lacey stirred, but didn't wake when Nell turned off the engine. "Do you come downtown often?" Elizabeth asked.

"About once a week. Maybe less in the summer. We go to the library and pick up groceries at the store."

"You should check those places. Anywhere else?"

Nell stared bleakly out the windshield. "There isn't much else. Oh." She jerked upright when she caught sight of the bus station. "The bus station. My truck isn't all that reliable, so sometimes we take the bus to visit Tony. Jacob would know his way around there, too."

She grabbed the door handle, then stopped and glanced over her shoulder. "I don't want to wake Lacey until I have to. Will you stay with her for a minute?"

"Of course." Elizabeth put her hand on Nell's arm. "Before you go, I need to tell you something. It's why I came to see you today."

Nell's heart froze. The social worker sounded so solemn.

"The complaint you made to the police about Stan Pugsley was in your file, and I decided to pay him a visit." Elizabeth tapped her pen against her notepad. "Stan was more than happy to spill the beans about what Tony had planned. According to him, and this was later verified by some of the other inmates, Tony was making plans to kidnap the children. He'd blackmailed Stan into agreeing to do it. Tony hoped if the children went missing, you would look incompetent, and he would regain custody. And of course get parole, which was his aim all along."

"Oh, my God!" Nell shoved the door open. "Stan has Jacob. Call the police. I'll look—"

"Nell—" Mrs. Cripps had to raise her voice to be heard "—Stan's in jail. The police are holding him as a person of interest at the moment. I doubt they can actually charge him with anything, but they wanted to give him a good scare. As for Tony Bleecher, he won't be getting parole for a long while. He'd already signed over his rights of the children when your sister died. And now all the complaints he lodged against you have been revoked. You're scheduled to appear before a judge tomorrow. She's going to approve the adoption. That is, if you can find Jacob."

The words came at Nell as if through a heavy fog. Jacob and Lacey were hers. The fight was over. Tears stung her eyes, and no matter how hard she scrubbed them away, they kept coming back. Finally, she rested her head on the steering wheel and sobbed as Elizabeth patted her arm.

"Nell," Lacey cried from the backseat. "There's Jacob."

Nell looked up and spotted Jacob running down the sidewalk toward the truck. She tumbled out the door, and raced around the truck to reach him. She couldn't grab him quickly enough or hold him tightly enough. He held on just as ferociously and fought the good fight against his tears.

"There's no one I love more in the world than you and Lacey," Nell began.

Lacey barreled into them, jumping up and down. "Nell's going to marry us, Jacob. That lady there—" she pointed to Mrs. Cripps who had remained in the truck "—she said we have to go to the judge tomorrow and tell her we want Nell to be our mommy. Is that like getting married, Nell?"

Nell pulled both children into her arms. "It's exactly like getting married. You're never getting rid of me now. Are you okay?" She pushed Jacob's hair off his forehead.

"I thought you'd be mad at me." He glanced at her, then down at his sneakers.

Not able to stop touching him, she squeezed his shoulder, hugging him with one arm. "Right now I'm just happy we found you. Don't worry. When I get you home safe and sound, I'll have lots of time to think up a suitable punishment." Hard to sound serious with a smile plastered across her face.

Jacob shoved his glasses farther up the bridge of his nose, looking far older than his nine years. "I'm sorry, Nell. You told me to face my problems and not run away from them. I won't do that again."

Had she said that? Heavy thoughts for a little boy. Maybe she should take her own advice.

"I know you really like Jordan," Jacob continued

with a determined look on his face. "He likes us, too, but Alex said Jordan doesn't want kids. At least, not Lacey and me. Maybe he could be your boyfriend until I grow up and get my own place. Or, you know, I could probably live with my dad when he's not in jail." He wrapped his arms around his stomach like he had a bellyache.

"Now you listen to me, Jacob Bleecher. After tomorrow, you're going to be my son, and no child of mine is going to grow up this fast. I plan on enjoying every day of your childhood. You and Lacey, you're right here—" She put her fist on her heart. "I love you, Jacob. I'll *always* love you. Jordan—" She waved her hand as if he were nothing more substantial than a dandelion weed that disappeared on a puff of wind. "I won't even remember his name a year from now."

Liar. She'd never forget Jordan Tanner's name. It was etched into her heart.

FIVE DAYS LATER, JORDAN wiped the last bit of dust off the dark walnut dining table and stood back to admire the latest treasure he'd unearthed in the old garage. When he'd complained to Nell about the emptiness of the three-bedroom apartment, she'd murmured something about having stashed most of Aunt Beulah's furniture in the garage. Who knew Beulah had a thing for antiques? So far, he liked most of the pieces he and Alex had dragged out. They were solid and better made than the expensive designer ones he'd been slowly acquiring the past three years.

"Your aunt had good taste." Alex carried in the last two chairs of a set of six that went with the table. "For a certified nutcase, she knew what to invest in. This stuff is worth a lot of money."

Jordan rolled his eyes. Alex was convinced Great-aunt Beulah had not been of sound mind. Big surprise there. Everyone, at one time or another, had related some far-out anecdote about his aunt. But, in her own way, Beulah had protected Nell, Jacob and Lacey. In Jordan's opinion that wasn't insane; it was the behavior of a kind, generous person.

"We should have a dinner party. Ask a couple of hot chicks over," Alex said from the living room doorway.

Great idea. Except they were both so depressed, it would be torture for anyone else to be around them. "I'd rather, I don't know, eat worms."

"That's a bit extreme."

Was it? Jordan went into the kitchen in search of a couple cold beers. He grabbed the bottles out of the refrigerator and brought them back to the living room.

He handed one to Alex. "You know the difference between you and me?"

"I'm better-looking?" Alex snickered.

Jordan sat on the black leather sofa, the only piece of furniture he'd brought from his condo other than his bed. "The difference is, as much as it sucks, I admit I'm in love. You, my friend, are still in denial." He toasted Alex with his bottle and drank deeply.

"You mean you're whipped. I'm not."

"No, I mean I know I love Nell. One hundred percent. You, on the other hand, are hanging around, hoping for a glimpse of Melody. Not that I don't appreciate your company. This house is as deserted as a boardroom on a long weekend."

He looked around the apartment. He'd spent all his spare time filling the rooms with Beulah's antiques, as if hoping that would also fill the empty spaces inside him. He'd thought they'd all celebrate Jacob's safe return and the adoption together, maybe go camping or something. But Nell had taken the kids to Rodney's farm for the last few days of summer. Rodney had said he wanted to clean out his house and needed Nell's opinion on what to keep and what to give away. But Jordan doubted that he was actually ready to do anything about the farm. The old man still walked with a shuffle and emitted the deep sighs of the exhausted and grieving. But in his own way, Rodney had given Nell what would help her most. He'd told her she was needed.

Jordan took another drink. Rodney had also given her some very necessary breathing room. Kind of what he'd had in mind with the camping idea. Unfortunately, that breathing room included getting away from him. Melody had waited just two days before she followed Nell. And when Rodney had come back to get some of the kids' toys and books, even Mrs. T. had packed a bag and gone back to the farm with him. Jordan was rattling around the big, old house by himself, except for Alex's daily visits.

A month ago if someone had told him he'd miss his

crazy tenants, he'd have thought they were certifiable. But now he swore even the old house was lonely for the sound of pipes groaning, phones ringing and the pounding of footsteps up and down the stairs. He shuddered, thinking of his sterile condo. Had he really believed he preferred its anonymity to the warmth and richness of Dunstan Lane? Yes, anywhere Nell lived was heaven for him, but beyond that, he'd discovered he relished being involved with people. He liked knowing Mrs. T.'s first name was Guinevere, despite also knowing spices gave her gas. And that Rodney preferred cleaning his nails with his knife because that's the way his dad had done it.

Jordan loved how Lacey threw herself into his arms, trusting that he'd catch her. And how, when Jacob forgot to be afraid of life, he acted like any other silly nine-year-old boy. But mostly he loved Nell. He flat out loved her.

Jordan stood, wandered from the living room into the small bedroom he was using as a home office. Before she'd left, Lacey had set up shop by the window, using an old TV tray for a desk and a folding chair. A box of crayons and her coloring book sat on the tray. He'd gotten a kick out of Lacy moving in on his territory until Nell had given the idea the thumbs-down.

He was a temporary fixture in their lives and the less contact the better. Okay, he got it. But what if he didn't want to be a temporary fixture? What if he…well, what if he wanted to make the relationship more permanent? What if he wanted to fall asleep every night with Nell in his arms? Wake up every morning to her beautiful face? Trip over toys and dogs and— What if he had a child with Nell?

What had he been thinking? No amount of money or prestige would compensate for not having Nell and the kids in his life. Yes, he still craved financial security, but he was exceptionally well paid for his work. They'd always have enough money. They wouldn't be rich, but they'd get by just fine. The real security, the one he hadn't realized he'd been searching for, would be knowing he could come home to their family every night. Overwhelmed by the revelation, he sank into his desk chair. He had no idea if Nell wanted the same thing.

"You couldn't get more pathetic if you tried," Alex said from the doorway.

Jordan straightened the papers on his desk. "I think I'm going to ask her to marry me."

"Seriously?"

"No, I don't *think* I am. I'm *going* to ask Nell to marry me."

"What about selling the house?"

Jordan stood. "I don't know. Nell and I will have to talk it over. But I've got a new idea." He circled the desk and leaned a hip against the front. "You said the land values are on the rise in this area. Makes sense, right? We're only a few blocks away from the ocean."

Alex stepped into the room. "I was just reading how a lot of people are retiring and they want to live in smaller communities like this one."

"Exactly. So as the value of the house and land go up, we can borrow on that. We'll buy into whatever we want to, and we're good."

"*We* meaning?"

"You and me. Nell could be a partner of some kind, but the business would be ours, like we always planned. Maybe Sandra would be interested, too. The three of us make a good team."

"Okay." Alex grinned at him. "Okay." He held out his hand to shake on the deal. "I'll see what I can find."

Jordan laughed, feeling younger and lighter than, well, ever. "Not going to hang around to see Melody?"

Alex rubbed the back of his neck. "I don't think Melody and I... I'll get back to you on that one." He studied the top of Jordan's desk. "I'm not good with this stuff, but you and Nell, you kind of make sense. I've seen the way you are when she's around, and I think you're wasting time hanging around here talking to me." He grinned.

"Just one little problem." Jordan finished his beer and put the bottle on the desk. "I don't know where Rodney's farm is. But..." He stood and rubbed his hands together. "I know exactly what I have to do before she comes back."

CHAPTER FOURTEEN

NELL SAT ON THE SHADY VERANDA of Rodney's farm-house, sipping her tea. She smiled as she listened to Jacob's giggle and Lacey's high-pitched squeal, followed by a splash of water. Melody had taken the kids for their third swim of the day.

Rodney's farm was a paradise for children. There was an ancient barn with several stalls and a hayloft, which Jacob had immediately asked if he could explore. She and Rodney had checked each and every timber to make certain it was safe before giving Jacob the go-ahead. He'd even tried to sleep in the loft once, but the nighttime sounds of the country were too much for him. Which was just as well. Rodney suspected skunks lived under the barn floor.

Lacey had found an old trunk of women's clothes from the twenties and spent hours dressing up and having tea with imaginary friends. Mrs. T. had appropriated the kitchen and spent her time concocting huge meals for everyone. After two years of feeding her at least two suppers a week, Nell had assumed Mrs. T. either didn't know how to cook or hated to. Clearly, she still had things to discover about her friends.

Melody had taken over Nell's original purpose for

coming to the farm. When she wasn't playing with Jacob and Lacey, she went through everything in the house, telling Rodney what he should keep, and what he should throw away. Rodney looked years younger— in the few days they'd been on the farm, he'd already gained weight and had color return to his face. Though he still grew tired in the afternoons and had to lie down for an hour or two.

When he'd asked her to help at the farm, she'd known he was throwing her a lifeline. Facing the past took a lot of energy, and he was still so weak, she'd almost refused his offer. But she'd been so overwhelmed that she agreed. Visiting the farm would be good for the kids, she reasoned. She hadn't really expected Rodney to start packing up his past. But when Mel and Mrs. T. showed up, the visit had taken on a bizarre party atmosphere. Rodney had a sparkle in his eyes that hadn't been there before, and he laughed— a lot.

Unlike Nell. She had many things to be happy about. The adoption, of course. Lacey and Jacob were her daughter and son now. If she didn't think it was a good idea for them to visit their father, they didn't have to. Although she had reservations, she hoped Tony would some day realize what he was missing and ask to be part of his children's lives.

She was happy Rodney was starting to feel better, and just this morning, she'd caught Mrs. T. waltzing around the living room with Jacob. Even Melody was making the best of the not-so-great situation with Alex.

But despite so many reasons to be happy, Nell felt like she was drifting. Whether her friends had conspired to give her time to think or it had come about naturally, Nell had been left with precious little to do since she'd arrived at the farm. She took another sip of tea, crossed and uncrossed her legs. What was the point of thinking about Jordan when she knew that was a dead end?

Jordan had been entertaining himself with her and the kids. They were a temporary distraction until he could get back to his real life.

More important than the different lifestyles, he didn't love her. She sighed and placed a hand over her heart, then embarrassed, glanced around, hoping no one had seen her poor-me gesture. She was better than this, stronger and smarter. She had a ton of things that demanded her attention; she didn't have the time to sit around feeling sorry for herself. So Jordan didn't love her. So she was head over heels in love with him. Nothing was going to happen. Get over it. She sighed again, sipped more tea. Her pep talk had absolutely no effect.

"You look like you're thinking hard thoughts." Rodney sat in the rocking chair beside her.

She summoned a smile. "I was thinking about all the things I should be doing. I've got to buy school supplies for the kids, and I'm sure after telling the Fitzgeralds I was taking a few days off on such short notice, I need to look for another job." She looked down at her teacup. "I think it's time I looked for a new apartment, as well."

"It's hard making changes." Rodney scratched

behind his ear. "I'm none too good at them myself. But I think things happen for a reason. You and the children can live here until you find what you want, if you like."

Nell blinked hard. She refused to cry yet again. "Thanks, Rodney. I appreciate the offer. But it's better if I find somewhere not too far from the old neighborhood, so Jacob and Lacey can continue going to the same school. They deserve to feel settled. Moving will be hard, but we'll get through it." And they would. She knew that. Yes, it would be sad to leave the old house. But maybe Mel would move with them, as she'd suggested. And they could always visit Mrs. T. and Rodney. As for Jordan, he'd probably already forgotten them.

"Lucinda and I sat on this porch, rocking in these chairs for years. I couldn't imagine things changing. It scared me to think of it." He studied his work-worn hands. "I think I got it wrong, hanging on to the way things were. You saw what it did to me. Sometimes I wonder if I had embraced change, instead of refusing to accept it, that things would have been easier."

Nell stopped her rocking chair. "You think I'm hanging on too hard?"

He shot her a sympathetic look. "I think you're afraid of taking a chance. Which is the same, if you think about it."

"You're not talking about finding a new job or a place to live."

"No."

She looked out at the grove of lilac bushes and wild apple trees in front of the house. "Jordan doesn't love me, Rodney. He doesn't have room in his life for us."

"Have you asked him?"

"I don't have to. He behavior has left little room for doubt."

Rodney stood. "You're selling yourself short, like you think you don't deserve to be happy. Life goes by so quickly, Nell. Don't waste a minute of it."

She kept her gaze on a red squirrel scampering up one of the apple trees. Other than Melody, it had been years since anyone had shown any genuine concern for her. She'd not only acquired a son and daughter, she realized with a start, she'd also inherited a father. "Thanks, Rodney," she managed to say.

"We can take care of the children for a couple of days if you need to go." He walked back into the house, leaving her alone on the veranda.

The squirrel resumed scolding her from its perch high in the branches of the tree. Could Rodney be right? Was she afraid of risking her heart? Her motto had always been to tackle things head-on. She hated cowards. Yet here she was, hiding.

She'd been willing to fight for Jacob and Lacey. For her sister, too. How many times had she rescued them? Begged Mary to leave Tony, offered to support all three? She'd fought for Rodney to stay at the house, and for Mrs. T.'s rent not to be raised. She'd been fighting for other people all her life, but never for herself.

Nell got up out of the chair and strode into the yard,

feeling the need to work off some energy. Was she turning into one of those sickening people who thought everyone else deserved good things, but not them? The thought was too pathetic for words. Of course she deserved to be happy.

Hell, she was the best damned thing that had ever happened to Tanner. If he didn't realize that, he deserved to live in a sterile high-rise that smelled of new paint, expensive leather and stale air. But to give him the benefit of the doubt, she'd tell him exactly why he needed her.

JORDAN GRINNED WHEN HE HEARD one of the sweetest sounds known to him—the roar of Nell's old truck pulling into the driveway. She'd come home to him, at last. Thank God. The last five days had been the longest of his life. He took a satisfied glance around the apartment, then waited by the door for Nell to call his name.

Okay, scream his name. It took all of five seconds after she'd entered her apartment. He worked hard at wiping the grin off his face as he listened to her race down the stairs.

"Tanner?" She hammered on the door. "You better be in."

He opened the door and tried to look casual as he leaned against it. "You're back. Where's your tribe of misfits?"

"What did you do with my furniture, you scum-sucking snake? You have to give a month's notice before you can get rid of me."

Uh-oh. His surprise was backfiring. "Nell, let me explain."

"You sold the house, didn't you? And now you can't wait to get rid of me. To think I came back here to tell you I love you, and why you should marry me. You deserve to live all by yourself in that soul-sucking condo building," she yelled.

Jordan grabbed her by the shoulders and dragged her into the apartment before the neighbors across the street called the cops. "It was a joke. I'm sorry."

"A joke? I go away for a few days, and you ditch my belongings, God knows where, and—" He relished her astonishment as she realized her favorite painting, the one from her living room, now hung on his living room wall. His heart skipped a beat, then started racing.

"What—" She'd noticed Lacey's toy tea set and her tiny foam armchair arranged in the living room. She looked at him, her face for once blank, as if what she felt was too much—or she was really going to blow.

Jordan couldn't hold back the smile that spread over his face. She'd always challenge him; never let him get away with anything. "Can we talk about what you said a minute ago? The part about you loving me?"

She pushed past him with a pitying glare. "What is my stuff doing in your apartment?"

Had he gone too far? What if she didn't like the idea? "Our apartment," he said.

He followed her into the kitchen where he'd organized her cookbooks on the shelf above the sink. From there, she wandered into his office, which was now

Lacey's bedroom, then into Jacob's room. She stopped outside the closed door of the master bedroom. She stood still, her eyes darting from the doorway to the hallway, then back to the bedroom. Anywhere but at him. "Look, Tanner," she finally said.

"Jordan," he corrected.

"Right. Jordan." She dragged a hand through her hair. "I…uh…I'm confused."

He took her hand, led her into the bedroom and sat her on the edge of the bed. He kneeled in front of her, all the while keeping her hand in his. Her eyes grew round and apprehensive.

"Nell Hart, will you marry me?"

A look of fear flashed across her face. "Why?"

"Because I love you. Because you fill up all the empty spaces in my life." Not able to stand being apart, he stood and pulled her into his arms. "Because I can't imagine my life without you. I want to be with you, always."

She burrowed her head against his chest. "Wow, that was great. I was just going to tell you I'd kick your ass if you didn't agree to marry me."

He laughed when he heard the smile in her voice. "Is that a yes?"

She looked up into his eyes. "Yes, I'll marry you. But what about the kids?"

"Well, it's a little early to be discussing children. I thought we'd need a year or two for the four of us to work out the family thing, but you know, now that you've brought it up, I'm thinking, four, maybe five kids total."

"And who do you think is going to take care of those children?"

He tilted her face up to his, lowered his mouth close to hers. "One of the perks of having your very own caretaker, I guess," he whispered before kissing her deeply.

After a couple of minutes, Nell came up for air. "In that case, I want to renegotiate my wages."

He drew her T-shirt over her head and tossed it on the floor. "Everything's up for negotiation, except for you leaving this room before I have my way with you. Unless, of course—" he hooked his finger through a belt loop on her shorts and pulled her back to him "—you want to go upstairs and find your overalls."

Jordan sucked in his breath as Nell slipped her hands under his shirt. "If that's your idea of kinky sex, I'm disappointed in you."

He tried to concentrate on what she was saying as her hands skimmed over his chest, then dropped to his belt. "I'm sure, given time, we could be a bit more inventive."

Nell sparkled up at him. "I'm counting on it."

CHAPTER FIFTEEN

Six Months Later

"DADDY, I NEED HELP GETTING dressed," Lacey yelled from her bedroom.

"In a minute, sweetpea." *Daddy.* He still wasn't used to Lacey calling him that. With a satisfied sigh, Jordan continued with his last-minute instructions to the caterers. Mrs. T., Melody and most of all, Nell, had been horrified when he insisted the party be catered. But he'd put his foot down. Aside from his marriage to Nell, this was the most important occasion of his life. It had to be perfect.

"Where's your mother?" Jordan asked a couple minutes later when he walked into Lacey's bedroom. He couldn't help smiling as he studied the pink, frilly room. He still couldn't get over how easy it was to make Lacey happy. Although lately he'd noticed she was a tad bit harder to please. Maybe Nell had a point when she scolded him about spoiling the girl. But what was he supposed to do? Lacey had him wrapped around her little finger.

"I seen her go to the greenhouse when she got back from her appointment."

"You *saw* her go to the greenhouse," Jordan corrected her.

"That's what I said. She's going to be late for the party if she doesn't get changed soon."

Sounded like a job he needed to take care of. Nothing he liked better than helping Nell out of her clothes. She'd been wearing her overalls this morning, hadn't she?

His smiled faded. That had been earlier, before she sped off to keep a doctor's appointment. She'd assured him it was a routine checkup, nothing to worry about. Over the past few months he'd learned to take some things on faith. Not an easy task for someone who had once thought he was in control of his life, though he was getting better at it.

But not this. He couldn't help worrying, although he'd tried to get himself busy with preparations for the party. When he'd asked Nell to reschedule her appointment, she'd refused, saying she'd had it booked for weeks and didn't want to miss it. If he needed help, Mrs. T. and Melody were only a shout away. But he wanted, needed, Nell by his side today. People would be arriving any minute now. Why had she gone to the greenhouse instead of coming straight to the house?

"Here you go." He slipped Lacey's new pink velvet dress over her head, zipped up the back and smoothed a hand over her messy curls. "You look like a princess."

"It's starting to snow." Her bottom lip quivered. "People won't come."

"Of course they will. I hear someone at the door right now. Let's go see who it is."

Jacob skidded into the hallway, followed by two friends who seemed to spend more time at Dunstan Lane than at their own homes. "Jordan, I invited Kyle and Paul."

They had so many adjustments to make learning to live together as a family, it had been easier on all of them to continue living in the old house. With three bedrooms and a large living room, the space should have been big enough. But he hadn't factored in the kids' friends underfoot, and now that they were feeling a bit more settled, Jacob had started campaigning for a puppy. Melody, Mrs. T. and Rodney dropped by once a week for supper, and even Alex had starting showing up, too. It was getting harder and harder to ignore the fact that the apartment wasn't big enough.

"Hey, guys. Thanks for coming. Is that what you're wearing for the party, Jacob?" Jordan checked that Jacob's jeans were at least clean. One of the first things he'd done after marrying Nell and starting life as a parent was to take Jacob to buy a new pair of glasses. The Harry Potter-style frames suited him much better than the heavy, black ones he used to wear. He'd even filled out a bit, and to both his and Nell's delight, he'd rebelled against wearing a shirt and tie to the party today. It was the first time since his birth mother had died that he'd dug in his heels about anything. That alone was worth celebrating.

"I changed my jeans. Where's Mom?" Both Jacob

and Lacey had started calling Nell "Mom" the day she'd adopted them six months ago. Jordan hadn't heard them use her name since.

Now it was his turn. Yesterday he'd signed the adoption papers. Today they were celebrating. He couldn't imagine a person less equipped than him to become a father. The thought should have scared him, but it didn't. He was crazy about Jacob and Lacey, and wanted to be part of their lives forever.

"In the greenhouse." Lacey sighed.

"Geez, Dad." Jacob stopped, his face turning a bright red.

Jordan's heart turned over. It was the first time Jacob had called him "Dad." He stuffed his hands in his pockets to stop himself from pulling Jacob into a hug and embarrassing the boy in front of his friends.

"I'm just on my way to get her now, son." They stared at each other with silly grins on their faces.

Lacey pulled on his hand. "You're my daddy, too."

"Yes, I am." He ruffled her blond curls. "The lawyer says we're officially a family now."

"And this is our first party as a family," Lacey said in a singsong voice.

"It will be if I can drag your mother away from her office. You two are in charge until I come back."

Just as Jordan was about to leave, Mrs. T. and Melody walked in without knocking. "I saw Nell go to the greenhouse," Mrs. T. said. "She's not working on a design today, is she? I thought you said two o'clock. It's ten to now." She strode over to the kitchen and stuck her nose in. "Those the fancy caterers?" She sniffed. "What's wrong with home cooking, I want to know."

Jordan suppressed a sigh. Mrs. T. added a dimension to his life he hadn't foreseen when he suggested they continue living on Dunstan Lane. He'd met Great-aunt Beulah only twice, but he bet Mrs. T. had been a match for the old girl. He didn't understand how, but he seemed to have inherited yet another cranky aunt.

He needed to talk to Nell again about at least starting to think about getting their own place. Over the past couple of weeks he'd caught himself slowing down in front of houses for sale to check them out. They'd bonded as a family unit more quickly than either of them had anticipated; they could handle a move.

Melody winked at him as he took Mrs. T.'s arm and led her to a chair. "This way none of us has to work, and we can all enjoy ourselves. Would you like something to drink?"

"A cup of tea would be nice, thank you. Lacey, dear, you look lovely, but you need your hair brushed. Pull that footstool over here for me, will you?" With barely drawing a breath, she continued, "Didn't you say you were getting Nell?"

"I believe I did. Jacob," Jordan called as the boy sidled toward his room with his buddies, "would you ask the caterers for a cup of tea while I find your mother? Would you like something to drink?" he asked Melody, who looked beautiful in black velvet pants and a sparkly blue top.

"Are the caterers doing the drinks as well as the food?"

"Indeed, they are."

"Excellent." She smiled. "I'm thinking it's an Irish coffee kind of day. I'll ask them if they can make one. Go dig Nell out of her office. Lacey." She held her hand out to the four-year-old. "Let's go do our hair together."

Jordan smiled his thanks and escaped into the hallway just as Alex walked through the front door.

"Hey. Congratulations. I brought you a present." Alex handed him a fine bottle of Scotch. "Thought you might need it."

"Very funny. Come in. I'm just on my way to find Nell." The longer she hid in her office, the more worried Jordan became. Something was definitely up.

"No problem. Where are the kids?"

Mrs. T. might be the cranky great-aunt, but Alex, much to everyone's surprise, had become the favorite uncle. "What did you buy them this time?"

"Tickets to the Cirque du Soleil for the four of you. And one for me. Hope you don't mind if I tag along."

"You were smart enough to buy one for Melody, too, weren't you? She'll have a fit if we go to the circus without her." Alex and Melody had formed a wary truce. They weren't exactly friends, but they weren't enemies, either. Jordan still hoped they'd see past their differences to what they had in common.

He'd tried to talk to Alex about his fear of commitment, but gave it up when Alex accused him of having turned into one of those nauseating people who tried to inflict matrimony on everyone else.

"I'm many things, but stupid isn't one of them. Go find your woman and leave me alone," Alex said with a smile.

Jordan made it out the front door, and when he saw Perry pull up to the curb, hurried around the corner of the house. He'd a hard time believing it at first, but Perry had found his perfect mate. Dana was a take-charge, no-nonsense woman who ran the diner down the street from the police station. Perry reveled in her bossiness, while she seemed genuinely affectionate toward him.

He headed for the greenhouse where Nell had her office. The first thing he'd done when he realized they wouldn't be moving was have the old garage demolished and a new one built in its place. Nell had filled the space with the equipment she'd purchased for her landscape business. Things had been slow over the winter, but they were confident the jobs would pick up come spring. And in the meantime she kept busy creating designs to tempt clients. Thank goodness Rodney was her business partner and foreman of the planting crew. He'd keep a watchful eye on her, make sure she didn't overdo it when the physical work started.

As if Jordan had summoned him with his thoughts, Rodney clambered down the stairs from his apartment above the garage. "I thought the party was starting. The kids must be some excited."

Even before Rodney had given Nell away at their

wedding, he'd become the children's surrogate grand-father. Jordan couldn't think of a better man for the job. "It is and they are. I'm looking for Nell."

Worry lines appeared between the elder man's eye-brows. When Jordan had first met him, Rodney had looked like an old, used-up man. It wasn't often he saw him frown these days. He'd sold his farm and used some of the money to invest in Nell's business, telling anyone who'd listen to never give up because miracles did happen. Nell was his miracle. Jordan's, too. She was everyone's miracle at Dunstan Lane.

"I didn't want to talk out of turn," Rodney said. "But there's something wrong with Nell."

"What do you mean?"

"She's not herself. It's like she'd drifted off some-where. I mean, you're having this party to celebrate you becoming a family, and she's shut up in her office. I checked the greenhouse in case she wanted to talk. She wasn't there, and the door to her office is closed." He shook his head. "That's not our Nell."

Jordan's heart pounded in his chest. He'd noticed her distance, too, but had put it down to being distracted by the second adoption and planning the party. "It's prob-ably nothing. I'll take care of it. Go to the party, okay? Make sure everything's all right."

Rodney put his hand on Jordan's shoulder. "Don't worry, son. Whatever it is, we'll all handle it together."

Jordan turned away before Rodney could see the sudden emotion in his eyes. It was a day for firsts; no one had ever called him *son* before.

Seven months ago, when he'd first moved to Dunstan Lane, he'd thought he had it all. But many of the things that were important to him then—his Lexus, his condo—he no longer owned. He figured he must be just about the happiest man in the world right now, because his life was filled with much more precious possessions. He had the love of a good woman, two beautiful children and an extended family that he still wasn't sure he wanted. But they were his, so he'd hold on to them.

The only problem now was that Nell was hiding in her office. But whatever had happened, they'd face it together. Because they were family.

"Hey there." Jordan tried to keep the alarm out of his voice as he swung open the door, and saw Nell huddled in her office chair, sniffling.

"Oh." She glanced up, her eyes full of tears. "Is it party time already?"

"What's wrong?" He wanted to go to her, put his arms around her shoulders, but fear kept him glued to the spot.

She wiped a hand under her nose. "Nothing. I just…" Her gaze drifted to the window as she blinked back more tears.

He covered the distance between them in two strides, whirled her chair around and squatted in front of her. He took her cold, trembling hands in his. "You're scaring me, sweetheart. What did the doctor say?"

Her bottom lip trembled, and she mumbled something he couldn't hear. Jordan felt a renewed sense of panic. Nell never had a problem telling him what was on her mind.

"Nell, please just tell me."

"I'm…I'm sorry. It's just…it'll all have to end. I don't think I can do it."

He scooped her up into his arms and sat in the chair with Nell nestled in his lap. She put her arms around his neck and sobbed, soaking the front of his clean, white dress shirt.

"What has to end, Nell?"

"I love this place. I love this office. You built it for me." Her voice rose in a wail.

"Is this about your company? Did something happen with a client?"

"No." She rubbed her tearstained face against his shirt and looked up at him. "Sorry, sorry, sorry. I just thought, you know…I thought everything was unfolding like it was supposed to. We got married and moved in together. I adopted the kids, then you did, and Tony can't ever take them away from us now. And then I started the landscaping business, and you and Alex and Sandra have your consulting business, and—"

"Nell—" he gave her a gentle shake "—you're babbling. Yes, things have changed a lot in the past few months, but we've handled everything just fine up to this point. Whatever this new challenge is, we'll handle it, too."

"Oh, Jordan." She sighed, laid her head against his chest. "I love you."

His arms tightened around her. "I love you, too, honey. Now talk to me."

She sat up and swung one leg over his thigh to straddle him. Looking him straight in the eyes, she tried to smile, but couldn't quite manage it. "Remember the night you helped me move into this office?"

"Yeah. We, uh, broke in your new desk."

A blush colored her cheeks. "Right. Well, I'm pregnant."

"Excuse me?"

"We didn't use protection, and now I'm pregnant."

"You're pregnant," he repeated.

"I'm sorry. I know this messes up all our plans and everything. We were supposed to live here another year or two, but honestly, we're already too cramped in the apartment. I love it and all, but where are we going to..." She bit her bottom lip before continuing. "Where are we going to put the baby?"

"Can we rewind for a sec? I'm still stuck on you being pregnant." He put his hand on her belly. "You're pregnant? Really? Are you okay?"

Nell's expression finally relaxed into a smile as she placed her hands over his. "The doctor said I couldn't be healthier. You're not mad?"

"About what? You want the baby, don't you?" His hand trembled as he ran it over her flat stomach, marveling at the miracle that was growing inside her.

"Of course I want him. Her."

He looked up. "Do you want to know which?"

"I think I want it to be a surprise. Seriously, Jordan,

we didn't intend to have a baby yet. You're not upset about all your plans getting messed up?"

He bent forward, caught her earlobe between his teeth. "You've been messing with my plans since the day I met you."

Her face lit up. "I'm pretty good at that, aren't I?"

"That's not the only thing you're good at." He undid the first button of her blouse.

She wiggled in his lap and laughed. "You want to do it on the desk again?"

"Absolutely."

"Dad, you're supposed to bring Mom back to the party," Lacey whined as she and Jacob stared at them from the open office door. "It's no fun without you."

Nell laughed again and collapsed against Jordan's chest. "More plans gone awry. I want a rain check."

He kissed the tender spot under her ear. "You name the time, I'll be there."

"I want a kiss, too." Lacey scooted across the room and leaned against Jordan.

He kissed his daughter on the top of her head. "Your hair looks nice, sweetpea."

She beamed up at him. "I know."

Jacob sidled up to Nell and put his hand on her leg. "Are you okay?"

Nell slung an arm around his neck and drew him closer. "I'm better than okay. Do you want to tell them?" She smiled at Jordan.

His heart swelled as he looked at his family. He didn't understand what he'd done to deserve such riches, but he knew he'd do everything possible to hold on to them.

"I have a story to tell," he began. "Once upon a time, there was a woman who liked to take care of people…"

* * * * *

HEART & HOME

Heartwarming romances where love can
happen right when you least expect it.

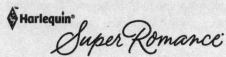

COMING NEXT MONTH
AVAILABLE JANUARY 10, 2012

#1752 A HERO IN THE MAKING
North Star, Montana
Kay Stockham

#1753 HIS BROTHER'S KEEPER
Dawn Atkins

#1754 WHERE IT BEGAN
Together Again
Kathleen Pickering

#1755 UNDERCOVER COOK
Too Many Cooks?
Jeannie Watt

#1756 SOMETHING TO PROVE
Cathryn Parry

#1757 A SOLDIER'S SECRET
Suddenly a Parent
Linda Style

SPECIAL EDITION

Life, Love and Family

Karen Templeton
introduces

The FORTUNES *of* TEXAS: Whirlwind Romance

When a tornado destroys Red Rock, Texas,
Christina Hastings finds herself trapped in the
rubble with telecommunications heir
Scott Fortune. He's handsome, smart and
everything Christina has learned to guard herself
against. As they await rescue, an unlikely attraction
forms between the two and Scott soon finds
himself wanting to know about this mysterious
beauty. But can he catch Christina before she runs
away from her true feelings?

FORTUNE'S CINDERELLA

Available December 27th wherever books are sold!

*Brittany Grayson survived a horrible ordeal at the hands
of a serial killer known as The Professional...
who's after her now?*

*Harlequin® Romantic Suspense presents a new installment
in Carla Cassidy's reader-favorite miniseries,*
LAWMEN OF BLACK ROCK.

Enjoy a sneak peek of
TOOL BELT DEFENDER.

*Available January 2012
from Harlequin® Romantic Suspense.*

"**B**rittany?" His voice was deep and pleasant and made
her realize she'd been staring at him openmouthed through
the screen door.

"Yes, I'm Brittany and you must be..." Her mind suddenly went blank.

"Alex. Alex Crawford, Chad's friend. You called him
about a deck?"

As she unlocked the screen, she realized she wasn't
quite ready yet to allow a stranger inside, especially a male
stranger.

"Yes, I did. It's nice to meet you, Alex. Let's walk around
back and I'll show you what I have in mind," she said. She
frowned as she realized there was no car in her driveway.
"Did you walk here?" she asked.

His eyes were a warm blue that stood out against his
tanned face and was complemented by his slightly shaggy
dark hair. "I live three doors up." He pointed up the street to
the Walker home that had been on the market for a while.

"How long have you lived there?"

"I moved in about six weeks ago," he replied as they

walked around the side of the house.

That explained why she didn't know the Walkers had moved out and Mr. Hard Body had moved in. Six weeks ago she'd still been living at her brother Benjamin's house trying to heal from the trauma she'd lived through.

As they reached the backyard she motioned toward the broken brick patio just outside the back door. "What I'd like is a wooden deck big enough to hold a barbecue pit and an umbrella table and, of course, lots of people."

He nodded and pulled a tape measure from his tool belt. "An outdoor entertainment area," he said.

"Exactly," she replied and watched as he began to walk the site. The last thing Brittany had wanted to think about over the past eight months of her life was men. But looking at Alex Crawford definitely gave her a slight flutter of pure feminine pleasure.

Will Brittany be able to heal in the arms of Alex, her hotter-than-sin handyman...or will a second psychopath silence her forever? Find out in
TOOL BELT DEFENDER
Available January 2012
from Harlequin® Romantic Suspense
wherever books are sold.